Stay this Christmas

GENNY CARRICK

Cover Design & Illustration by Melody Jeffries

Edited by Zee Monodee

ISBN (ebook) 978-1-957745-06-0

ISBN (paperback) 978-1-957745-07-7

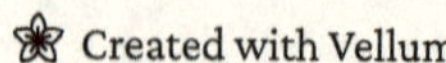 Created with Vellum

*For everyone who needs a second chance romance.
I know I sure did.*

ONE

harper

THEY SAY you can't go home again. Wish someone would have told my ex-boyfriend.

Sam Donnelly had been off exploring the world for eleven years—long enough for me to assume he had no intention of ever coming back to sleepy little Magnolia Ridge to stay. Not that I wanted him to come back, or thought about what that might be like.

I didn't. He could have stayed in New Zealand or Colorado, or wherever his latest impulse had taken him, for all I cared.

But he'd turned up here about a month ago, and not long after, started volunteering at the retirement community where I work. In a room separated from me and my physical therapy patients by a glass wall. Where he encouraged groups of seniors into yoga positions he also demonstrated in painstaking detail.

Twice a week, I played the *Ignore Sam Donnelly* game.

I lost every time.

"Let's do one last set of the calf stretches." I stood beside my current patient, Diana, as she lowered into a partial lunge, her fingers lightly touching the back of a chair to steady herself. Most of my patients at Fiesta Village knew the move designed

1

to help with mobility, and I liked to finish up routines with it when I could. I tailored every session to each person's particular needs, but some conditions became pretty universal with age. "We're almost done."

She counted under her breath before straightening again and switching legs. "You spoiled my view."

"What view?"

Looking at me over her shoulder, she revealed a cheeky grin. "Don't think it slipped my notice we're facing the wall with these awful inspirational posters on it, and not the exercise room. I like watching hot yoga every Friday afternoon."

The inspirational posters were awful? I'd picked them out myself. What other aspects of the PT room weren't quite doing it for my patients?

Nope, let that go.

"I think hot yoga is when they turn the temperature up so you sweat."

Her smile grew wider. "Oh, Sam gets it pretty hot in there."

I swallowed down a sarcastic retort. Nobody here knew Sam and I had dated an age ago, and I wasn't about to release that particular cat from its bag. I'd learned early on that in a group of people living in a relatively contained community, gossip swept through like a river in a flash flood. Every resident would know our history in under five minutes flat, and I would drown in embarrassment.

"The class is a distraction." For my patients *and* me. Hard to focus on PT with Sam doing sun salutations twenty feet away.

Not that I was looking, but he drew the eye. Him and his skintight shirts.

"Mmhmm." Diana sounded like she had the same image in her head. "Keeps it interesting, though."

Shutting my own imagination up, I tried to steer the conversation in a new direction.

"I'd better change your sessions if you'd rather watch other people do yoga," I said around a laugh. "We can always crank it up a notch if I'm going too easy on you."

She turned her head again, her mouth pulled in an exaggerated scowl. "Don't you dare. You're wearing me out as it is."

"You're doing great. I'm impressed at how much better you're walking lately."

"Well. I do have an excellent physical therapist."

That compliment swirled around in my chest, puffing me up. I'd pursued PT to help people improve the quality of their lives and loved seeing just how much I truly could. My patients' progress made all the hours I spent here—and the hours doing paperwork at home—worth it.

"I might even be able to keep up with my grandsons when I visit them in Hawai'i for Christmas."

"I'm sure you'll have a great trip."

"I expect so." She counted out another slow stretch. "Do you have holiday plans?"

"My parents are hosting a big family get-together. My sisters and all my cousins will be there." Most prized among them, baby Maisie, my cousin Wade's littlest. I couldn't wait to get that cute bundle of pudge in my arms again.

The rest...well, I wasn't looking forward to it as much this year. I adored Christmas, and was absolutely devoted to my family, but with just about everyone paired off and grotesquely happy, big family get-togethers didn't have top spot on my list of favorite activities anymore. I'd managed Thanksgiving okay, but it'd been hard to know where to look to avoid witnessing starry-eyed gazes and adoring kisses. Christmas seemed guaranteed to bring out even more PDA from my loved-up relatives. Let's not even think of all the mistletoe hanging everywhere. Only my cousin Jed and I were still single—maybe we could form an alliance and distract each other from the non-stop love-fest.

"Sounds like a good event to bring a sweetheart to."

Her lilting hint held a question I wouldn't answer. The same question my mother peppered me with every time we spoke.

"Could be." I tried to sound both positive and noncommittal without giving actual information. Impossible not to be friendly and grow to care for my clients after working here over three years, but I couldn't share too much about my personal life. I still needed to be professional, and discussing my love life would cross a line somewhere—even if there wasn't much to discuss.

"Did you ever go rock climbing like you wanted to?"

Ugh. Case in point. I should *not* have mentioned that. Not because it was unprofessional, more because people kept bringing it up.

It had recently come to my attention I *might* have dedicated myself a little too much to my work. I'd been so busy helping the residents of Fiesta Village improve their lives, I'd kind of forgotten to live my own. My social circle didn't extend much beyond my sisters, Eden and Eliza, and our cousin, June. I basically lived my life within a three-square-mile radius. My hobbies had begun to overlap with those of my elderly patients, and while I could crochet with the best of them, I wasn't exactly raising the roof. I needed something more.

Just what that something was...I hadn't figured out. Rock climbing had seemed far enough outside of my norm to shake up my routine. Just needed to get around to it.

Eventually.

"I haven't gone yet, no."

"Maybe you need an instructor."

"Probably would be best." I shuddered, imagining the

carnage if I tried without even taking a class. Broken legs every-where. "That's ten. I think you're good for today."

Diana turned on the spot to look past me. That little grin returned to her face, her bright pink lips set off by her stylish silver pixie cut. "I might have to try the yoga. What do you think?"

I moved the chair she'd used back into its usual spot and straightened up the PT room. We had a few exercise machines, a weight rack, and various sized yoga balls, with a privacy screen on one end of the room and my desk in the far corner. I'd felt right at home the last few years, sure of my work and my place here. Right up until *hot yoga* started in the next room.

Over time, I'd convinced myself I'd forgotten about Sam, and maybe I'd even occasionally succeeded, but his return had brought everything back out into the light. Our teenage friend-ship that had been my most important relationship in high school. The single, marvelous year that friendship developed into more. The day I'd lost both friend and boyfriend, when he said he couldn't date me anymore, only to turn around and start dating someone new two weeks later.

Sam showing up again had taken my neat little world and shaken it like a snow globe, my heart rattling around in pieces like so much falling glitter.

"I think yoga could be good for you." I shifted, allowing myself to look through that dang glass wall into the exercise room beyond. Sam had his class lying on their mats, finishing up their session. A few of the residents sat in chairs to avoid getting up off the floor, but had their eyes closed along with everyone else, exuding peace. A muffled snore drifted through the wall. "It might help you feel more limber. Stretching could be really beneficial."

I had to admit, Sam seemed to know what he was doing. From everything I'd seen, his gentle routines were well-suited to our residents' abilities, and his enthusiasm couldn't be denied. Certainly, I'd heard no complaints. Quite the opposite.

So much the opposite.

If gossip was a flash flood, praise for Sam Donnelly had become the never-ending *drip-drip-drip* of a leaky faucet I couldn't fix.

"What a kind young man."

"So good to volunteer his time."

"Aren't we lucky to get him?"

Sam had become a minor celebrity, the residents of Fiesta Village his adoring fans.

He'd always been that way, though. His outgoing nature, quick smiles, and infectious laugh made him an irresistible force. Once, I'd been drawn to him right along with everyone else. I liked to believe I had immunity now, like a vaccine against some deadly disease. My heart would recognize him, and reject him outright. My Sam-suppressants would eradicate all possibility of ever crushing on him again.

"Ooh, they've finished up," Diana said. "Let's go see what Sam thinks about your yoga plan."

My yoga plan?

She grabbed my hand and dragged me to the PT room door with a vigor she rarely displayed in our weekly sessions. In the next room, Sam helped a couple of the residents to their feet while others rolled up their mats and wandered out into the main hall. Everyone greeted me as they passed, since nearly all of the Village residents had seen me a time or two for physical therapy.

Although, they didn't smile like this after *our* appointments.

I smothered the jealousy trying to spark to life. Not that long ago, I'd been the new young thing the residents had *oohed* and *aahed* over.

"Sam!" Still gripping my hand, Diana pulled me into the exercise room behind her. "Do you have a minute?"

After seeing one of the chair yoga residents off, he turned to us. Our eyes locked, and my breath got lost somewhere on its way to my lungs. Lucky I didn't stumble over my own feet like I had the first time I'd run across him here. I'd looked up, seen him standing five feet away from me, and promptly tripped like some klutzy romance novel heroine. If my director hadn't been there to grab my elbow, I would have wound up on the floor. Not the high ground I might have hoped for in a first interaction with my ex-boyfriend.

I'd gotten used to his presence since then, but not by much. Seeing him made me feel like I'd just stepped off a merry-go-round—dizzy and a little nauseated. I positively hated that he still had that effect on me, but time had been oh so good to Sam Donnelly.

Five-foot-eleven, wavy blond hair mussed to perfection, those pale green eyes full of mischief—it all spoke of the boy I'd once known. But the man—*oof*. His body had filled out with glorious muscles stretched across wide shoulders down to abs scandalously defined by his workout clothes. Golden scruff covered his jaw, the beginnings of lines traced the corners of his eyes, and I did *not* need to see that hint of chest hair peeking out from the vee of his T-shirt.

He was supposed to be gross and disheveled, a pathetic heap of a man without me in his life, and instead, he'd turned into a freaking cover model. Not fair that the guy who'd broken my heart had come barging back into town to flaunt his gorgeousness. He could at least wear looser shirts.

Tone it down, buddy. You're hot, we get it.

I cringed over my stupid thoughts. This right here? This was why my PT routines now faced the wall instead of the exercise room on Mondays and Fridays. You don't get burned and then admire the beauty of the fire. No matter how sculpted that fire had become in the last decade.

Sam put the yoga mats in a plastic tub before approaching Diana and me. "What can I do for you ladies?"

She moved us even closer. "Harper was just telling me the benefits of yoga."

He turned to me, and I swear the light in his eyes twinkled. *Twinkled.*

"Did she, now?"

I shook my head, wondering why I had followed Diana in here at all. She didn't need me with her to ask Sam about yoga. "I only said—"

She squeezed my hand twice, a silent signal to shut my mouth.

"She said I should give it a try," Diana cut in, "but I don't know. I've got arthritis in my knees, and I can't stand for a long time like some of the others in your class."

"We can do whatever modifications you need," he said. "You can sit in a chair as much as you like, and follow along from there. I won't ask you to do anything that makes you uncomfortable or causes injury, I promise."

He gave her his full attention, his warm smile like a little sunbeam just for her.

I used to think his interest in people genuine, but after the way he'd treated me—not to mention the eleven years apart—now I couldn't be sure he wasn't just snowing her, a smiling conman pitching the wonders of yoga.

"Oh, that sounds like a good idea, I'll try that." Diana urged me forward, practically shoving me against him. "Do you know Harper, Sam?"

I managed to avoid slamming into his chest, but then he almost knocked me down with the grin he flashed. This close, it proved a deadly weapon, murdering my pride at point-blank range.

"I do know her."

I forced a smile even as that four-word summary of our history resurrected my pride just to strangle it into oblivion again. Diana sure didn't need to know the details, but Sam and I had grown up side by side, been inseparable best friends through high school, and eventually each other's first loves. *"I know her"* felt like a pretty shoddy sum-up.

"Are you a rock climber, by any chance?" she asked.

Oh, no. No, no, no. Dread barreled through my stomach like a train going straight off the rails. She wasn't about to do what I thought she was about to do, right? I squeezed her hand, telegraphing my own desperate pleas to keep her mouth shut.

"I am," he said. "Are you looking to learn?"

"Oh, not me. Harper." Diana nudged me even closer to him, like playing with dolls and saying *Now, kiss.* "She's the one who wants to learn. You two should have a chat about that. I'll run out and sign up for Monday's yoga class and give you a chance to talk."

She turned and shimmied her way to the door, flashing a quick wink—at me? at Sam?—before disappearing down the hall.

Well. It could have been worse. She could have invited the resident retired pastor over to 'have a chat' with us, too.

I shouldn't have been surprised. Residents here had tried to play matchmaker for me several times, to varying degrees of awkwardness. From eager introductions to indifferent grandsons, to blundering conversations with the new security guard, not a single person had ever been subtle about it. Kind of sweet they wanted me to find love so badly, but this particular love had already gone down in flames.

"Should we talk about rock climbing here, or over drinks at

The Broken Hammer?" he asked, the dimples in his cheeks on full display.

Too much to hope Diana literally throwing me at his feet would have escaped his notice. His rakish grin did something stupid to my insides, but I stomped on that like a cockroach. His personality had always been 105% flirt. Like everything else he did, this meant nothing.

"I think people lose nuance with age." I crossed my arms over my chest, achingly aware of my Christmas tree-printed, deeply unflattering scrubs while his form-fitting workout clothes made him look like a demi-god.

Normally, this would be the point where I slunk back to the PT room. So far, I'd put on a mask of detached politeness with him for work's sake, but we didn't really talk. Standing around with my former best friend-turned-boyfriend like we'd just been introduced made me supremely off-balance, like I wanted to pull a privacy screen around myself and catch my breath until he left.

No. Screw that. He was the one in the wrong here. If anything, *he* should be afraid of *me*. He should be the one with sweaty palms and a prickle of anxiety gliding through his stomach like Jaws on the hunt for a struggling swimmer. Not standing there wearing an unfazed grin.

"Nice scrubs. You fit the theme."

He gestured past me to the main hall. Christmas trees stood guard at both ends of the lobby, red and green decorations festooned tables and hung from the walls, and if I listened hard enough, I could just make out the Christmas-themed muzak they piped through the common areas.

"'Tis the season."

"Kind of early, isn't it?"

I scoffed. "It's December first."

"Exactly. It just seems early for all of this. That should be more of a Christmas week thing."

The. Nerve. Stealing my distraction-free work environment and my patients' allegiance was one thing, but I would *not* let him steal my holiday joy.

"I'll have you know, I've been watching Christmas movies since October."

He laughed, the sound thrilling through me in a way both familiar and unwanted. Incidentally, also two apt descriptors for the man himself.

"You're the reason stores are overrun with Santa stuff the minute Halloween is over."

I would not admit to how many Christmas goodies I'd already bought this year. "I don't see the problem."

He shook his head at me, but his smile sparked with amusement. "You wouldn't."

I glanced around the exercise room, counting down the seconds until I could exit this conversation while still saving face. If I ever stood any chance of that to begin with.

"Looks like you're getting more residents in your classes each week."

His grin shone out again all bold and bright, a naughty boy who didn't care if he got caught red-handed. "Aw, Harps, are you jealous?"

His old nickname for me smothered the feeble embers of my instinctual attraction. This was why I kept that glass wall between us. Sam just couldn't turn off the charm. His flirty conversations brought all that hurt right back to the surface, tiny little icicles digging into my heart with every casual remark. Did he really think we could pretend we'd never had a history? Maybe what we had was long gone and meaningless to him now, but I couldn't just forget it like he had.

He'd dumped me and our plans for college with zero explanation, traveled the world for eleven years, then mysteriously returned to Magnolia Ridge and thought we could just be friends again? What next? Drive out to a field, throw a bunch of blankets down, and—

I swallowed hard. I would *not* think about that. I'd been inoculated.

"Why would I be jealous of them?"

His naughty grin twitched. "I meant jealous of me stealing your patients, but interesting that your mind went there."

I willed the heat spreading from my chest up my neck not to color my cheeks for once. My red hair and freckled skin helped me stand out from my blond, blue-eyed sisters, but it also put all my emotions on display. Embarrassment, anger, annoyance over close proximity with someone I'd resented for the last decade—it all showed up in bright red splotches on my face.

"I actually think yoga is good for the residents." My voice came out a little lofty and judgmental, but better that than cracking under his relentless gaze.

"That's good, because Olivia bumped me up to three times a week. I'm adding a session on Wednesdays now."

My mouth popped open, but not much I could say if Fiesta Village's director had arranged it with him. Certainly nothing that wouldn't make me sound exactly as bitter as I felt. I'd handled seeing him on the regular pretty well so far, but I could only swallow down so many feelings in a week.

"I can rearrange the class schedule so you could join in, too."

I snorted. "Pass."

Let Sam Donnelly teach me yoga? I'd seen the moves he did. No way would I have my butt that much on display around him.

His hands went to his hips, making his shoulders look impossibly broad. "Come on, you could help them do their stretches and maximize the good they get out of the class."

"That's..." Not a bad idea, actually. I sometimes helped out with activities, encouraging small changes using pastimes residents already enjoyed. People who didn't think they needed physical therapy were often more willing to let me help with their bocce toss or little movements during Village trivia night than a full PT session.

Still. Admitting that would feel like a loss, and I'd already lost enough to Sam.

"We'll see."

He nodded as though my wishy-washy response had been an enthusiastic reply. "So, was that a yes to drinks at The Broken Hammer tonight?"

Heat flashed again over my cheeks. "*No.*"

"Busy?"

"Yes, actually."

His flirty gaze didn't alter. "Anything I should know about?"

Going out for a girls' night, if we were being honest, but I didn't feel like being that forthright.

Since the three closest women in my life had paired off in the last year, we didn't make time for girls' nights the way we used to. I liked their partners, and sometimes they included me in their plans, but I didn't love the awkwardness of being the odd one out in a group of couples. Tonight, I would soak up my time alone with the girls.

"Not really."

"Fair enough." He watched me with that stupid twinkle in his eyes. "So. You want to learn rock climbing."

I edged toward the door, ready to end this conversation ASAP. This was already much too close to our old dynamic than I liked—him encouraging me to try something new, and me getting swept up by his enthusiasm. I needed to shut this whole thing down. Getting swept up by Sam Donnelly again was a giant *NO* in my book. "It was just an idea."

"I could teach you."

I backed up another step. "Nope."

No way would I subject myself to spending time with Sam again. Seeing him through the exercise room wall twice a week was plenty. Ugh—apparently, soon-to-be three times a week.

His cheerful attitude didn't fade even as I shot him down. "I'm a fully-certified instructor."

"Good to know."

I'd tried not to keep up on all the Sam-related gossip through the years, but the pattern had been pretty clear: he liked travel and adventure. He'd left Magnolia Ridge the week after high school graduation and set off around the world. I'd heard about trips to New Zealand and Australia, Vermont and Wyoming, doing everything from running ski lifts to giving local tours. Rock climbing would be right in his wheelhouse. The yoga maybe came as a surprise, but still in the right vein.

"You know where to find me if you change your mind."

"I won't."

"It might not be so bad," he said. "Learning from a friend."

Annoyance flared to life in the pit of my stomach at how casually he'd slipped on a label he hadn't worn in over a decade.

"We're not friends." The ice in my tone could have chilled all the sweet tea in Texas, but I couldn't keep pretending we'd started from scratch four weeks ago when he walked through Fiesta Village's doors. We had a history, and if ninety-five percent of it had been wonderful, that last five percent had knocked me down hard. Acting like the last bit hadn't happened only served to make me feel rejected all over again, a reminder that it hadn't been all that important to him.

That *I* hadn't been all that important to him.

His smile slipped a touch, his cheery expression almost strained. For a second, I felt bad for being so blunt about it, but then I remembered just who I was talking to. Sam Donnelly, heartbreaker extraordinaire. The guy I'd cried my eyes out over, who had loomed over the rest of my dating life as Villain Number One, the only guy I'd ever let into my heart enough to crush it. Not going to feel sorry for that guy.

I hooked a thumb over my shoulder. "I have paperwork to do."

He nodded, his smile back in place. Real or fake, I couldn't tell anymore. Didn't matter anyway—not my problem.

"Okay. See you around, Harper."

I darted through the door and back into the PT room, ready to throw myself head-first into an abyss of soul-sucking insurance forms. Fiesta Village had been my happy place for the last three years, but now, with the arrival of one volunteer yoga instructor, I'd rather be anywhere else.

Reminding myself this was only temporary, I tried to shake him from my mind like an Etch-a-Sketch. Sam had traveled the world seeking out new adventures—he would leave sleepy Magnolia Ridge again sooner or later. I would just have to wait him out.

sam

HARPER MADE her quick escape into the next room, insulted by the term I'd used.

Friend.

Clearly, I'd overshot. I'd known getting back into her good graces would be an uphill climb, but I hadn't thought she would shut me out so thoroughly. Not that I really deserved open arms after the way I'd left things between us. I should probably be grateful she spoke to me at all.

I'd meant to jump right in with an apology, try to start fresh and get to know each other again. I hadn't expected her to be happy to see me, but I'd still hoped. But the shock and bitterness in her eyes my first day here had crushed those hopes down to a superfine dust. Since then, her thinly-veiled aversion to me had knocked my confidence down a few pegs, and I'd avoided mentioning our past.

Like a chicken.

In the PT room, she sat at her desk and opened her laptop. Her auburn hair fell in a braid down the middle of her back, a sliver of her face visible at this angle. We were only separated by about twenty feet and a pane of glass, but it might as well have been twenty miles.

You ever make a mistake, and you know it's the wrong thing when you do it, but then you go on making it anyway?

That had been me the day I walked away from Harper Webb.

My best excuse? I'd been seventeen and stupid. Harper and I had been everything to each other, but I'd decided breaking up with her before she went away to college would be best for both of us. She could focus on her studies, and I could do my thing without anybody being tied down. High school sweethearts didn't last, anyway, so better end things sooner than later. Give us a clean break, and we could move on.

I mentioned I was seventeen and stupid, right?

"You're running late today," a voice said from behind me.

I wiped the moony look off my face and turned to find my grandpa Glen shuffling into the exercise room, his cane in one hand and a wooden box under the other arm. Today, he wore trousers with a belt and suspenders, which seemed overkill. Did Fiesta Village have a pantsing problem I hadn't heard about? He also wore a blue fleece jacket over his plaid flannel button-down. Just looking at him made me sweaty. Although December, temps still climbed into the mid-fifties most days, but the residents here dressed as though they were preparing for the Iditarod.

His gaze went straight to the glass wall, and Harper beyond. He smiled as if I'd made an emotional confession.

"I see. You're thinking about what a fool you've been."

His laughter didn't take away the sting of his words. I *had* been a fool, a thousand times over. I'd come home to try to repair the damage, but didn't know if I could yet. Hard to know where to start when I'd made such a mess of things.

"I'm always thinking about that."

I pulled the wooden backgammon box from under his arm. Double-checking I would leave the exercise room as tidy as it had been when I arrived, I turned back the way he'd come. He didn't have much interest in the yoga I taught here, but he liked playing backgammon with me after. Our twice-weekly sessions gave me plenty of quality time with my grandpa, along with the added bonus of lessons on how to lose with grace.

I kept my pace slow to match his as we headed to one of the free tables in the main hall. When Grandpa first announced his intention to move into Fiesta Village three years ago, I hadn't been on board with the idea. I'd never been to a retirement community before, and my expectations had been fairly pitiful. Think uncomfortable rooms with stale meals served by frowning employees who couldn't wait to quit. But the Village very nearly qualified as luxury—certainly more luxurious than any place I'd ever lived—and now that I'd been here a while, I wouldn't want to see him anywhere else.

"You fall on your knees begging forgiveness yet?" he asked.

"Not yet."

I wouldn't exactly say I'd had the opportunity. Harper made sure we spent as little time together as possible, speaking to me only when given no other choice. Seeking her out outside of Fiesta Village seemed a sure way to get a door slammed in my face—or worse. She'd never held back from punching me in the arm when I deserved it, and I definitely deserved it now. If I'd immediately agreed to Olivia's suggestion to add another session to my volunteer schedule last week, well, I guess I still had a spark of hope left, after all. Tiny, maybe, but holding out.

"Dragging your feet isn't like you."

I hitched a shoulder. "I'm turning over a new leaf. I'm patient now."

He laughed again, well aware my default decision-making

setting was just a huge red button with the words *Do it!* emblazoned on it.

"Sensible, too."

"Nice to meet you, Sensible Sam. Does this new leaf of yours include winning at backgammon, for a change?"

"Unlikely."

We sat down at a table, and I laid the board between us, preparing myself for another tally mark in a long streak of backgammon losses.

Grandpa's mouth pulled into a smile, accentuating every wrinkle on his face. My chest constricted at that harsh reminder of just how long I'd been away from Magnolia Ridge. Eighty-five was worlds away from seventy-five, and I hated how much time with him I'd lost. We'd kept in touch, mostly through phone calls and the occasional video where he faced the camera the wrong way, but it didn't compare to actually being here together.

I had plenty to make up for on all fronts.

He laid out the pieces on the board, his fingers sure despite their tremble. "You have a plan for getting your life in order yet?"

He'd asked some variation of that question twice a week for the last month, and I still didn't have any better answer than I'd had the day I first got back in town.

"I'm winging it."

He arched a brow, shaking the dice cup. "That's been part of your problem all along, hasn't it?"

Maybe. I'd never been good at planning ahead. *Act first, think it through later* was more my speed. After high school, my only goal had been to put as much distance between me and Magnolia Ridge as I could. I'd needed to get away from my dad, and the constant reminder I'd royally screwed up in ending things with Harper. Thanks to gifts from my grandpa and more savings than I knew what to do with, I'd followed my thirst for new views and experiences from Stowe to Jackson Hole to Queenstown, New Zealand, never thinking further than what I wanted in the moment. Schooling and certifications were only to get a job—or more likely, a location—that sounded fun. Rock climbing, ski patrol, yoga instructor, none of it came out of a big plan. I wanted to do it, and that was enough motivation for me.

My decision to come back to Magnolia Ridge hadn't been quite so spontaneous. Grandpa had planted the idea a couple of years ago—the moment he'd mentioned Harper Webb worked in the Village, to be exact—but I hadn't seen it as a real possibility. In what universe would she ever want me back? I'd held out up until the summer, when my mentor's life-altering accident flipped my perspective on its head. In what universe shouldn't I try?

My guiding lead in Colorado had built a life around climbing I envied, but one careless wreck had taken his leg, and along with it, his vision for his future. Seeing my hero broken and alone, pushing everyone who cared about him out of his life, had rattled me like a knock to the head. Non-stop travel and adventure hadn't seemed so all-important after that.

"Maybe it's time to sit down and work out a plan. You need to win that woman back, get a job, and put your life together."

I laughed at how easy he made it sound. Just three steps, right?

"I don't think Harper's interested in being won back." Anyway, planning how to get my ex-girlfriend back sounded a little creepy in my book. I'd come home hoping to reconnect with her, along with Grandpa and the rest of my family. But winning her back was about a thousand steps away from reconnecting, considering she'd run from the room when I'd called her my friend. She wasn't exactly giving off warm fuzzy vibes.

The job part probably did require more thought than I'd

given it. Currently, I slept on my sister Georgia's couch. Generous of her, but not ideal. After years of shared apartments and couch-surfing, I wanted my own place. That meant solid work—stringing together part-time jobs only got me so far. But I wasn't really built for longevity in the workplace, as my patchy resume would confirm, and so far, I hadn't found a good fit here. My skill set was better suited to seasonal work in tourist towns than setting down roots in Nowhere in Particular, Texas.

"You could always ask your dad for help finding work. He's got connections. Maybe even something at his firm." He laughed. "A nine-to-five job might not be so bad after years of working crazy hours."

The hours weren't the problem. I bit my tongue as I moved my pieces around the backgammon board, unwilling to spoil the afternoon by telling him Christopher Donnelly would be the last person I asked for help.

My parents' split had been messy, and although my mom made her share of mistakes, they didn't total up to much compared to Dad's. The lies upon lies, the affair, his total lack of shame for my half-brother's arrival three months after his divorce from my mom finalized—yeah, Christopher Donnelly wasn't my favorite person in Magnolia Ridge.

He reached out regularly, eager to share whatever latest shiny thing was going on with his new family. *"Finn's a T-ball champ." "Willa built a Lego set all by herself."* To any outsider, he sounded like an invested dad, but the less forgiving side of me chafed at how he wanted applause for doing all the things he'd missed out on with Georgia and me. With us, he'd been around but not involved, spending more time in the office than at home. Now, he spent his days coaching Little League teams and having tea parties like his life's goal was a *World's #1 Dad* mug.

Throw into the mix the fact he'd never acknowledged his divorce from Mom might have been hard on us. Never apologized for what we went through, or conceded he might have gone about things completely backwards. His arrogant insistence we not only accept but be happy about the new normal added one more layer of hurt and anger to an already complicated situation. He stood in the middle of the chaos he'd created and wanted us all to cheer his good fortune.

"There's always that outdoors store downtown," Grandpa said.

I pushed away thoughts of my dad's self-indulgent choices as another one of my pieces came off the board. One of these days, I'd figure out the strategy to this game. "No openings, I already asked."

He nodded, plotting his next move. "It's a long drive to the nearest ski resort."

He joked, but I'd had the same thought several times these last weeks.

Once again, I'd moved to a place without any clear idea of what I would do for work when I got there. I'd only known I needed to come back and try to reconnect with the people I'd left behind. My mentor's accident had woken me up and made me see I needed more than just a place to live—I needed a home.

But I'd been back over a month and didn't feel any closer to that goal than the day I first left town. The job situation looked bleak, I still held onto mountains of resentment toward my dad, and my ex-girlfriend glared at me as if she'd like to toss me off the nearest cliff.

Grandpa chuckled. "It's not so easy starting your life over, is it?"

I'd started my life over several times. I knew better than most how to pack up my things and hit the road running. Starting over would be no problem—it was starting over *here* I wasn't sure I could do.

harper

"WHICH MOVIE ARE WE WATCHING?" Eliza stood in front of Eden's television, remote in hand, her red and green highlights making her look like a Christmas elf. "The one where she falls in love with a ghost? Or the one where she falls in love with a time-traveling knight? Vote now or forever keep your trap shut."

The four of us voiced our choices at the same time, split straight down the middle.

She rolled her eyes. "I guess I could have called that. Eden and I voted for the hot, sensible guy, and June and Harper voted for the rugged, outdoorsy type."

I ignored her and buttered another slice of thick, homemade bread. We'd opted to stay in for girls' night, and we'd each brought something to make a cozy winter meal. June's butternut squash soup, my bread, Eden's banana-ginger muffins, and Eliza's molasses cookies were better than any night out at The Broken Hammer.

Honestly, I might vote we make it a girls' night *in* from now on.

"Sensible and outdoorsy aren't mutually exclusive," June

said. "But you're right, the knight has a certain something…"

"Yeah, yeah, you've got a thing for guys with horses. We know." Eliza made a face at our cousin, who grinned back.

Since June's boyfriend, Ty, owned a horse ranch, it probably did make sense she'd lean toward that in a romance hero. As for me, I would go on ignoring Eliza's hints about *outdoorsy* types.

"Your theory is ridiculous," Eden said from her spot on the couch. She had a pillow in her lap and had picked at a little bit of everything. Her morning sickness had turned into a round-the-clock upset stomach, and I hadn't seen her eat a full meal in weeks. "Booker is nothing like that ghost. If you think he would *ever* go behind my back on some bootleg moonshine operation—"

"Fine. Forget the ghost." Eliza threw her hands in the air and grabbed another cookie. "I really just wanted to get Harper talking about Sam."

I stared her down even as heat crept up my neck. Best part about girls' night? Spending time with my closest friends. Worst part? Getting grilled by them.

June and Eden weren't that bad, but Eliza had no more subtlety than the residents of Fiesta Village. She'd been pushing me in Sam's direction ever since he'd shown up in town, pulling his name into conversations he had no business being included in, and generally making him impossible to avoid. No matter what I said to try to dissuade her, nothing could shake her ridiculous notion he'd come back to Magnolia Ridge for me.

Clearly, she'd watched too many cheesy romance movies. Maybe we should have picked a different activity for the night. Monopoly didn't give anybody starry-eyed notions about reuniting exes.

Not that the girls had willingly played Monopoly with me in years.

"How are things at the Village?"

June asked so gently, I knew we were still talking about Sam.

I hadn't told them much about it, just that he'd started volunteering there. All my inner turmoil over it, I'd kept to myself. Not that I didn't trust them—I had implicit trust in all three of them, and even Eliza would keep any secrets I shared. I just didn't trust myself to talk about Sam without diving back into *feeling* things about Sam, and I would never cross that line with him again. Much better to pretend total indifference to his existence than allow the possibility of any emotional response to his return.

"It's not that big of a deal." An irritation, yes. A big deal? Absolutely not. Seeing my ex through a window for one hour twice a week would be a silly thing to get worked up about. "And anyway, I'm dating someone."

Sort of. Dating-lite. We were taking things slow, like adults. Not everyone rushed head-first into an epic love story after knowing a guy for a few weeks, the way all the other women in this room had done.

We'd met at a PT conference in Round Rock over the summer. After sitting together through several speakers, we'd gone out to dinner, and our relationship had progressed from there.

Although, relationship might be a strong word.

Eden and June shared a look, but Eliza huffed out a breath.

"Yeah, I forgot about Trevor."

"Travis," I corrected.

She jabbed a finger my direction, triumph all over her face. "Exactly my point!"

I splayed a hand. "What point?"

"He might as well be Trevor. We've never met him."

Guilt and a little bit of unease swam around inside me. "He's been really busy."

All three of them shared a look I knew too well. We used to look at each other like that whenever Eliza pretended to get moony over her latest diversionary tactic, made-up feelings over made-up guys so we wouldn't realize she'd boarded up her heart.

"He's been busy for an awfully long time," she said.

"Travis is real." Saying it only sounded even more like I'd made him up.

"We believe that he's real," Eden said, shooting Eliza a glare before our youngest sister could argue. "We just want to be sure you're happy with that whole situation."

"I am."

"Could you say it in a full sentence, please?" Eliza said.

My turn to glare, but I would do it, if only to move the conversation along.

"I'm..." The word sat *right there*, ready for me to say it, just tell them what they wanted to hear and be done with it. Pretend I was happy with Travis, just like I pretended I never thought about Sam at all. But regret wiggled around in my chest like a porcupine, poking and prodding tender spots, and I couldn't do it. "I'm not unhappy."

"But—?" June prompted.

I sighed and sank onto Eden's velvet desk chair. "I'm not happy with him, either."

"Step one," Eliza said, sitting on the floor at my feet. "Get rid of Trevor."

"Travis," I said automatically.

"What's wrong with Travis?" Eden asked.

I hitched a shoulder. "Nothing. Everything. We barely see each other. When we talk, it's kind of...clinical? Like he's only talking to me so he can check it off a to-do list somewhere. I don't feel like he's very invested."

After our first two dates mid-summer, things had slowed

down between us. Phone calls had dropped down to once every week or so, and texts weren't much better. Our third date had been almost two months ago.

Wait, had we really only had three dates in six months? I thought back, but we'd definitely only seen each other in person three times aside from the conference, and I wasn't desperate enough to count a professional meeting as a date.

Three dates in six months wasn't just dating-lite, it sat on the edge of dating-free.

"It doesn't sound very promising," June said softly.

I'd mostly avoided talking about Travis with the girls, but laying it out there now, it crossed from *not promising* into *pathetic.* A made-up boyfriend would have been slightly better than whatever this was. I'd been preoccupied with work, sure, but so much I hadn't even realized my supposed boyfriend was more of an indifferent acquaintance?

"Are *you* invested?" Eden asked.

I didn't have to search my heart all that hard for the answer. I'd kept telling myself I was being sensible about romance and moving at a normal pace, that all the stars and butterflies would make their appearance once Travis and I spent more time together. But we *didn't* spend more time together. And clearly, the time apart hadn't made our hearts grow any fonder.

"I'm not invested, either." Probably should have felt like a weight had lifted, like I'd been freed after accepting something I'd been ignoring for months now. The only thing I really felt was how much time I'd wasted. Kind of fit. "That's one more thing I need to change up."

"What do you mean?" June asked.

They waited wordlessly as I gathered my thoughts. I'd been agonizing over this for so long, you'd think I'd have been a little more prepared to talk about it. "Do you remember our conversation a few weeks ago about our lives being messy?"

"The one where I had a crisis because I was in love with my boyfriend but I was afraid to be in love with him because maybe I was too messy?" Eliza smiled sweetly up at me. "Sure, I remember that one."

The others nodded. We'd each reassured her that we were all messy in our own ways. It'd taken her a few more days, but she'd figured things out for herself and with Dean. They'd become a couple, he'd become a fixture at our family dinners, and now Eliza couldn't shut up about how wonderful her boyfriend was.

But my part in that conversation had stuck with me, a bothersome splinter I couldn't quite forget. My messiness had been my *lack* of mess. My lack of really living. The half-hearted attempt at dating Travis went right along with the pattern I'd fallen into: bland and faded out. Plain white bread with nothing on it.

"I can't stop thinking about that. I realized just how insulated I've become at Fiesta Village. I meant it when I said I don't go anywhere or try new things. My life is kind of...stagnant."

I hated that word, but it still fit.

"How do you mean?" Eden asked.

I kind of loved that she seemed honestly to not know. Me, as soon as I'd seen it, I couldn't *unsee* it. That word had followed me around for weeks now, flashing like neon every time I took the same roads to and from work or cooked the same meal for dinner. Every time I sat down to watch Netflix by myself or crocheted a scarf on a Friday night, the word glowed bright again.

"My patients at Fiesta Village are having more fun than I am. Mrs. Lopez goes to Costa Rica twice a year. Jerry still runs marathons. Edith just learned how to brew beer. Diana's going to Hawai'i for Christmas." I sank my face into my hands. "I'm almost twenty-nine, and my life is more boring than most eighty-year-olds."

Eliza shook my knee. "We can fix that, though!"

I dropped my hands, buoyed a little by her optimism. I'd figured she would poke some fun about me becoming as snoozy as my patients at the retirement center she liked to call *Siesta Village* before she rushed in to help. She usually doled out her love with a big side of affectionate teasing, but maybe I'd underestimated her.

"All you need is a game plan," Eden said.

"Spoken like a true coach's wife," June said beside her.

From Eden's sweet smile, she still got a thrill out of the reminder. Married less than six months and newly pregnant, she could have been the poster child for *Marital Bliss*.

Except for the morning sickness, which sounded like a whole big bag of misery.

Eliza leaped up and clapped her hands. "That's it!" She rummaged around behind me in Eden's desk and sat down again, a notebook and pen in hand. "We'll help you come up with a list of things to do."

"Like a bucket list?" I asked.

"Sure, but not, like, for your whole *life*. Let's say, before your birthday."

I choked on a laugh. "That's less than a month away."

She flashed a cheeky grin. "Then we know you'll work really hard at it."

"But they have to be things *you* want to do." Eden spoke to me, but her eyes were on Eliza like she wanted to put our youngest sister in a time out.

"Step one: kick Trevor to the curb."

"That's a given now." I didn't even bother to correct his name. Trevor, Travis, it didn't really matter if neither of us were actually invested in this pseudo-dating we were playing at.

"Do you have anything else in mind?" June asked.

I hesitated, words stuck in my throat. I'd thought of things I could do to break free of this rut, but actually saying them out loud would add a new pressure to actually *do* them. Especially with Eliza waiting to write them all down.

But it was either this, or continue down my path to becoming the world's saddest thirty-year-old.

"I want to take a yoga class."

"Ooh," she cooed up at me. "Does this have anything to do with—"

I lifted a hand to cut her off. "*No.* I suggest it to my patients all the time lately. It's natural I'd want to give it a try, too."

Anyway, that was how I'd justified it to myself. There *were* benefits to yoga. This had nothing to do with Sam. It was all in the name of self-care.

She clamped down her smirk, scribbling a line on the paper. "Okay. What else?"

"Classes could be good. I want to learn something new." Village residents were always rotating through new activities and interests. They said it kept them young, and I had to agree. Some retreated to familiar routine, but the ones who chose variety and new experiences seemed happiest. I'd been choosing routine for way too long.

"I could teach you to make soap," she offered.

"That's kind of putting her back in her comfort zone, isn't it?" June asked.

Eliza shrugged. "She doesn't know how."

I liked the idea of totally customizing soap bars, but I already had someone willing to make my vanilla-spice soaps for me. The things I wanted to try were in a whole different sphere from arts and crafts.

"I've been thinking about rock climbing."

Eliza's eyes lit up again, but I just shook my head at her.

Yes, Sam had been on my mind lately, but this wasn't about *him*. Not precisely. From all I'd heard, he'd changed jobs as often as he'd moved, hopping from one adventure to the next. Mountain climbing to wilderness rescue to swimming in oceans—he'd been out there all this time really *living*, and I'd been...not doing that.

My work achievements gave me a glow, but I wouldn't say I'd been having a lot of actual fun. My daily life sat so far away from adventure, the two weren't even on the same Venn diagram.

"What else should I write down?" she asked. "Maybe you want to learn how to operate a chair lift? Get certified in CPR?"

I ignored her. I needed to try a few new things. If some of those things overlapped with a guy who had done practically everything, well, I couldn't exactly reinvent the wheel.

"I also want to try one of the kickboxing classes at the gym on Third."

Eliza's mouth snapping shut gave me a whirl of satisfaction. For a minute, the three of them just stared at me in silence.

Okay, yeah, maybe it seemed out of character, the unassuming woman in scrubs wanting to learn the proper way to punch. Every day, I passed the studio on my way home from work, driving without thinking, going through the motions of my routine. The people in the classes working up a sweat and kicking the crap out of a punching bag didn't look like they were living on autopilot. I wanted to mix it up a little, too.

"I. Love. It." Eliza's pen scratched over the paper.

Peeking over her shoulder, I saw she'd written *'learn to kick some butt'*. Fair description.

They waited for me to share the next thing, but after those few, I didn't have other big ideas stored away. Little ideas, maybe, things I'd enjoyed once but hadn't thought about since my Doctor of Physical Therapy program and eventual job at Fiesta Village had sucked up all my energy.

"I haven't gone stargazing in a long time," I finally said.

Eliza paused, and I could practically hear her mentally debating whether or not to give me crap about this, too. Back in the Before times, Sam and I used to go stargazing all the time. We'd drive into a field somewhere, pile blankets in the back of his station wagon, and just snuggle up. It was where we'd have our deepest conversations and share our most secret selves. Unsurprisingly, it was also where we got into the most compromising positions.

Just thinking about those nights under the stars could still make me blush, stolen moments I'd never shared with anyone else.

My desire to go again didn't have anything to do with reminiscing about that, though. I'd always loved how peaceful it could be in the dark of nowhere, watching the canopy of stars slide across the sky. I wanted a place to get away from my stresses at work, and lying out under the stars would do it. No rule stated I had to look at stars with a man, and certainly not with Sam.

Luckily, Eliza wrote it down without commentary.

"What else?" June asked.

I thought about how much Sam had to have seen and done in all his travels. So wrong to keep using him as a frame of reference, but hard not to when I had a literal globe-trotter in my midst. Gossip had put him in a dozen cities spanning states and continents—his return only highlighted the fact I'd never left Texas. I'd gone to college here, spent another three years getting my Doctor of Physical Therapy degree, and the last three working at a local retirement community. I couldn't very well plan a trip to Italy in the next few weeks, but even a short trip would be something.

"I need to get out of Magnolia Ridge, at least for a night."

"What about…" Eden started, drawing my attention back to her. "Giving yourself permission to make a mistake?"

"Pot, meet my friend kettle," Eliza muttered as she wrote on the notepad.

"I make mistakes all the time." Exhibit A: talking to or about Sam Donnelly.

"I mean more like going into something that's uncertain, knowing you might not get things right."

One big caveat to hanging out with Eden was the way she saw right through me and had no problem calling me out. She was uncanny that way, and I kind of hated it, but I couldn't argue the point, either. Not convincingly.

Uncertainty and I were not friends. I liked to know what was coming, and how I would handle it. I liked predictability. But that was part of the whole *stagnant* problem, wasn't it? I could predict exactly what was coming, every day of my life: more of the same.

I nudged Eliza with my knee. "Okay, write that down."

"How about conquering a fear?" June suggested.

"That's the whole list," Eliza said without looking up.

"I'm not *afraid* of doing these things. I just haven't done them yet." I sounded too defensive for it to be entirely true.

The implication I'd been cowering in my house afraid of the world irritated me, but I couldn't fully refute it, either. Whatever I'd rather call it—dedication to my work, comfort in familiarity, simply being too busy—a dull thread of fear wove through it anyway. Fear of failure, fear of letting people down, fear of looking foolish—all still real and valid fears, even if they weren't the stuff of horror movies.

"You're not afraid," Eden agreed, picking at a muffin. "You're like I was a year ago. Happily living in a little bubble world. It's not *bad,* but you want better."

"Or like I was," June added, "living in the too-big bubble of Austin, not seeing the ways I wasn't being fulfilled. But you see it now, and you're making changes."

Seemed a rosy view, considering the only change I'd made so far was admitting that I *needed* a change. Still kind of a big deal, though.

"Wow. Everyone's so serious," Eliza said. "I was thinking she'd conquer her fears by riding a motorcycle or something."

She scribbled away, but when she went on writing for too long, I peeked again.

"Naked Twister?" I screeched.

Over on their couch, Eden and June laughed at Eliza's saucy suggestion.

My youngest sister's haughty expression reflected zero remorse. "You said you want to learn some new skills."

"Cross that off."

She drew a line through her improvisation, and wrote *Kiss a stranger*. Hardly an improvement.

"Eliza!"

"Would you rather it said *Kiss an old friend*?"

Of course she would circle back to Sam. "It's not supposed to be *that* kind of a list."

"Fine," she grumbled. "How about *Kiss someone under the mistletoe*?"

My instinct was to tell her no way, but I closed my mouth. Mistletoe would be unavoidable throughout Magnolia Ridge. I could probably cross that one off tomorrow if I walked slowly enough through town and didn't get too choosy. Nobody said the kiss had to mean anything.

"I guess it can stay."

"Anything else?" June asked.

I thought for a minute. "How about...make a new friend under sixty."

Couldn't think of the last time I'd spent quality time with someone other than the three women in this room. Probably had something to do with the whole *not leaving my house except for work* thing.

"Sounds perfect," Eden said.

Eliza handed me the paper with a flourish. "There. Your list of things to do before your birthday at the end of the month."

She'd written *Harper's New-Me List* across the top. I read through the items, excitement mixing with a hint of dread with each addition. "This is a lot to do in a few weeks."

I'd been slipping deeper into the predictability of my routine for the last couple of years—suddenly, I thought I could just shift gears and tackle all of this in twenty-five days? Dread overtook excitement, and my stomach seized up.

"It's ten things." Eliza batted away my concerns. "Anyway, you can always double up on some of them. Combine getting out of Magnolia Ridge with naked Twister."

She gave me a slow wink, and laughter bubbled out of me against my will. Eliza could be a flirty goof, but I loved her.

"I get it, I get it. I'll see what I can do."

Her eyebrows shot up.

"With everything else, I mean."

Her eyebrows fell again. "I swear, I'm the only fun one in this family."

Eden chucked a throw pillow, hitting Eliza's shoulder. "We're all fun. And we're all behind you, Harper, whatever you need."

"Thanks, guys. Now, let's watch that hot ghost fall in love."

I swiveled my chair to have a better view of the TV, but my eyes stayed glued to the list in my lap. Just ten things. I could do this.

If I couldn't, I might as well give up now and move into Fiesta Village myself.

sam

I SPUN a slow circle in Georgia's front room, taking it all in. When I'd left her place this morning, it had looked normal. A little cramped, maybe, but nothing I hadn't lived with before. But now? Red and green everywhere, tinsel flashing all around like miniature paparazzi, with a handmade paper chain strung in gentle waves around the ceiling.

"It looks like Santa exploded in here," I muttered.

Georgia popped out of the kitchen brandishing a spatula. "You take that back, Scrooge McDuck, or no dinner for you."

I raised my hands in surrender. "On second glance, this room is quite tasteful. Not at all the type of thing to make someone's eyeballs bleed."

She looked around, and both of us took in the dazzling, mismatched array of Christmas decor. Elaborately carved candles, a delicate miniature village, vintage Christmas postcards hung on a string. Some items I recognized from our childhood home, but most of it might have been rescued from a thrift store's bargain bin. Knowing Georgia, it probably had. Somehow, she made it work.

"I think it looks good," she said, ever defiant. "You just have no taste."

"I have taste."

She flashed me a *Get real* look and disappeared into the kitchen. Since I'd never lived in any place long enough to bother decorating, I didn't really have a strong defense there. Plain white walls and furniture I found on the curb didn't make for stunning decor.

I followed her into the kitchen, drawn by the spicy scents wafting through the air. Leaning over a bubbling pot, I took a long inhale.

"Curry?"

She nodded and passed the spatula to me. "Give it a stir, please, while I check the bread."

I did as she said, mixing the veggies in the green sauce. White chunks bobbed around with the broccoli and carrots, and an unsettling shiver wormed through my stomach. "Tofu again?"

We'd traded off dinner duties since I'd been crashing with her, and it more or less worked. Except for tofu nights.

Sometime in the last few years, Georgia had become a vegetarian. I couldn't say I wholeheartedly approved. Don't get me wrong, I didn't think eating meat was a necessity due to some physiological or moral requirement. I'd eaten all sorts of foods on my travels, and living the way I did, meat was often out of my budget. But I'd never been a fan of tofu.

"It's good," she chided, flipping a golden-brown flatbread in its pan.

"It's colorless, odorless, tasteless, and has the consistency of a wet sponge. Explain how that's good."

"It's good *for you*," she corrected. "And who is sleeping on whose couch?"

"You're right, I apologize." I gave the curry a sideways look, stirring it again. "I'm sorry, tofu, I was wrong to disparage your rubbery good name. I'm sure, to some people, you're actually edible."

"Worst tofu apology ever." She handed me a square of cork board she used as a trivet. "Let's eat."

We took the meal my sister had kindly made to her table: green curry, white rice, and flatbread cooked to perfection. A delicious sort of Indian-Thai fusion, I shouldn't complain, even if I would leave the tofu cubes untouched on my plate.

She made a face as though she didn't like the taste of the tofu, either.

"Ava wants to know if you're coming to their house Christmas morning."

Ah. So, not the tofu making her react that way, but our stepmother. I'd missed out on the brunt of it, but Ava had taken to her role in the family with gusto. Considering she was only ten years older than Georgia, her enthusiasm for mothering us came across a little overzealous.

"And what else after?" I'd learned Ava never had just one thing in mind.

"What do you think? Family photos for their New Year's cards."

Yeah, should have called that. "Does she have matching outfits for Finn and me?"

I could just imagine her trying to dress us both in little red and green suits and ties. I'd seen their cards through the years —their outfits usually hit the garish end of the holiday attire spectrum.

Georgia rolled her eyes. "She hasn't said, but I wouldn't put matching jammies past her."

"She makes it real hard to avoid them." Since I'd been back, Ava had found excuses for a whole raft of get-togethers, most of which ended with dinner at their upscale house in one of the swankiest neighborhoods in Magnolia Ridge. Mom had sold our old childhood home next to Harper's a few years after the divorce and moved to Houston—meanwhile, Dad had bought Ava a McMansion. "Their perfect family image is a lot to take."

"I know," Georgia conceded. "It's a little tone-deaf sometimes."

A little. Dad had never acknowledged what he did, never sat down and said, *Hey, kids, I know this is tough on you, but...* He just expected us to pretend we were all fine. He wanted all of the benefits of having a new family, and none of the fallout. He'd had plenty of chances to apologize to any of us, but never so much as hinted at one, the coward.

A cold ache worked its way down my ribcage, settling into a hard knot in my stomach. I knew another chicken—I looked him in the mirror every day.

Dammit. If Dad was a coward for never admitting he'd made mistakes in his relationships, what did that make me with Harper? I hadn't apologized to her yet, just carried on pretending things were fine when I knew they couldn't be if I didn't acknowledge how badly I'd ended things between us. I'd figured I would get to the apology after she'd warmed up to me, but how could that ever happen without her knowing how awful I felt for the way I'd treated her? And how did that make *her* feel in the meantime?

The knowledge I hadn't behaved any better than Dad solidified my impulse to mend things with Harper as soon as I could, screw waiting around. If it meant a swift punch to the arm, so be it. Hopefully, she wouldn't aim any lower.

"I'm taking the littles to see Santa downtown in a couple of weeks," Georgia said offhand. "Thought you might want to come."

The *littles* being our half-siblings, Finn and Willa. Eleven and six, they looked a lot like us when we were that age, except they had their mom's straight, jet-black hair instead of my mom's curly blond hair like Georgia and me. I'd barely been a blip in their lives, stopping in town once or twice a year for a few days, but you'd never know it from the way they piled on me whenever I saw them.

Surprisingly, I liked spending time with them, too. Whatever my feelings were on the way my dad had handled himself, none of that was their fault. Anyway, what would that make me if I held a grudge against two little kids?

"Dad and Ava are going Christmas shopping while I take the kids off their hands. You know they'd love to spend the day with you, too."

"I should be able to make it." She knew as well as I did my schedule was wide open. "Maybe we could find something else to do with them, like paintball or go-karts."

Georgia's look was pure unimpressed. "Sure. Paintball or go-karts in the middle of Christmas season. What a great idea."

"You know they'd love it."

"Maybe, but Ava asked me to take them to see Santa."

I could just imagine downtown Magnolia Ridge all lit up and sparkly for Christmas. They used to have Santa set up in Town Square, with real reindeer to look at while you waited your chance to sit on the big guy's lap. All part of the show. Wasn't sure what all had changed in the last ten years, but if the increase in lit-up wreaths and snowmen around town were any indication, it'd only become a bigger production.

"Aren't they a little old for that?"

She set her fork down, glaring at me as if sizing up whether she could still give me a charley horse. I had a lot of experience with this look—I often brought out her scolding scowl, as though she were the older sibling and not the younger.

Of everyone I'd left behind here, I'd kept in touch with Georgia the most. Impossible not to, with her penchant for twenty-four-seven texting and late-night calls about nothing. She'd visited me over the years, spontaneous trips to wherever I'd settled for the moment, reminding me that our family hadn't completely shattered. We still had each other.

Even if we had ongoing debates about major holidays.

"I know you have a whole thing about Christmas being a big con, and I get it. After everything that went down with Mom and Dad, it makes sense." She hitched a shoulder as if unsure of her own words. "I guess. But I don't agree with you."

"I didn't say—"

Her eyes flashed fire. "And I won't let you pass that attitude on to the littles."

"I wasn't going to try to. Sheesh, suddenly you're the Christmas police over here."

"When it comes to you, I am." Her gentle smile contrasted with the anger that had flared up a second ago. "You came away from what we went through believing it's all lies. I prefer to think of it as a time where we can set aside all the bad stuff, if only for a little while."

"That's just it. It's all temporary." That last Christmas together *had* only been for a little while. Mom and Dad had lied to us, put on one last big display of family togetherness, only to pull the rug out from underneath us a few months later. I didn't get how Georgia could come through that thinking any of the empty spectacle a good thing.

"Temporary doesn't make it bad. Look at your life." She picked up her fork, smirking as if she'd won a conversational point somewhere.

"Ouch. Say what you really feel, why don't you?"

"What's the longest you've ever lived in one place?"

I stilled, disliking where this was headed already. Using my life as an example could never be good. "Two years. In Durango."

"And you enjoyed yourself there?"

I had to smile just thinking about my time in Colorado. Two years working for Vaughn Mountain Views, moving up from a virtually unpaid gofer to a full-time assistant tour guide. The Vaughn brothers had taken me in, shown me the literal ropes, and shared what they knew about the adventure tour industry and mountain guiding. Those months exploring the Rockies were unmatched in my travels. Unmatched in my *life*.

"You know I did." I couldn't count the times I'd called her needing to share my exhilaration over my most recent achievement. The heights, the views, the pure adrenaline—she'd listened to me rave about it all.

"But you left to come here."

My adrenaline-fueled nostalgia slipped away as regret wrapped tight around those memories. Not for leaving, exactly, but I couldn't deny missing what I'd left behind. I'd created a stability there I'd never had anywhere else. My work life and even my home life had settled into something almost *normal*. If it hadn't been for Ian Vaughn's accident, I might have gone on working there indefinitely. I would have tried for my mountain guide certification and moved up to lead runs. But after seeing what he went through, I'd come back to Magnolia Ridge looking for a different sort of stability altogether. One I'd never built before, and wasn't sure yet could truly last if I tried.

I wanted a home. A place where I belonged. Partnership. Family.

Just a small ask.

I'd always thought those things would come along in their own time, something for my thirties, maybe. But seeing Ian wiped out after one accident, I'd realized I couldn't count on somedays and maybes. I only had right now.

"All I'm saying is, just because Durango didn't last forever, doesn't mean it was all a scam, right?"

I let my thoughts about Colorado go. Looking back wondering if I'd made the right decision wasn't me. Forward was the only direction you could ever go, anyway.

"This is a terrible analogy."

She made a face. "Yeah, I hear it. Still. My point stands that something being temporary doesn't automatically make it bad. You of all people should know that."

No, temporary wasn't bad. I'd lived the proof out several times, just as she'd said. But I'd come home to try to build something permanent. And if I wanted to do that, I knew where I had to start.

Time to stop being a chicken.

harper

I WALKED down Center Street shivering slightly in the evening breeze as Eliza ranted beside me.

"This is a baby step," she said. "We should be mixing it up with all the sweaty MMA guys, not taking *gentle yoga* like a couple of old ladies. No offense to your old ladies at Siesta Village."

Her ongoing joke about Fiesta Village's name barely elicited an eye roll now.

After movies last night, Eliza had pushed me to start my New-Me list as soon as possible. Even Eden and June had agreed I should take action rather than marinate any longer in my stagnation stew. I'd eventually agreed, but yes, I'd chosen a baby step. I wasn't Eliza—I couldn't just leap right in and mix it up with the sweaty MMA guys on day one.

"I never said you had to come."

"It was implied," she said.

We walked through Lotus Flower's doors, and she shot me a dirty look. Her old lady assessment had been pretty spot-on. Most of the people in the lobby putting their shoes and purses in the cubbies were women a couple of decades older than us.

They could have been our mom and her girl gang out for an evening of yoga and wine.

So. I probably wouldn't make my under-sixty friend here, then.

We filled out the free trial paperwork with the receptionist at the front desk, Eliza scolding me under her breath the whole time.

"It's because you chose the *gentle* option. I bet *hard yoga* would have a totally different demographic."

"Easing in is smarter than going straight for the advanced classes," I whispered back.

I'd seen more than enough clients with pulled muscles from diving right into activities they were unprepared for, so no way would I risk doing the same thing. I liked my joints, thank you very much.

I stopped cold. Wait—had I just complained about my joints like my eighty-year-old clients? One more indication this New-Me list was the right choice. Although, maybe the *gentle* part hadn't been. Really, I should do the kickboxing class next, just to remind myself that although my patients were geriatric, *I* wasn't.

We trailed the other women into one of the studio rooms, where more students were laying out mats and gathering up straps and blocks. Everyone seemed to know what they were doing, and I followed along, trying not to look like a total novice. Waiting my turn to pick a strap from a bin, Eliza nudged me hard in the ribs.

"Oh, wow," she said, sounding like we'd just sat down to watch her favorite Chris Hemsworth movie. "This is going to be awesome."

She nudged me again and again until I shifted out of reach of her elbow.

"What?" I hissed.

She stared at the front of the room, and I slowly swiveled my head, realizing too late just who I would see leading the class. Of course. Sam stood in front of a bank of mirrors, grinning at me as if he'd been handed a million dollars.

My stomach turned like sour milk as heat washed up my neck and over my cheeks. "No. No, no."

Oh, Lord, I had not considered this. Why hadn't I *considered* this? Of course he had to have a job somewhere. Why wouldn't it be related to what I already knew he did? I couldn't have been less prepared to run into him, in my skin-tight top and leggings, my hair in a severe bun, and my face already washed clean of makeup. Not my best look.

Not that it mattered—I didn't care what he thought of me. Still, would have been nice to look decent when confronted with his gorgeousness.

Gorgeousness I needed to ignore.

He sauntered over, satisfaction spelled out all over his toothy grin. "Welcome to Gentle Yoga."

His eyes stayed stuck on me, and, like it always did when I stood this close to him, my breath sort of faded out. *Just a physical response*, I reminded myself. This had nothing to do with Sam personally—it was just being in the immediate presence of an overly-attractive man.

One I used to know embarrassingly, intimately well.

"I didn't know you taught yoga," I blurted as if my mouth weren't connected to my brain.

"I teach yoga twice a week at Fiesta Village. I'm surprised you hadn't noticed." He grinned even wider.

I pursed my lips, willing my cheeks not to flare bright red. He would poke fun at me when I was already off-balance. "I meant here."

"Side gig." His eyes drifted next to me, and his smile lost its teasing. "Eliza, it's great to see you again."

"It's really good to see you, too." She grinned up at him, her cheeks practically bursting with joy at this awkward turn of events.

See, if I'd come alone, I could have pretended I'd forgotten something in my car and just got the heck out of there. But with Eliza? No such luck.

"I hope you have a good time tonight."

He winked at me, then turned and went back to the front of the room to greet the last stragglers walking in.

My heart raced liked crazy, my stomach churning at the prospect of the next forty-five minutes in close proximity to Sam. I didn't like the idea of doing new things in front of strangers in the first place, but doing new things in front of *him*? Gentle yoga wouldn't be relaxing at all.

I followed Eliza to a couple of spots way too close to the instructor for my liking. I hoped she'd give it a rest with the saucy looks she kept shooting me, but understated had never been her style. Every time I glanced up, I found her waggling her eyebrows or staring expectantly, as if I should have thrown myself at Sam's feet by now.

"Stop," I hissed.

Bad enough just being here, but with my baby sister in tow, I didn't even have a chance to get my tangled emotions in order.

Taking the cue from the others in the room, we laid out our mats and sat cross-legged, listening to the soothing music playing overhead. Everyone else had their eyes closed or were doing gentle neck and shoulder rolls, getting ready to relax into the session. Meanwhile, all my muscles had gone tight like rubber bands ready to snap.

"Weird coincidence, right?" Eliza whispered.

I stared straight ahead, refusing to take the bait. I wasn't sure how tonight could be any more embarrassing, but putting my sister in a headlock would probably qualify.

Eventually, Sam returned to the front of the room to start the class. He led us through easy stretches wading in, and though I'd feared some sort of smug awkwardness, he took his job as seriously here as he did at Fiesta Village. He spoke in low, soothing tones, encouraging us into each pose. After a while, my anxiety over the situation unwound until I almost relaxed.

Not quite, though. As the class went on, he wandered among the students, lightly offering suggestions and helping people shift deeper into their poses. Keenly aware of everywhere he moved in the room, my heart thumped faster the nearer he got like some kind of ex-boyfriend sonar. At one point, he touched my shoulder blades to bring my arms back into a stronger Warrior pose, and I nearly lost my balance. My attention zeroed in on the tiny spot he'd touched, my skin alight with electricity that pulsed outward, as if his fingertips had started a chain reaction inside me at a molecular level.

I drew in deep breaths, trying to look as calm and unflustered as I could while a nuclear bomb went off beneath my skin. If I turned my head, we'd be eye to eye. I'd face those pale green eyes, see the way his too-long hair fell over his forehead, scan his biceps bulging below his shirt sleeve. Absolutely none of which was okay. Staring at the wall in front of me, I counted down the seconds until he turned his attention elsewhere.

After a while, he walked away to assist someone else, and my breathing came easier again. So ridiculous. I should have been past all this by now, shouldn't I? I'd had eleven years to get completely and totally over Sam Donnelly, and yet somehow, I was right back to responding to him the way I had at seventeen.

I hated it.

Even if a tiny, unrepentant part of me loved it.

By the time the class ended, I'd boomeranged between high anxiety to near-peacefulness and back to anxiety again. Eliza and I followed the rest of the group, wiping down our mats and stowing the gear we'd used. I turned to whisper that I wanted to get out of there as fast as possible, but she'd disappeared.

When I found her, my heart slid through a trapdoor in my chest to the deepest levels of mortification. She stood with Sam at the front of the room, grinning wildly. Of course she'd had to stop to talk to him, the little chatterbox. I couldn't just walk away—I'd driven us here, and leaving her would be an awfully petty response to her chatting up my ex. But I couldn't very well go join in their conversation, either. Not when my stupid shoulder blades still burned as though his innocent touch had marked me.

"How are you adjusting to Magnolia Ridge after traveling the world?" she asked. "Pretty big change, right?"

"It's not so bad. And I wouldn't say I traveled *the world*."

"You left the country, though."

He nodded, and she gestured as if to say, *See?*

"So why come back? I mean, I love Magnolia Ridge, but it's not very exciting."

Annoyance squirmed around inside me, making me antsy for her to wrap up this conversation. No, Magnolia Ridge wasn't bursting with tourist attractions and wild nightlife, but she didn't need to go around pointing it out, either.

Sam glanced at me for the barest second before turning his attention back to her. "I've missed the people here."

A tingly something started up in my chest, but I did my best to ignore it, focusing instead on Eliza's gigantic, satisfied smile. It probably wouldn't really matter what he said or did, she'd find a way to link it to me in the end.

"You picked the best time to come back. You'll have to check out the Christmas market downtown on Saturday nights. It's a great time. I've got a booth there selling my soaps, FYI."

His ready enthusiasm faded a touch, like dialing down the sun. "Not really my thing."

Undeterred, she plowed on. "You don't have to be into arts and crafts to enjoy the market. There's all kinds of great food, and the Christmas tree will be lit up and everything. It's a must-see."

"I'm not really a Christmas guy."

His casual response rocketed around in my brain, searching for something to slow it down and make sense.

"Since when are you not a Christmas guy?"

Sam and Eliza turned to me before I realized I'd said that out loud. Apparently, mindless blurting was my thing around him tonight.

He didn't look all that concerned about my shocked reaction. "It's arguably the worst holiday."

I worked my mouth but couldn't find the words. The worst holiday? Who was this man?

"Sure, I can see what you wouldn't like about it, what with all the cheer, goodwill, and the cozy times." I didn't even know what I was saying. Sam didn't like Christmas? When had that happened?

His grin warmed me up better than standing in front of an open fire. I wanted to stick my hands out and toast them in his glow.

"I am intrigued by the cozy times."

Ugh. His cockiness doused that fire with a bucket of ice water. "Never mind. Come on, Eliza, I need to get going. Mrs. Palmer has an eight a.m. appointment tomorrow."

She looked confused. "On Sunday?"

"She decided she'd rather do PT before church." I shook my head. My work schedule wasn't really the point of any of this. "We should go."

"Okay." She turned back to Sam. "Thanks for the class, Sam. I'm sure we'll *both* be back."

It took superhuman strength not to roll my eyes at her obviousness.

"No problem, I'm glad you were here." He glanced at me, looking almost as satisfied with the night as Eliza did. "*Both* of you."

"Yeah, thank you." So eloquent, look at me go. I gave a silly little wave and made for the door.

In the lobby, I grabbed my things and slipped on my shoes without bothering to tie the laces. Eliza seemed tempted to hang out a little longer, but I encouraged her through the door with some light shoving. Just before it closed, I made the mistake of looking over my shoulder.

Sam stood in the lobby, a small smile playing along his mouth. He raised a hand in farewell, and I could only gulp down a cocktail of embarrassment and reluctant longing as I darted out into the night.

sam

I SHOWED up at Fiesta Village bright and early Sunday morning hoping to catch Harper after her appointment to finally give her the apology she'd deserved for the last eleven years. With no confidence she'd ever show up to my gentle yoga class again, ambushing her here seemed my best bet. Unfortunately, my Swiss cheese brain forgot my dad sometimes took Grandpa to his house for breakfast on the weekend, and I ran into them as soon as I walked through the doors.

"Sam!" Grandpa said when he saw me. "Are you angling for some waffles, too?"

"Sam probably doesn't eat anything as unhealthy as waffles," Dad said with a laugh. "Too much butter and sugar, right?"

For some reason, he'd conflated my high activity level—and probably my side hustle as a yoga instructor—with being a health food fanatic. Didn't matter how many times I contradicted him or how many fattening foods he'd witnessed me eat, he still brought it up, the joke that wouldn't die.

"Waffles sound terrific, but I already had breakfast." Eggs

and cold cereal, for the record, but Dad would probably find a way to turn that into a well-balanced meal.

"It's awfully early for you to pop over here just to lose at backgammon," Grandpa said.

"I'm not here for that, either. I was—" Yeah, no, I would not be finishing that sentence in front of either of them. I preferred to keep Dad blissfully ignorant of my intentions with Harper, although Grandpa guessed plenty whether I admitted it or not.

Right on cue, his eyes lit up as though eager for me to confess my true reason for dropping by Fiesta Village on a Sunday morning.

Just here to fall on my knees begging for forgiveness from my ex-girlfriend like you've been pushing me to do for the last several weeks. Didn't really roll off the tongue.

"I need to check on something in the activities room," I said instead. A passable lie. Dad didn't have much notion what I did here anyway, even if Grandpa saw right through me to the street beyond.

"Sounds urgent," he said, a gloating smile tugging at his mouth.

Glancing toward the closed PT room door, I nodded. "Very much so."

"I'm glad we caught you," Dad said, ignoring my make-believe emergency. He wore a casual long-sleeve shirt and jeans, but from the change in his tone, he might as well have been leading a business meeting in a suit. "From all your grandpa's told me, you still don't have a real job yet."

I loved my grandpa, but he could gossip right along with the best of them. It wasn't malicious—he just didn't have enough entertainment to fill his days, and other people's lives proved a ready source. Mine, most of all.

He could have led with anything else. One of my successful climbs, the stranded hikers I'd helped rescue, even my impressive skills operating a tow rope line would have been something. But no. He'd gone with current employment.

"I'm working at Lotus Flower." Which Dad knew, for all the little verbal jabs he'd made about it.

"Full time?"

No point in lying—then he'd just want to know why I hadn't moved into my own apartment yet. I still had some money left over, but I couldn't safely get a place until I had more coming in. "Not right now."

"We have an opportunity for you at Donnelly & Burke."

He said this as though he'd just saved my life, like maybe I should break out into applause. I glanced around the main hall looking for whoever he thought he was impressing.

"I can't think anyone in Magnolia Ridge would like me in control of their finances."

Not that Dad needed the reminder, but I hadn't even gone to college, and despite his constant droning on about them, I didn't know the first thing about stocks. Pretty sure I would tank everybody's portfolios on my first day.

"You wouldn't be."

He laughed like the idea was absurd, which only irritated me. I hadn't come to him asking for a job; he'd brought this to me.

"One of our admins is moving at the end of the year. Typing, filing, managing databases. All very doable. Might be a good opportunity for you if you're really here to settle down."

My eyes went to Grandpa without thinking, afraid he'd gone and spilled the beans about Harper. The gentle shake of his head confirming he hadn't set me at ease, even if Dad's offer managed the opposite.

Accept a desk job at my dad's firm? Couldn't think of a worse combination. I'd go stir-crazy working in an office every day, typing up notes and looking at databases. Wasn't even one hundred percent sure what databases were, and that right there said it all.

"I don't think I'm your guy."

His expression fell like I'd snuffed out his last dying hope. Didn't make a lot of sense, since I couldn't imagine he actually wanted to work with me, either. That disappointment crystallized, his briefly warm gaze turning hard. Now *this* look I understood. I'd seen it my whole life.

Behind him, Harper walked out of the PT room, headed our way. That was my cue to exit this conversation of fake interest and bad ideas.

"It's been good running into you, but I've got to go. Enjoy your waffles." Catching Harper's eye, I moved to step around Dad, but he grabbed my arm.

"You can't keep running from responsibilities forever, son."

My eagerness to get to Harper blasted apart. He wanted to lecture me about responsibility? The man who abandoned his wife and children to build a new life in a new house one mile over? This guy?

Harper flashed me an almost-smile before escaping through Fiesta Village's front doors. Terrific. Dad had busted out his condescension over my job *and* ruined my plans to apologize. Might as well slash my tires next and be done with it.

Grandpa put a hand on Dad's arm, easing him away. "That's too harsh, Christopher. Sam's had plenty of responsibilities, including keeping people safe on mountainsides. Might not be the same as sorting their financial futures, but just as important. Maybe even more."

Dad didn't seem impressed by Grandpa's defense, but I sure appreciated it. Probably more than I deserved, but it warmed me up all the same.

"Fine, I'll concede that being a mountain guide involved responsibilities." Even saying that much made him squirm.

"Then I'll amend my statement to say it's time he quit running, period. This job would be a good step in that direction."

"I'll take it under advisement." I clapped them both on the shoulder. "Good seeing you, but I've got to go."

I turned and beelined for the door.

Grandpa called out, "What about the activities room?"

"I just remembered it's fine. All good."

Rushing out into the cold, I scanned the lot for any sign of Harper or her little car, but she'd already gone. At least I could be glad she'd finished her work for the day. Probably. Couldn't be sure she wouldn't turn up again later for someone's post-church PT session.

My shoulders sagging, I headed for my station wagon. Dad was right about one thing—time for me to stop running. I might not be looking for a desk job, but I was ready to settle down here for the long-haul, hopefully, eventually, with one particular redhead.

If only she would stop running from me.

harper

MONDAY MORNING, I tried to keep my expression light and neutral, my smile sincere, even as everything inside me wilted like a time-lapse of a flower decaying.

"You want to try on-call physical therapy?" I said to Olivia Cruz, Fiesta Village's Executive Director.

Usually, that meant a physical therapist who covered shifts at multiple sites, accepting appointments as they came up. Pretty sure that wasn't what she had in mind. Olivia had a surplus of enthusiasm for taking care of our residents' needs, but not a whole lot of first-hand knowledge of what bringing a medical practice into the center involved. She'd apparently started out in marketing here, and worked her way up to Director. When she first brought me on, I'd been given freedom to carve out how my practice would work, but in the last year or so, that freedom had been swallowed up by her urge to offer new and unusual services to the Village residents.

No shocker her switch in attitude coincided with a new retirement community opening up just south of town. A bigger facility boasting state-of-the-art technology and on-site medical care of every stripe anyone over fifty-five would want, the competition had directly influenced most of her decisions over the last year.

Olivia smiled as though my clarification meant I was on board with her plan. "It'd be a great perk, don't you think? Being able to say our residents have access to a skilled physical therapist twenty-four-seven?"

I couldn't help the weird way my lip curled up. Hopefully, she read it as an awkward smile and not the horror it truly was. "Twenty-four-seven?"

Did she think one of the residents would feel the urge to do calf raises and bicep curls at three a.m.?

"You wouldn't be working the whole time, obviously. But what a marketing tool. We could have a special phone line just for you, and they could call you with any questions or concerns."

Giving my patients unlimited access to me for questions or concerns wasn't really the draw Olivia seemed to think. "I'm already available to them all week."

"Sure, but this way, they'll know they'll be taken care of even when you're not on site."

Twenty-four-seven access made sense for emergencies or skilled nursing staff, but PT? The residents didn't need me around the clock, and I didn't want to encourage them to think they did.

"I don't think anybody else offers something like that." Hedging, but still true.

"Exactly! This will draw even more residents to Fiesta Village."

And away from the other retirement community. Because of course.

"Your presence here means so much to our residents, Harper. This would remind them how much we really care about their health, and provide reassurance whenever any issues come up. We want what's best for our residents, right?"

Right. We just had slightly different definitions for that.

"Can we talk about it more later? I have an appointment soon." I needed to figure out how to respond to this in some way other than the *Oh, hell no* I wanted to answer. Twenty-four-seven access to a PT was absolutely absurd, and way outside of my original job description. But I wasn't ready to start that long, uncertain conversation right now.

"Of course. I was thinking we could trial it the first of the year. I'll need to arrange phone lines and all of that. We've got time to work out the details. Thanks, Harper!"

She walked out of the PT room, leaving me in a whirl of dread and confusion. My dream job just got a little bit of nightmare fuel laid on it.

It took a few hours to mentally recover from her unusual proposal, but by lunch, I'd mostly come to terms with it. I might not be able to avoid her latest plan for the community, but the end result probably wouldn't be as bad as I feared. A lot of the residents were what I called unwilling patients—they didn't even like PT with me; they wouldn't call me day and night just for the sake of complaining.

Actually, the ones who disliked it the most would probably light up my phone line the most often.

But if I refused? Just because I was their sole PT didn't mean I was irreplaceable.

Trying not to let dread show on my face, I encouraged Arthur to spread his arms to make a T while he held an elastic stretched between his hands. The move helped prevent stooped posture, a common problem among seniors, but it worked best when my clients actually participated. Arthur usually mimed the moves, putting in as little effort as possible, and keeping the elastic too limp to do any good.

A great example of an unwilling patient. He, at least, wouldn't call me at all hours of the day.

"Pull your arms wider until you feel a good stretch." I touched just beneath his collar bones. "You want to feel it here."

"You know, I don't really need the physical therapy," he fussed. "It's all a bunch of bunk."

I smiled sweetly at him, well aware of his views on PT, since he voiced them every time we saw each other. But his doctor had convinced him to do sessions with me twice a month, at least for a little while, so every other Monday morning, he enlightened me on how very worthless he found what I did.

Joy.

"It can help strengthen your muscles."

His bushy gray eyebrows twitched like two huge caterpillars in a gyrating dance. "Who am I, Arnold Schwarzenegger?"

I put on my most encouraging smile. "Maybe one day."

He ignored me, as he often did. Most of my patients at least pretended to appreciate our time together, but a few got through our sessions fighting and grumbling the whole time. Arthur grumbled loudest of all. Thank goodness he'd reached the end of his appointment.

"That's ten." I held my hand out for the elastic, hoping he couldn't see evidence of relief on my face. An overly-enthusiastic goodbye could be as bad as an indifferent hello. "You're good to go until next time."

Dropping the elastic in my hand, he turned to leave without a second glance. Shouldn't have been worried he'd notice anything about my reaction, since he rarely looked at me at all.

"I might not feel like it next time," he muttered.

I followed him to the PT room door, assessing his gait even though he thought it *bunk.* "If you do, I'll be here for you."

He flicked his hand over his shoulder as if I were a particularly troublesome fly he needed to get rid of. I watched him go, wishing he'd let me help him just a little bit more. Only so much I could do for residents who didn't think they needed me, but it still irritated when people flat-out refused. What else was I here for but to help them?

"That man is a *delight*."

I turned to see Sam leaning on the exercise room doorframe, separated from me by less than a foot. I must have been getting used to him, because seeing him so close only gave my heart a tiny flutter. See? The Sam-suppressants were doing their thing.

"He's been to yoga?" I could hardly believe it, considering he called physical therapy 'hocus-pocus.' Surely, yoga would be a step down on Arthur's credibility scale.

"I think his words were, *"I'd rather hit myself over the head with a ball-peen hammer"*."

Now *that* sounded like Arthur.

"He's told me three times how useless yoga is, so yeah, I expect him to wander in for a class any day now. He'll be doing headstands with the best of them."

I started laughing before I caught myself and paused, frozen in place, staring at Sam. Dangerous stuff, being so close to him. Memories of when he used to be mine came rushing back until I could almost touch them. Once, I'd been ready and willing to let him shake up my plans—impromptu dates had been the norm with him. Catching a glimpse of mischief in his eyes had been an adrenaline rush back then. I didn't care what we did or where we went, as long as we were together.

Now, he didn't move, just held eye contact as though waiting for something. Once upon a time, we played our own version of staring contests. We'd see how long we could gaze into each other's eyes before one of us cracked. Sometimes, we'd break into laughter, the seriousness too much for us. Other times, we'd crash together in a kiss.

I could crash into him now. See if he'd really forgotten

everything.

No, Harper. Just no.

I took all my pathetic thoughts, crumpled them into a ball like a fitted sheet, and shoved them into the deepest, darkest corner of my mind.

Clearing my throat, I tried for some composure. Or something composure-adjacent. "I'm on my way out for lunch."

He watched me as if he knew all the thoughts that had been chasing around inside my head. "Me, too."

I nodded, not trusting myself to say anything more. Instead, I crossed the room and grabbed my purse and fleece jacket from my desk, only to find him still standing in the doorway when I returned.

"I'm walking to Homegrown," I said. Was that information? An invitation? I didn't even know.

"That sounds good. Can I walk with you?"

Could he? Part of me wanted to switch on the snark and tell him he could walk right off a pier. But the time to take my anger out on Sam Donnelly had passed eleven years ago. Now, it would just make me sad and bitter, and after spending forty minutes with Arthur, I didn't have much desire to act like him.

"Sure. We can walk together."

His bright smile reappeared. "Great."

He seemed to relax, as though he'd been tensed up, expecting a curt refusal. Guilt twisted through my stomach as I thought over my behavior with him these last few weeks. I hadn't exactly been sunshine and daisies with him so far, had I? If my New-Me list was all about changing for the better, maybe I should put that on there, too. *Let go of animosity.* I'd been carrying that weight way too long.

We walked through the Village's main hall and out the front doors, managing to be seen by only a handful of people. The last thing I needed was for us to become the main feature in

Fiesta Village's gossip mill. They already paired me up with every available man they saw—if they actually thought something was going on, they'd be meeting up with my mom to plan our wedding.

Outside, a chill December wind blew around us until I almost wished I'd worn my big coat. I zipped my fleece to my chin, trying to decide in advance what I would order at Homegrown, and generally pretending Sam wasn't walking right next to me.

"So, what did you think of yoga?" he said, ruining my game.

I thought he'd done an excellent job teaching the class—I'd felt somehow both relaxed and invigorated by the end—and I really wanted to make it a weekly thing, but no way in heck would I tell him any of that.

"So, when did you start hating Christmas?"

He laughed at my random question. "I knew you wouldn't let that go."

"It's kind of hard to forget. *'Christmas is arguably the worst holiday'*? When did you start thinking that?"

"A long time ago." His laughter died off, and his voice came out sounding more serious than I'd heard in ages. "It's not all everybody makes it out to be, you know?"

"Uh, no, I absolutely do not know." I gestured at the shop windows we passed, all decked out in their Christmas finest. Tiny trees, faux snow, and glittery baubles as far as the eye could see. "This is the most magical time of year."

He made a face as if I'd just told him I'd personally seen Santa put toys in my stocking.

"It is! It's like we get a little slice of childhood innocence back every year. There's so much goodness wrapped up in the holiday."

He had the audacity to laugh, which only made me more insistent.

"It's the time of year people are most generous and give to charities—"

"Because they want their tax deduction."

I scowled at him. "It's *beautiful*, with all the trees, the lights, the—"

"Mistletoe," he put in.

"Sure, mistletoe, but there's also wreaths and—"

"No," he said, drawing to a stop on the sidewalk. We stood beneath a gift shop's dark blue awning strung with red and gold tinsel garlands. Looking me in the eye, he pointed straight up. "Mistletoe."

I tilted my head to find a sprig of green with white berries hung from the center of the awning. Right. Mistletoe. Anticipation shivered through my stomach. Licking my lips, I dropped my gaze to his, thinking of my New-Me list.

Kiss someone under the mistletoe.

His mouth quirked, his eyes on mine, waiting.

I could check another item off my list right now. Just lean in, give him a quick peck on the lips, and move on. We were right here. He was obviously willing.

But after? We would kiss under the mistletoe, and then what—pretend that had never happened, either? Throw it on the pile of things we didn't talk about? No way.

I jerked myself out of the mistletoe's gravitational pull and walked on.

Sam chuckled low at my side. "Why'd you change your mind, Harps?"

I ground my teeth together at his continued use of the old nickname I used to love, the one only he ever called me. The one that used to send curls of delight through me every time he whispered it. The one that, even after all this time, sent little shivers up my spine as if testing to see if they'd be welcome to blossom into more.

"Because second chance romance is my least favorite trope."

"All I heard was *romance*."

I shook my head, my eyes glued straight in front of me. "Nothing. Never mind. Forget it."

Forever, please.

We'd almost reached the safety of Homegrown when Sam stopped me.

"Harper."

Just that one word, and everything shifted. No more teasing, flirty persona, just my name spoken with utter reverence. My legs stopped without me thinking to do it, and I faced him again.

"I'm so sorry."

I stilled as those words I'd been waiting eleven years for washed over me. I struggled to catch my breath, waiting to see if his apology would cleanse me, or drown me.

"I broke up with you in the most immature way possible. We'd been best friends for years—" He paused, the seriousness in the cast of his eyebrows and down-turned mouth making him look torn apart. "*More* than best friends, and I ruined everything."

I couldn't seem to form words—I just listened to his confession and begged myself to hold it together. Forced myself not to do something stupid like reach out to him, or, God forbid, cry. I'd cried so much over Sam Donnelly in the years after he went away, I wasn't sure I had any tears left to spare on him. If I did, though, they'd probably come now, when they'd be the most humiliating.

"I should have apologized to you then, and every day after. You deserved better than how I treated you, and I am sorry, Harper. I'm sorry for hurting you, and I'm sorry for being gone for so long without a word."

Even in my confusion over this apology, I recognized that

part wasn't entirely true. He'd called me once, the night after high school graduation. I'd let it go to voicemail, thinking maybe he'd butt-dialed me. When I listened to the message, my heart had cracked open all over again.

"Harper, I need you."

Just that, nothing else. But I'd still been so angry with him, I'd deleted the message and hadn't called him back. By the end of the week, he'd left town. He never tried to get in touch again, confirming my initial suspicions he hadn't needed me all that much.

"I…" The rest wouldn't come. I *what*? I forgive you? I'm sorry, too? I missed you until I thought my withered husk of a heart would never love again? My brain had gone blank, every thought in my head replaced by *I'm so, so sorry* on repeat. Words I'd longed to hear, and now that I had them, wasn't sure what to do with them.

"You don't have to forgive me, you don't even have to say anything. I just wanted you to know."

He'd said I didn't have to say anything back, but he watched me with a sort of cautious hope, as if he expected something, anyway.

"Okay." I had nothing else. Not a single thing.

"I was an idiot at seventeen," he said, his low voice strained, his mischievous eyes gone somber for a change. "I wouldn't make the same mistake at twenty-eight."

My mouth dropped open like a gulping fish, my brain twisting and tangling over that weighty remark. I tried to swallow, but my heart had lodged somewhere in my throat. He couldn't mean what this sounded like. *He couldn't.* He was Heartless Sam, Selfish Sam, Traveling the World Sam—I'd never expected him to be Apologizing Sam. I'd cast him as the bad guy for so long, I didn't know how to deal with him rewriting his role.

And I sure didn't have the mental or emotional capacity right now to deal with the hint he might want me back.

He opened Homegrown's door for me. "Should we get a table or a booth?"

Choosing a table or a booth seemed like a huge decision when I no longer knew which direction was up.

I walked through the door and into the sounds of the other diners on numb legs, my heart still flickering on and off trying to restart itself, my brain on lockdown. Looking around Homegrown as if I might find the answer to all the questions crowding my mind, I spotted June's brother, Jed, sitting alone in a booth. I sighed in relief.

U.S. Army to the rescue.

"I'm having lunch with my cousin." I didn't quite look Sam in the eye. Couldn't.

His gaze moved from me to Jed and back again. I spotted the moment when his carefree persona switched back on, his smile widening without any heart to it, his head ticking down in a nod of acceptance he didn't seem to actually feel.

But if I stood here any longer contemplating Sam's reaction, I risked saying more to him, and right now, I didn't have any clue what I might wind up saying. That sounded like a sure recipe for regret.

Needing time to process, I left his side and clumsily barreled toward my cousin.

"Jed!" Hopefully, it came out more of a greeting and less of a cry for help. "Thanks for meeting me here."

He looked up from his menu to see who'd called his name, clearly not expecting me. I opened my eyes wide, begging him to play along. My little ruse would either soothe my embarrassment or double it, wasn't sure which yet.

Without missing a beat, Jed stood up and threw his arms out. "Harper! You made it!"

He wrapped me in a big hug, the wonderful man, engulfing me in flannel.

"Can I have lunch with you?" I whispered.

He pulled back, scanning over my shoulder. I could tell when he zeroed in on Sam because his whole expression seemed to go to battle stations. The usual friendliness in his eyes hardened as he assessed the situation.

"You want me to get rid of this guy?"

He sounded casual, almost joking, and yet I had every confidence he'd escort Sam outside if I asked him to. More, if it came down to it.

"No, it's fine, but can I please sit with you?"

He waved me into the seat across from him. "I'd be honored."

"You sweet talker." I scooted into the booth, but stopped cold. Jed *was* a sweet talker. I looked on either side of me as if I'd somehow sat on his date. "Oh, crap, you aren't here with someone, are you?"

His easy laugh rang out, his wide mouth showing off his teeth. "Not today."

I clasped my hands in front of me on the table, watching Jed size up Sam. He didn't hide it, either. After twelve years in the Army, he didn't seem to have much concern about taking Sam in a fight. Sam was in great shape, but if worst came to worst, my money would be on my cousin. Six-three, lean muscles beneath his long-sleeve shirt, dark scruff along his jaw—Jed was the epitome of fighting shape, even if now, he mostly used that to wrangle fruit boxes in his family's orchards.

"What's he doing?" I asked softly.

"Watching you."

Oh, everything inside me wanted to turn and catch him at it, but I wouldn't.

That couldn't possibly lead to anything good.

harper

"HE'S GONE."

At Jed's announcement, my shoulders relaxed, and I loosened the death grip I'd had on my paper napkin.

We'd been served our lunches, a surprisingly healthy steak salad for him, and a bacon, lettuce, tomato, and avocado sandwich for me. The side of crispy fries were exactly what I needed to soothe my jagged nerves.

"Are you going to tell me what's going on there?" he asked after a while.

"Nothing's going on," I said on autopilot.

"Uh huh. You sound like June when she told me she wasn't interested in Ty."

I nearly spat out my bite of avocado. "You shut your demon mouth."

He laughed again, setting me more at ease. I'd always found Jed a little intimidating, and not just the learning-ten-ways-to-kill-stuff-in-the-Army part. With messy dark hair and kind hazel eyes, a sharp jaw and devastating smile, Jed was truly beautiful to look at. My cousin, too, so obviously I never thought of him like *that*, but being around a man that good-looking was just off-putting.

Although, probably all the other women in Magnolia Ridge would disagree with me on that.

He wiggled a fry in the air. "Defensiveness is not a denial."

I sighed. "No, it's just…I've already got the T-shirt for that disaster, you know? We were good friends in high school. Best friends."

Sometimes, it still hurt to think of that relationship being gone. Sam had been more than just the boy next door—we'd shared everything together, from first dances to first awkward kisses to first *not* awkward kisses. We'd teased and argued and meant more to each other than anyone else.

And then one day, we just *didn't* anymore.

"We dated senior year. We were serious. But after almost a year together, he dumped me and took another girl to the prom two weeks later."

Honestly…saying it out loud, I felt kind of foolish about the whole thing. Almost thirty years old and still twisted up over a high school boyfriend? Seriously, Harper? Maybe if I'd ever truly dated anyone else in the intervening years, I would have been over it by now.

But nobody else had ever made me feel so free, so comfortable. Nobody else had ever slipped into my heart so easily. After him, it'd seemed smarter not to risk it. I hadn't thought of myself as hung up on him all this time, but I'd sure never quite gotten over him, either.

"That sucks. No reason why?"

"Nope. Just *'I can't do this'* and that was that."

As though, after so many years, he'd just changed his mind. Switched it all off and walked away without a glance back. Like nothing we'd shared meant anything to him. Taking Madison

Morgan to prom right after had been a blow, but the break-up had been the real sucker punch.

"I guess he wasn't ready to be serious, after all." Understatement, but I had no explanation for what he'd done, despite years of considering the possibilities.

Jed, that sweetheart, listened without judgment or advice. One thing about sharing this with the girls, I really didn't want advice on what to do now that Sam was back in town. I had *no idea* what to do, but I didn't want to be told what they thought would be best, either. I liked that Jed could listen without feeling he had to fix everything for me.

"Anyway, that was a long time ago. We've barely seen each other in the years since graduation. He's been traveling all over, and now, he's back for some reason, and volunteering at Fiesta Village."

"Stepping on your toes?"

"You could say that. Some of my patients would rather do downward dog with him than PT exercises with me."

Jed choked on a sip of water before I heard the unintended innuendo for myself.

"That's not what I meant!"

He swallowed with difficulty, but his eyes shone. "Now that would be cause for concern."

"Anyway, it's not important."

"Seemed important."

My still-tangled heart agreed.

I leaned closer, my voice a whisper. "He just apologized for all of that."

"Just now?"

"Yeah." I sat back, toying with my fork. "And I kind of ran away."

He nodded, dipping one of my fries in ketchup before popping it into his mouth. "Bold choice."

His easygoing attitude about the whole thing helped me relax some. Hard to stay wound up about it with Jed remaining firmly unruffled.

"I don't know how to be around him anymore. It's been over ten years. Can we be friends? Does it even matter anymore that we dated? Is it weird that I still care?"

Would not add *Does he actually want me back?* to the list. That question would crack open a Pandora's box I wasn't ready to face.

"You'll figure it out."

I blew out a laugh. "I like your confidence."

He grinned again, and I swear, the woman at the table across from us fanned herself.

"I hear it's one of my better features."

I shook my head at him. "Okay, my pity party's over. Thanks for listening."

"Anytime, Harper. Folks do call me the Love Doctor."

I snort-laughed at that. "I don't even want to know."

He just smiled mysteriously, as if he were made of secrets. Mostly naughty ones.

"What's new with you, Love Doctor?"

He wiped a napkin across his mouth, some of his teasing fading out.

"Not much new. The orchards are put to bed for the winter, so I've got plenty of downtime right now." He shot me an exaggerated nervous look. "Why, what did June say?"

"Not a lot. Just that your dad wants you to take over the farm."

"That little gossip." He grinned again. "That'll probably happen in the next year or so. Pop wants to retire from thinking about worm spray and crop yield. Mostly, he wants to spend time with Marilyn."

June and Jed's mother had passed away a couple of years

ago, and their father had recently started seeing someone new. The scenario had been tough for June at first, but she and Marilyn worked together now, so safe to say she'd made her peace with her father dating again. The times I'd seen them together, my uncle and his new lady love couldn't have looked happier, holding hands and sharing sweet little moments together.

Geez. My sixty-something uncle had a more exciting dating life than I did.

"Looks like we're the last hold-outs in the family," I said, a little unfairly looping Jed into my circle of sadness. "The last singletons of the Evans-Webb clan."

He pressed his palms together in front of his chest, turning his eyes to the ceiling. "Praise the Lord above."

"You really don't mind it? Being alone? Or...whatever?"

Wasn't sure what to call it. Jed hadn't been shy about dating around since he'd been home from the Army, never settling on any one woman long enough to introduce to the family, but he seemed happy that way. Certainly, the man saw no rush to head down the aisle. I didn't know all the details, but I didn't think he'd had a real relationship in the almost three years since he'd been home.

I hadn't, either, but pretty sure we had different feelings on the matter.

"I don't know any other way to be."

He'd tried for carelessness, but something in his eyes told me he felt that loneliness just the same as me.

"Well, we can be happily single loners together." I offered him my fist to bump.

He bumped it, but light danced in his eyes. "The way that guy was watching you just now, I have my doubts about how long you'll stay a single loner."

harper

NOTHING LIKE GETTING STOOD up in a public place to make you feel like a single loner.

I avoided the waitress's eyes as she walked by my table for the fifth time. With each pass, her expression filled with more pity I really didn't want to see. Soon, she would probably get all weepy for the sad Hallmark card commercial turn my evening had taken.

I sipped at my water glass and nibbled from the bread tray she'd brought out when I arrived half an hour ago. Staring at the empty chair across from me, I accepted the same cold, hard truth my waitress had: Travis wasn't coming. Honestly, I would have felt nothing but pure relief if not for the way she kept sad-eyeing me.

I should have just taken Eliza's advice to text him a simple *It's not working out* and leave it at that. But no, I'd had to take the high road and invite him down for a mid-week dinner so I could have this conversation face to face. At first, he'd seemed genuinely excited by the invite, and I'd questioned if we really meant as little to each other as I'd suspected. But his enthusiasm had faded about halfway through the conversation, and I think he just hadn't known how to back out of our plans.

Kind of a snapshot of our short-lived relationship, really.

Picking my bread into tiny pieces, I tried to find an acceptable reason I'd let this nothing relationship carry on for six months. I'd never been giddy over Travis or full of butterflies when I thought about him. I hadn't talked him up with my family or told all of Fiesta Village about my supposed man—I'd kept him almost entirely to myself. Probably a good thing, since it made tonight's mutual dumping that much easier, but that weak interest hardly seemed like a recipe for a love match.

The guy didn't even like snuggling during movies—could we ever have been compatible as a couple?

A loud, emphatic *No* rang in my mind. Still, dating him had been safe enough. No chance I'd fall head over heels and then he'd take off to climb the Matterhorn or something.

Wow. Didn't love what that said about me. Had I really picked my dating partners specifically so they wouldn't be like Sam? The short answer...yes. I had. Even though absolutely none of them had ever done a thing for me, they'd seemed like good choices in the moment. Solid, safe guys who wouldn't get my heart worked up, and definitely wouldn't break it when things fell apart.

Maybe I should try Eliza's old method and just make up boyfriends on the spot.

Resigned to my dinner alone, I looked up to flag my waitress over, but she had already shuffled to my table, her eyes shining with pity.

"Honey, your dinner's on us tonight."

I stared at her. "Pardon?"

She gestured at the empty chair with a half-hearted wave as though not quite wanting to draw attention to it. That didn't stop her from speaking at full volume, though. "I hate to see a nice girl get stood up like this. Your meal's on the house."

My hands clenched around the napkin in my lap, my stomach lurching over being called out. I didn't like the spotlight on me in the best of times, and right now was a *very* bad time. "That's not necessary."

"Oh, it's the least we can do, honey. You've had a rough night. We'll take care of it, whatever you want."

Her generous offer only made my rough night rougher. Couples at two tables nearest mine watched me with unabashed interest, and I caught others sneaking glances my way. A free dinner sounded great in theory, but in practice, the truly generous thing to do would have been to bring me my ravioli and let me pretend I'd intended to eat alone all along.

"I'd really rather you didn't."

"It's no trouble, these things happen sometimes. Such a shame, too, bless your heart."

Oh, she did not just *Bless your heart* me. My date might not have showed, but I wasn't as low as all that. And anyway, *I* was going to dump *him*.

"You know what—"

A blur streaked past my vision, clarifying to reveal Sam sidling past the waitress and dropping into the seat across from me, all eager enthusiasm and dazzling smiles. My breath hitched in my throat, because of course it did. Caught off-guard like this, my heart picked up its pace, giving fluttery little reminders it liked being around him.

My heart had bad, bad judgment.

"Sorry I'm late." He flashed a lightning-fast wink. "I was pulled into a work meeting and didn't have time to text you to let you know I was running behind."

I stared at him a beat as I scrambled for something to say.

What are you doing here? fought with *What work meeting?* so my dumb brain popped out with, "We're doing a meeting?"

The surprised little grin that pulled across his mouth qualified as adorable, but didn't make me feel like any less of a doofus.

He looked up at the waitress with nothing but politeness, as though ignorant of her scowl over his late arrival. "Hi. Could you give us a minute, please?"

She raised her eyebrows but wandered away as asked. The little audience I'd collected during the pity meal offer went back to their own conversations, leaving me and my unexpected companion to ourselves.

He leaned closer across the table. "You looked like you were thinking about burning this place down if she didn't stop offering you free food."

I leaned closer, too, dropping my voice to a hiss. "What are you doing here?"

He raised a finger. "I believe the proper phrasing is, *What are you doing a meeting here?*"

Annoyance tried to kick into gear, but a laugh bubbled out of me instead. Much better than feeling sorry for myself because I apparently didn't even rate an in-person break up from Travis.

"If you really don't want me to stay, you can always fake break up with me. I'll walk away crying and really sell it. You would look pretty badass if you did, I admit." A hint of fear shone in his eyes, his expression just slightly apologetic. "Unless someone is going to turn up, after all, and I have to walk away looking like the fool that I am."

My phone pinged in my purse, and I raised a finger indicating he should wait as I pulled it out, checking the notification. Speak of the no-show devil himself.

Travis: I think we both know this isn't working out.
Good luck in all you do. Best

Best? Who signed off a break up text with *Best*? Best stood out as a disingenuous closer in any context, but this crowned a whole new level of insincerity. I slipped my phone back into my purse and shoved it under the table by my feet.

Best. Right. Whatever.

"Yeah, he's definitely not coming."

"Sorry about that."

I waved away his consolation. "Don't be. I think he knew I was going to end things with him if he showed up. I guess he saved us both the hassle."

Would have been nicer if he'd made that decision sometime before I wound up looking like a sad, lonely woman in the middle of Bella Italia, but at least it was done now. Mark it off my New-Me List.

Sam's apologetic expression cleared. "You were going to end things?"

I debated the wisdom in telling him anything about Travis, but quickly saw I didn't stand to lose much if I did. I hadn't cared for Travis, and he hadn't cared for me. No sob story there —really, barely even a story.

Our waitress returned, we placed our orders, and she walked away again, shooting daggers at Sam the whole way. I couldn't tell if her unhappiness with him stemmed more from him making me wait, or because he had ruined the perfectly good spectacle of me getting stood up.

"There wasn't much to end," I said once she'd gone. "We weren't serious."

As evidenced by the *Best* text and my *Whatever* response to it.

Sam nodded, a satisfied expression tugging at his mouth. "Good."

Not going to think about what that meant, or the way my stomach dropped a touch, as if preparing to swoop. I still had a ban in effect on that whole thing. Absolutely no swooping over Sam.

I'd had forty-eight hours to process his apology for the way things had ended in high school. I'd turned his words over, examined them from every angle, scoured them for any hint of insincerity or a game, but found nothing. All signs pointed to a legitimately contrite Sam.

And me? I'd found myself willing to forgive. I'd been holding onto those hurts longer than anybody should. Pretty sure most twenty-eight-year-old women weren't still dealing with getting dumped when they were teenagers. Long past time to let it go. I'd been mad at him for eleven years, and it hadn't gotten me anywhere. Maybe putting it in my rearview would help me move forward.

Didn't mean I was ready to get all *swoopy* over him, though.

"What are you doing here, really?"

"Picking up dinner for Georgia and me. That reminds me." He pulled his phone from his pocket and shot off a text. "Just letting her know I'm going to be a little late."

"You don't have to stay if you had plans with your sister."

"Oh, Harps. Nothing beats saving the day for you. I'm staying."

I rolled my eyes. "You did not save the day. You made an uncomfortable situation slightly less uncomfortable."

"Dead-on rescued your night is what I'm hearing."

I laughed so loudly, I startled a woman two tables over. Being with Sam certainly was a good antidote to getting stood up. Or pre-emptively dumped. Whatever you wanted to call it, Sam made the situation much more bearable.

"So," he said, a grin splashed across his face. "What was wrong with Mr. Break-up Text?"

I ran a finger through the condensation on my water glass, mentally picking over my encounters with Travis. Not much stood out one way or the other, positive or negative. "Nothing's wrong with him. He's nice."

Sam looked unimpressed. "Burn on that guy."

"What? Nice is a good thing."

"Nice is the bare minimum. My grandpa's nice, but that doesn't mean you should date him."

"I'm going to tell Glen you said that."

He smiled but leaned back, hands raised. "I'm just saying. Nice is a pretty low dating bar."

Agreed, but I really wasn't in the mood to get into the specifics of my sorry dating history with Sam. I'd dated a little bit in college and grad school, but those relationships hadn't gone much better than the one with Travis. Nice guys who'd seemed like a match on paper, but in person, I'd felt a whole lot of nothing for.

For a long time, I'd thought something must have been wrong with me. Maybe my heart had been permanently damaged, and it couldn't work up more than a mild interest anymore. Maybe I would just have to live with lukewarm romance for the rest of my life. Become the queen of tepid dating.

But judging by the way my heart hurtled around in my chest with Sam sitting across from me, it wasn't so broken, after all. If only I could redirect its frenzy to someone I could trust to actually stick around.

sam

I'D NEVER CRASHED a date before, but for a first-timer, I'd done pretty well.

The waitress wouldn't stop shooting me dirty looks, and I figured I stood a forty percent chance somebody had spat in my food, but aside from that, a successful night.

Harper savored a bite of her pasta. "So glad I didn't burn this place down."

"You would have regretted it the next time you wanted four-cheese ravioli."

We ate our meals, the sounds of the bustling restaurant humming around us. Even if she hadn't told me anything about the guy who hadn't showed tonight, I knew enough. Dude must have been completely ignorant to not know what he had in front of him. She practically glowed. Kicking a guy to the curb looked good on her.

The thought of her dating anybody right now left me a little queasy, but seeing her utter indifference to him? Perfection.

Stumbling upon her here was great, but I needed a way to spend more time with her beyond crossing paths at Fiesta Village or a random restaurant. Wasn't entirely sure yet if she'd welcome a scenario like that. She'd defrosted to me a bit after the long overdue apology, but asking for more still seemed a stretch.

Not that I didn't want to ask for more at every opportunity. Just needed to find the right one.

"How *are* things going work-wise?" she asked.

That question poked a tiny pin in my joy-balloon over my good fortune of running into her.

"I've picked up several yoga sessions at the studio, but it's still just part-time." Would not mention crashing with my sister until absolutely necessary. Shouting about my status as a couch-surfer would kill the buzz of this spur-of-the-moment date.

"Are you looking for something else?"

I set my fork aside, already more stuffed on pasta than I normally let myself get. Still wasn't the health fanatic Dad thought, but this dish held more cheese than I typically ate in a week.

"I'm looking, but it's, ah—" I couldn't stop my sheepish grin. "It's slow going. Finding work here is different than other places I've lived."

She nodded, staring down at her plate, and I had the feeling I'd said the wrong thing. It reminded me of the way she'd looked in the yoga studio when Eliza wanted to talk about traveling the world. Just one more indication of all the time I'd spent away from Magnolia Ridge.

Time I'd spent away from her.

"But I should come up with something here soon." Wasn't sure if I'd laid on my confidence so thick for her or for me. I'd been looking longer than I liked already, and I doubted the holidays would be the ideal time to find a career match. But if I wanted to stay—and I did—I needed to find work.

"You've had a lot of different jobs. Are you looking for anything in particular?"

"I'm not too picky." Using my skills or certifications would be ideal, but as long as a job didn't require following mundane routines or anything to do with databases, I'd be just fine. Pretty sure a desk job would drive me insane within days.

"Okay."

She sounded like I was swinging nothing but strikes, but I couldn't imagine going into detail about my lackluster career plans would impress her any more than my vague answers had done.

"How did you get into yoga?"

I shrugged. "I worked at a lot of resorts, and yoga was always on offer. It seemed like a good way to pick up extra hours here and there. I took the teacher training about four years ago, and I've been doing it part-time ever since."

"Yoga seems pretty low-key for you. You're a lot more..." She studied me, searching for the right word. "High-energy."

"I choose to take that as a compliment." Not that she was wrong. Settling down for yoga always required a mental and physical shift. "A friend of mine first suggested yoga as a meditative practice. A way to find a little peace from my rapid-fire thoughts."

"Does it work?"

"I don't think I'll ever be cured of my high-energy ways, but I like practicing it. Having the chance to teach others is an added bonus."

"Well, you're good at it."

My grin must have made me look especially stupid. "Yeah?"

"The residents would have eaten you alive if you weren't."

"Bonnie and Vivian give me a rough time, if it's any consolation."

"Criticizing is their greatest skill."

We both laughed over that. I liked those two, but man, did they believe in brutal honesty. Everything from my pose choices in any given session to the way I looked in my workout clothes was up for grabs with them. So far, no one had literally grabbed me, but I wouldn't put it past them.

"What's been your favorite job so far?" she asked after another minute.

"No question: working as an adventure guide in Colorado."

Her eyebrows ticked up. "That was fast. I'd expected you to debate a little more than that."

"Nope. I've liked most of my jobs, but that one stands out as the best."

She tilted her head to the side. "Tell me."

Those years at Vaughn Mountain Views were never far from my thoughts, the good and the bad.

"I think it was one part place, one part people. Every day, I found new things to love about those mountains, rivers, and lakes we explored. Views to take your breath away around every corner. And I've never worked with a better, more giving group of people."

"So why did you leave?"

My excitement in recalling those days dimmed as another memory roared back in stark contrast. Seeing Ian Vaughn in that rehabilitation center after his accident, broken and alone. The realization it could just as easily have been me, with no one by my side. The crystal-clear understanding I needed something more in my life, something lasting. For the first time in eleven years, the urge to have a true home again had overpowered me.

Not the conversation for this faux-date, though. It would spoil the dinner I'd salvaged, and I still wasn't quite sure how to put all my feelings over that experience into words. How to explain the gut-punch of having a mirror held up to your life and seeing abject misery? I wanted to share it with her, but not right now.

Instead, I flashed what I thought of as my most charming smile. "I always dreamed of one day teaching yoga to the elderly."

She laughed at my silliness. "A noble dream."

"Not as noble as being a doctor."

As though I needed to point out that yawning gap between us. I'd never given a lot of thought to my haphazard work history—*Obviously*, as Georgia would say—but sitting across from Harper put it in a new, unflattering light. A few certifications here and there, other work I'd learned on the job—all just grains of sand compared to the mountain of her accomplishments. Having done most of my jobs in beautiful locations didn't make them sound any more significant.

"I'm not a physician," she said.

"Sure, downplay it." I gave her a slow, sarcastic nod. "You have a doctorate, though, right? I can legally and technically refer to you as Doctor?"

Her true smile peeked out again, spearing me straight through the ribs.

"This is all true, but I can't diagnose illnesses or anything."

"No, but you can help people improve their day-to-day lives. You help people like my grandpa recover from their injuries. That's pretty big, too."

Her expression brightened, but landed somewhere between pleasure and confusion. "You know about that?"

Grandpa Glen had taken a pretty bad fall in his apartment at the Village last year. No broken bones, thank God, but the resulting injuries and muscle strains had made simple activities like walking or getting dressed painful productions. Sessions with Harper had seen him through his recovery to the other side. Still an eighty-five-year-old man, but able to get around on his own without pain meds—I called that a land-slide win.

"He never stopped singing your praises. He's been talking you up ever since you started working at Fiesta Village."

"Really?"

"Believe me. He was always giving me updates on how you made everybody's day. You're everybody's favorite PT."

"That can't possibly be true. Have you seen how crabby some people can get when they're injured?"

"He never mentioned them, only how thoughtful and encouraging you were. How much all the ladies dote on you, and all the men try to hit on you."

She made a face. "That happened one time. I didn't think Glen even knew about that."

"My grandad's a pretty big gossip. Anyway, after a couple of years of Harper reports, I had to come check it out for myself."

She pursed her lips, doubt written across her face. Probably not the time to tell her just how true that was. Grandpa had peppered stories about her into every conversation, sprinkling bits of Harper trivia around like fairy dust. Even a thousand miles away in Colorado, I'd become not just interested, but invested, needing to hear his next tale about what Harper had said to him in the hallway, or who else raved about how much their resident physical therapist had helped them. My mentor's accident had cemented my decision to come back to Magnolia Ridge, but Grandpa's non-stop sharing about Harper had laid the foundation.

"That's sweet of him."

"He's not the only one. You've got a lot of admirers over there."

She flashed that skeptical look again as if I were talking crazy.

"Hey, you've got an admirer right here." Too much? Maybe. But one hundred percent true.

She made a face and forked up another bite of pasta, thoroughly unimpressed.

"I mean it, Harps. I admire the hell out of you. How many people have the kind of dedication you do? Not just college, but a whole doctorate program? That's huge. And now look at you, going above and beyond every day for patients who don't always appreciate just how much you do for them."

No need to call out Arthur specifically, he of the crabby attitude and dismissive waves, but I'd seen a couple of others with similar responses to her never-ending sweet nature. She could bend over backwards for those folks, and they'd only complain she hadn't gone far enough. Most of the residents seemed to love her, but those few I'd seen who didn't made me want to shake some sense into them.

She fidgeted in her seat like she was about five seconds away from bolting. From me? From the way I'd shoved her amazing qualities in her face? Couldn't say.

"I'm not a saint or something. I just do my job."

I relaxed my posture and leaned in over the table, wanting to grab her hand and comfort her from—well, my overzealous appreciation of her, I guess—but knowing I couldn't do it. Pretty clear she wouldn't let me yet.

"I'm sorry I'm making this weird. I just—" I ran my fingers through my hair, tugging at the curls to try to get my tangled thoughts straight. "Moving around the way I have, working the jobs I have, I've met a lot of people who did exactly and only what they wanted. People who worked as little as possible, just enough to support their climbing or skiing habit. People who would never in their life say they chose to do something based on how much they could give back to others. Good people, most of them, but nowhere near what I'd call selfless.

"You're not like that. You're special, Harper. That's all I'm trying to say."

She seemed to process that, her eyes sharp on me. "Do you include yourself in that description? Someone who does exactly and only what he wants?"

Her question twisted like a knife in my ribs. From breaking up with her the way I did, to abandoning my college plans and taking off after high school graduation, to every single one of my travels, I'd been pretty well focused on what I wanted. What I thought would be the most fun or offer the most opportunities. Looking back now, I had a lot of great stories to tell about a lot of great places, but I wasn't proud of the way I'd lived.

"I have been that guy," I admitted. "But I'm trying to be better."

harper

IF ANYTHING'S MORE awkward than being a seventh wheel, I'd love to hear it.

Creatures of habit, we'd wound up at The Broken Hammer yet again on a Saturday night, at two wooden tables pushed together, couples taking up each of the sections. Except for mine, where I valiantly held up my side of the table by myself. Going it solo. A lone wolf. Just me, myself, and I.

I should mention I'd had a bit to drink already. With Eden pregnant, I'd given up my faithful post as our group's default designated driver and had made short work of a bourbon. It might not sound like much, but for someone who rarely had more than the occasional glass of wine with dinner, the bourbon had quickly loosened me up to have a good time.

Except for the tricky little bit about being surrounded by happy couples.

Conversations about Booker's undefeated high school basketball team and Ty's plans for a gazebo on his acreage whirled around me, but I mostly just listened. Partially because my brain had already gone fuzzy from the bourbon, but I also liked to watch them.

Kind of made me a weirdo, but I did.

Seeing my three closest family members and best friends in love was a trip. They couldn't get enough of each other, and it was adorable to see. When Dean tugged lightly on Eliza's multi-colored braid, looking at her so full of devotion, I died a little inside. Booker had one hand on Eden's knee while he talked, and in a few months, that hand would be on her growing belly. Ty kept his arm around June, their chairs snugged up close and their sides pressed together like he'd never let her go again.

I loved to see it...and it kind of broke my heart at the same time. I know: weirdo.

"That gazebo sounds like a piece of craftsmanship," Dean said to Ty. "I'm planning to put a pre-fab shed on my property, but I think the hardest thing will be pouring the concrete slab."

Eliza grabbed his arm, leaning into his side. "I can't let you do the she-shed thing."

He smiled down at her but turned his attention back to Ty. "We're working out the details."

"A shed would be no problem." Ty took a drink of beer with one hand while his other lightly trailed along June's arm. "You need any help with that, let me know."

"I will, thanks."

"I think the she-shed for your soap business is a great idea," Eden said between sips of ginger ale.

"So do I, but it's the principle of the thing." Eliza shot Eden a look, but her gaze turned moony when it hit Dean again. "It's too much."

"No such thing." He leaned down to place a sweet kiss on the tip of her nose. She gazed back at him like she owned the whole world.

Jealous tentacles squirmed inside me, squeezing and poking until I couldn't sit still. Maybe I'd watched the love-fest a little too long tonight. I grabbed my purse and stood. "I'll be right back."

I beelined for the bar. The Broken Hammer was stuffed to the rafters, but I found a couple of empty barstools and ordered another bourbon, trying to squash down the bitterness caroming around inside me. I was happy for the girls—I was. I delighted in their joy as much as anyone, but seeing all three couples at once could be a lot to take.

Too much, really. Like getting the triple-scoop sundae with all the toppings and extra whipped cream. Sweetness overload.

The bartender slid a small glass of amber liquor my way, and I knocked half of it back in one go.

"That was impressive."

My shoulders sagged even as my heart rate kicked up at the caramel-sweet sound of his voice beside me. *Of course he would be here.* I hadn't been able to escape him lately.

Sam slid onto the barstool next to me, a small smile curving along his lips. I swiveled to face him, taking in everything from his dark blue long-sleeve T-shirt and jeans to his black Converse he'd propped on my stool's footrest. He leaned one elbow on the bar, his body angled toward me, that smile growing wider the longer I looked him over.

"Ugh, don't," I said, fiddling with my bourbon's paper coaster. "I can't take it right now."

He toned down his smile, his eyes shifting past me to the couples I'd left behind. "Sorry. Looks a little awkward over there. When did all this happen?"

"In the last year. Eden met Booker last fall and fell madly in love. They got married this summer. June and Ty reconnected during the lead-up to the wedding, and they fell madly in love. Then Eliza started working with Dean and went from wanting to strangle him to—"

"Let me guess: they fell madly in love."

I had to laugh at the silly expression on his face. I'd missed this, how Sam could take a bad day and turn it around. Just like the other night at Bella Italia, he'd flipped the script on my less-than-stellar evening.

"They did," I agreed. "I'm happy for them. I'm glad they've found love."

His shoulders shook, his laugh seeming to reverberate through me even though we weren't touching.

"Sure sounds like it."

"What?"

He dipped his head in a stern little look. "You said that like they'd caught some terrible disease."

I sighed because he wasn't wrong. I *was* happy for them. But I was also sad for me. And I hated that I would take their happiness and turn it into some kind of statement on my life. I loved my life.

Mostly.

"It's just a lot of change to take in all at once," I said.

"And you don't like change."

I didn't. Not really. Which was why all week, I'd carried my New-Me list around in my purse but hadn't actually tried anything else since the gentle yoga last Saturday. But at least I'd had it on me to read through whenever I wanted to feel even more overwhelmed about my upcoming birthday.

"You like change a lot." Much rather shift the focus onto him than my sad-sack night out on the town.

Sam ordered a beer and turned to me, his smile dialed up again. "Guilty."

"Why are you back here, really?"

He laughed again, and it seemed to loosen something in my chest. I'd always loved that laugh, and it sounded even more wonderful now, all delicious and rumbly. Why did the extra years have to make everything about him so much better?

"You're not on the Magnolia Ridge welcome committee, are you?"

"You could be anywhere right now, but you're here. It's not the Rockies or New Zealand."

His eyes lit up. "Harps, have you been asking about me?"

Ignore the nickname-shivers.

"I live in a small town. I don't have to ask, I'm just told."

"You forgot Hawai'i."

I sipped at my bourbon. "I hadn't heard that one."

He hitched a shoulder as if living in a tropical paradise was nothing to get excited about. "I didn't last long. It's a lot more expensive than I expected. But those were a fun few months on the beach."

I tried to imagine what that might have been like. I loved Magnolia Ridge, but Eliza had been right the other night—not much here to draw in someone like Sam, who seemed to live from one adventure to the next. Not much to keep him here, either. Not when so much more waited *out there.*

I still couldn't figure out why he'd come back. It couldn't have been to volunteer at the retirement community, so what had prompted the big change of heart?

"Was it because of your grandpa?"

His eyebrows lifted at my half-formed question. The bourbon wasn't helping my conversational skills tonight. Probably should have stopped at one.

"I mean, did you come back to spend time with your grandpa?"

He watched me way too closely, but seemed to consider. "He was one reason. He'd been asking for a while. And Georgia pretty much never shut up about me coming home to stay."

Georgia reminded me a lot of Eliza, with her younger sister eager interest in everything Sam and I used to do. She worked at the local bookstore, and I saw her sometimes when I stopped in at Dogeared to pick up the latest rom-com release. We'd talk books, or about whatever latest festival or event was happening downtown. I never asked about Sam, but she'd drop hints about his latest whereabouts or job situation, little tidbits I'd filed away with the rest of the info I'd heard about him over the years.

I hadn't gone there for the gossip, but I didn't mind that she'd handed it out for free.

Anyway, she proved a far more reliable source than the person I'd overheard once at Homegrown claiming Sam had joined the literal circus. Not that I would put anything past him, but contortionist? He'd much more likely be the trapeze artist. Especially with those arms...

No. Snap out of it.

"What were your other reasons for coming back?" Way to beat that horse, Harper. "You've never really said."

His brow furrowed, the tiniest dip pulling in the center. "What, people don't move back to Magnolia Ridge because they want to?"

"Maybe. Probably. I'm just trying to understand why you would—"

Leave. Even my tipsy brain understood the real question I wanted answered. The mystery of his return might make a whole lot more sense if I could just wrap my head around what had taken him away in the first place.

He leaned closer, a subtle shift of his body, a tilt of his head, but I felt it as though he'd pulled his arms around me. His hand brushed against mine still fiddling with the coaster, his fingers lightly grazing my skin. That minuscule touch sent bottle rockets off in my chest, their sparks growing bigger like they needed to take up all the available space in my ribcage.

The noise of the bar crowd seemed to thin, my attention riveted to his eyes. His mouth. His lips.

"I realized that what I'd gained by traveling to new places didn't compare to what I'd left back home."

I stared at him, my half-drunk mind wanting answers to more questions I couldn't ask. Hard-hitting questions like *What?* and *Who?*. But my dad had always told us not to ask questions unless we were sure we could handle the answers.

Typically, that referred to gross technical questions about his large-animal veterinary practice, but the principle still applied.

One side of Sam's mouth curved, and that hint of mirth made me realize just how horrifyingly obvious I was being. Straightening up, I tried to shake myself out of the Sam-induced fog. Probably it was the bourbon messing with my thoughts, making me do ridiculous things like stare at his lips, wondering how they would taste. Wondering if he still kissed the way he used to, or had he gotten even better at that, too.

Nope, I couldn't sit here any longer, my heart roller-coastering around and my body practically sweltering from the sudden blast of heat scorching me.

"I should probably get back to the others."

Right. Because going back to the couple's table would definitely take my mind off of kissing. I could hope.

I searched through my hemp bucket bag, but the ten-dollar bill I'd had at the ready had vanished. Pulling out receipts and slips of paper like a magician with her never-ending scarf trick, I came up empty.

"I've got your drink," Sam said while I emptied my purse on the bar in front of us.

"I can get it." Buying my drink was a tiny step short of a date, and we'd already had one fake-date at Bella Italia. Where he'd also picked up the tab, by the way. We didn't need to slip further down this slippery slope.

"What's this?"

"Hmm?" I looked up from the mayhem of my purse in time to see him slide the New-Me list closer to him. An avalanche of embarrassment crashed through me for every last item Eliza had written down. That list said way too much about my life.

Snatching it out of his hands, I crumpled it in my fist. "It's nothing."

He stilled, his eyes wide like I'd just leapt onto the bar and shimmied around for everyone to see.

Raising his hands, he drew back, giving me as much space as he could. "I didn't mean to cross a line."

I exhaled, coming back to my senses. Okay, yes. My knee-jerk, crazy-lady reaction had been completely out of left field, and probably no less embarrassing than the list itself. Guilt pinched at me for how hard I'd been trying to ice him out since he first arrived back in Magnolia Ridge. He hadn't done anything to deserve my snippy attitude. Even after his apology, my behavior hadn't been the best. What did I want, eleven years of penitence?

Sighing heavily, I slipped the paper back over to him. "It's a list of things to do before my birthday."

He hesitated a second, then flattened the paper out on the bar top. His eyes drifted over it as he read, his face moving from a solemn seriousness to appreciation, finally switching into something I'd describe as impressed. Which didn't make a lot of sense, considering how basic most of the things on the list must have been to him, but I liked looking at his impressed-face.

Probably should *not* look at his impressed-face, given my current penchant for moony stares.

"This is a lot to do before the twenty-sixth."

A weird curl of warmth spun through me that he'd remembered my birthday. A small thing, really, but that didn't stop the little buzz of pleasure.

Birthdays next to Christmas were often ignored in the

tumult, but my family had always gone the other direction, making sure my presents weren't pulling double-duty. Kind of made the holiday that much more special, getting an extra day to bask in the excitement. But it was easily overlooked outside of the family, making the fact he remembered that much sweeter.

"How many of these have you done?"

I grabbed one of the pens I'd pulled from my purse and uncapped it. Sliding the list closer, I crossed out two items: Travis and yoga.

He re-read the things I'd marked, and his expression sobered a little. "What's next?"

I lifted a shoulder, reading back over the items. "I don't know. There's not a lot of time left, anyway. It's not a big deal, it was just an idea."

Days had whittled by, and still, I procrastinated. Couldn't say exactly why. Eliza's comment echoed in my head, but I rejected it outright. I wasn't *afraid* of the list. But maybe I feared just a little bit what it would mean if I tried to do those basic things and failed.

"There are some great things on there. I especially like the naked Twister."

I pulled the list back and stuffed it into my purse, my neck hotter than the surface of the sun. "That was all Eliza, and I crossed it out."

He smiled, undeterred. "Still. If you ever need a partner."

The casual offer warmed me up like a stove set on high. Yes, please. Sam still held his title as the single greatest kisser I'd ever known, and that had been back in high school. Twister with Adult Sam would probably have life-changing effects.

But—no. This couldn't keep happening.

I didn't love the rapport we'd fallen into, where it constantly felt like he was flirting. Where he leaned in and said soft things about missing people in Magnolia Ridge and I got all drunk on him. Well—drunk*er*. Where he made me think he truly wanted me back. This was just Sam's default; he tackled life with a grin and a cheeky remark. Thinking that meant anything more would just wind up biting me in the butt.

"Can we not do this?" I said.

"What?"

"This thing where you flirt and tease and joke around like you're interested? It's just..."

Too hurtful of a reminder of what we used to have. And too tempting for me to slip back into it for however long it would last.

"Can we just be friends? I could really use a friend right now."

His smile faded a touch, his eyes softening. "Sure, Harper. I can be your friend."

I shivered at his use of my full name. Honestly, it didn't matter what he called me, my body responded to it all.

"Great. Good."

"As your friend, I'd like to help you out with your list."

I rolled my eyes. "Not the naked—"

"Not that part. Having new adventures is kind of my area of expertise. Maybe having someone with you would help you tackle them. Like you said, it's not a lot of time." He seemed to consider. "Unless the point is to do it on your own."

Torn, I debated his proposal. Obviously, I didn't have to do the list by myself, as yoga with Eliza had proved. And having a literal adventure guide with me would come in handy. But doing the list with him could get tricky. I'd have to be careful I didn't take his friendship as anything more than just that. As long as I reminded myself that whatever happened, it was all just temporary, I could probably handle it.

Probably.

And...it might be good for me to spend time with Sam again. Maybe I could get past this hang up about him and finally move on. I could finally accept that what we'd had was long gone. That might be the best birthday gift of all: *Get over my ex.*

I didn't like the balance of the scales in this scenario, though. We would be doing things that made me uncomfortable or nervous or just slightly off-center while he would be entirely in his element, doing things he'd probably done dozens of times before.

But...maybe I could change that.

"I have one condition."

He grinned again. "You wouldn't be Harps if you didn't. Name it."

"We have to tackle your list, too."

His dimples shone out, proving him perfectly unfazed. "I don't have a list."

"You will. The one I'm going to give you to make you like Christmas again."

sam

I HEAVED A FULL-BODY SIGH. Should have seen this coming. Harper always had been sharp. Competitive, too. No way would she just accept a scenario that put her at a perceived disadvantage.

"You can't make a person like Christmas. Could I ever make you like pineapple on pizza?"

She grimaced, and we might as well have been at Slice of Delight years ago when I tried to convince her that the tropical fruit was just as worthy a topping as Canadian bacon or, God forbid, spinach.

"Heck no. Fine, you don't have to *like* Christmas, but you need to participate in some of the Christmas traditions around town. You can't just bah-humbug your way through the season."

I groaned, letting the sound drag out. I'd hoped to avoid as much of that nonsense as I could this year. Especially here, where I'd first seen behind the tinsel, so to speak.

"How many traditions are we talking?"

"One for every item we do off my list."

"I try to do a nice thing, and this is my reward? Karma is a lie."

She smiled sweetly in response, and that right there made me decide to agree to her trade. She'd given me so few true smiles like that since I'd been back, I was hungry for them. I would have agreed to pose as Santa himself and sing Christmas carols in town square if only she'd keep on looking at me this way.

"What do you have in mind?"

"I don't know yet. The usual. Baking cookies. Watching a few select Christmas movies. The holiday market downtown. Decorating a tree."

I banged my head on the bar top. I was hosed.

"I mean, it's either that or a haunting by three spirits type thing, and I don't have those kinds of connections."

Smart-aleck Harper had come out to play right when I needed to stay strong. I straightened up and stared her down, narrowing my eyes on her as if I could get her to relent. I'd never had that much sway over her, though, not when she dug in her heels. I would either endure a little Magnolia Ridge Christmasing in exchange for helping her with her adventures, or I'd get nothing.

"Those are my terms."

Oh, that sassy little twitch at the corner of her lips. Yeah, I was definitely hosed.

She couldn't possibly understand just how much I disliked Christmas, or why. Couldn't know she was asking me to do things that just a few years ago actually turned my stomach. But if it meant spending time with her? Being close to her? I could only give one answer.

"Okay, yes. I'll do it."

She did a little fist pump like she used to whenever she beat me at something. We'd played a lot of board games back in the day, and she rarely lost. Her brain was just too good at puzzles and strategy while mine always had about a hundred tabs open so I could barely focus on each move. Ordinarily, I didn't even like board games, but for her? I played.

I'd just wanted to spend time with her. Even as a kid, I'd recognized that being with Harper was a rare privilege. She didn't let many people in, but once she did, you realized she'd given you the key to a kingdom you didn't ever want to leave.

And, like the ultimate fool, I'd abandoned it.

She pulled her list back out of her purse and read over it again. Then she got out her pen and started making additions.

"What are you doing?" I tried to see over her shoulder, but she twisted away from me, blocking my view.

"I'm writing down the conditions."

After a minute, she swiveled back around, and her knee knocked mine. A jolt shot through me at that small contact, my body waking up even though the smarter side of me knew it meant nothing. She adjusted back so we no longer touched, but the damage had been done.

I wanted to touch her again.

"What do you think?" she asked.

I tore my gaze away from her deep brown eyes and focused instead on the paper between us. She'd made additions to one side, scrawled notes about my part of the bargain.

Sam's Christmas list:
Go rock climbing: Decorate a tree.
Learn to kick some butt: Bake cookies.
Stargazing: Holiday market.
Conquer a fear: Ghost romance.

Sounded fair. Kind of.

"Should I ask what a ghost romance is?"

She flashed a haughty smile. "If you want to know, you'll help me conquer a fear."

"Which would be?"

Her happy little smile drooped. "I haven't decided yet. The rest of the list, I can do on my own."

"Harps, that's not real Twister."

She rolled her eyes, but a pink flush swept up her neck toward her cheeks. I'd missed this, too. Making her blush over the smallest things had been my primary motivation for being such a flirt with her.

"I've already established I'm skipping that one."

It was the best one on there. I'd just said I could be her friend, so I probably shouldn't tell her all the things I wanted to say. Like how I'd kiss her anytime, anywhere, no mistletoe required.

"Shame."

Her mouth twitched, all pert and lovely.

"To the list." She held her hand out to shake on our deal.

I clasped her hand like we'd finalized a formal business transaction. Nothing very formal about the way her hand felt in mine, exactly where it should have been all this time. Or the way our eyes held, and the crowded bar might as well have disappeared into nothing. Her lips parted, but she didn't speak. She didn't pull her hand away, either.

For a moment, this was more than just shaking on an agreement to self-improvement, or a bid to spend time with the woman I desperately wanted back in my life. A spark of something ignited between us—faint, maybe, but there. It gave me hope that what we'd had all those years ago hadn't been completely lost.

That would be worth all the Christmas crap this town could throw at me.

I finally released her hand before I could do something

stupid like spill my guts and send her running from The Broken Hammer once and for all. I laid some money on the bar for our drinks and stood from the barstool.

"There's just one thing," I said, close to her ear.

Her throat worked as she swallowed, and she moved her head as though to clear it.

"Oh?"

I pointed at the paper still in front of her. "The 'New-Me list.' You don't need to be a new you. You're perfect just the way you are."

Not over the line. A friend would tell her something like that. Although probably not while fighting the urge to brush a finger across her lower lip to test its fullness.

She drew in a sharp breath as though debating what to say, holding my gaze. The moment went on, and whatever she might have been thinking, she kept to herself.

"You good with a ride here?" I asked. She nodded. "Good. I'll see you on Monday."

I dragged myself away from her, weaving my way through the other bar patrons to the door. Before I stepped out into the night, I looked back at Harper.

She watched me from her seat at the bar, that look of surprise still dancing across her face.

That tiny spark of hope inside me blazed bright.

sam

I COULDN'T ESCAPE the Christmas-themed hellscapes.

They'd given Fiesta Village the holiday treatment the weekend after Thanksgiving, with two huge trees covered in fake snow, and fake presents and tinsel strands scattered throughout the lobby. Tinsel, incidentally, is fake ice. Everything in the place was shiny and fake.

But this? This was something new.

The PT and exercise room had been strung with lights, garlands, and oversized ornaments. Propped in the space between the two room doors stood a four-foot-tall plastic Santa, its bold red and white colors looking as though a jittery child had painted it.

In the far corner of the PT room, Harper leaned up on tiptoes to secure the last section of garland, her height at beautiful advantage as she stretched out. In keeping with her holiday spirit, she wore dark blue scrubs printed with white snowflakes. Not ashamed to say I committed the view to memory. Popping her heels back down, she surveyed her work, an adorable smile on her face.

Adorable but devious. I hadn't seen this side of her in way too long.

"Did you do all this?" I asked.

She startled as she spun, one hand raised to her heart. "Geez, warn a person."

"I could say the same to you. What's with this abomination?" I pointed at the plastic Santa whose wide eyes and open grin could have featured in creepy campfire stories.

"That's just Saint Nick."

"More like Saint Nightmare."

She walked over, that smile back on her face, the one she used to wear when she was about to beat me after slogging through hours playing Risk. The one that said she knew she had the upper hand.

"Don't you like him? I think he's cute."

"You think this is cute? I'm pretty sure he's plotting where to hide my body."

She looked at him fondly and patted the thing on the head. It rang with a dull, hollow sound which really didn't help his image. Less silver bells, more death knell.

"Just part of the magic of Christmas."

"I won't sleep for a week."

"Okay, if you really don't like him, I'll keep him with me."

She picked up the plastic horror show and set it fully inside the PT room. He looked like he was ready to make her next patient run on the treadmill until they had a heart attack. Even if I hadn't had an aversion to Christmas already, that Santa would have made me check under my bed at night.

Tearing my eyes away from the cursed thing, I focused on Harper. "When do we start working on your list?"

"How about tomorrow?"

"I've got a yoga class at three, but after that, I'm open. What's first?"

"A kickboxing class at the MMA gym on Center." She fiddled with the ID badge clipped to the hem of her scrubs shirt. "I've wanted to go since they opened, and I never have. So that's what I'm doing."

A slow smile worked over my face. *Learn to kick some butt.*

"I can see that for you." She'd always had a protective streak to her, and she'd never shied away from a good jab at me when I needed it. "I'm in."

"Great. Do you want to do your thing after?"

My enthusiasm faded a touch. *My thing.* Which meant whatever demonstration of Christmas cheer she had planned. Hopefully, nothing involving her so-called Santa. "We don't have to do it after."

Her mouth tugged to the side, unimpressed. "We're doing your thing after. At my place."

Well. If you insist.

"I have a session in a few minutes, but we should exchange numbers. I can text you the details on the class."

She retreated to her desk and rummaged around in her purse before returning with her phone. We relayed our info, and I tried not to get excited about entering Harper's phone number in my contacts like a teen boy with a crush. Tried —failed.

"Do you want me to pick you up? It might be easier than both of us driving."

Sure, yes, that made sense. I'd offered for the ease of it. Or, another, more likely scenario, I'd offered because I wanted to maximize my time with her, and she probably knew it.

No, she definitely knew it. She pulled her bottom lip into her mouth, looking past me. When her eyes returned to mine, that hesitance peeked out again, like maybe she was rethinking this whole arrangement.

"We can meet there."

"No problem." As though a dealbreaker existed when it came to her. "Text me the info, and I'll meet you there."

Rather than hang around and risk saying something stupid, I went into the exercise room to prepare for my class. Shifting the chairs around to make enough space in the center, I reminded myself not to get too amped up over tomorrow night. Not a date. She'd asked for friendship, and friendship only. So friendship's what I would give her.

But the minute I thought I had half a chance at more with Harper Webb, you better believe I'd take my shot.

A couple of early-bird residents wandered into the exercise room, giving themselves plenty of time to get ready for class. Fifteen minutes early seemed about average here, and Bonnie and Vivian didn't let me down.

A few steps into the room, Vivian made a strangled sound. "Good gracious, what is that?"

I followed where she looked and had to take a step back, too. The creepy plastic Santa had been turned around to peek in the exercise room window, his staring eyes and wide grin looking more like one of Chucky's relatives than Kris Kringle's.

Shaking my head, I stifled a laugh. Maybe this Christmas thing would be fun, after all.

* * *

Tuesday night, I stood in Rumble Room's lobby area waiting for Harper to show. As much as I wanted to support her in her list of adventures, I wasn't convinced this was it. Most of the people milling around were dudes, and even if some of them looked like they'd just clocked out at their desk job, it still amounted to a lot of testosterone. Knowing Harper, she might turn right around and choose something else.

Ignoring the guy across from me flexing his biceps in the

mirror, I frowned to myself. I *didn't* know Harper anymore. Not really. I knew who she'd been years ago, but I had plenty to learn about present-day Harper. She might not be fazed by a room full of sweaty guys.

Doubtful, but in the realm of possibility.

Still, I would take every opportunity this list exchange gave me to get to know her again, Christmas and all.

When she walked through the doors, windswept and pink-cheeked, all eyes turned to her. I'd kept my composure the week before because I liked my job at Lotus Flower and didn't want to lose it for staring at a patron. But here? Off the clock, I would stare until I burned her into my retinas.

Harper's workout gear wasn't provocative, yet everything about it did something for me. From her racerback tank to her green leggings all the way down to her sneakers, the woman made my day.

Her gaze clouded as she took in the room. She paused halfway through the door, and if I had to guess, she was trying to decide whether or not she could leave without being noticed. She had no idea *everyone* had noticed her.

Some things hadn't changed, then.

In high school, she'd been oblivious to just how many guys had crushed on her, including me. We'd been best friends, but I don't think she'd realized just how wound up over her I'd been, or for how long. It took me months to work up the nerve to ask her out, worried I'd ruin our friendship if she said no, and equally scared I'd regret it forever if I didn't try.

Adrenaline shot through me now as if I were about to ask the same question all over again.

"What do you think about dating me?"

To the point, even if my confidence had all been fake.

I stepped forward, drawing her attention to me. Relief crashed over her features, and she broke into a huge smile as she rushed my way. My heart spasmed in my chest that she would find any kind of comfort in being with me. A week ago, she would have run in the other direction.

"This is going to be interesting," she said under her breath.

"You aren't kidding."

"Maybe I should have tried something easier." Her voice came out barely a whisper. "Something less...dangerous."

I wouldn't have called half these guys dangerous-looking, but a few qualified. Lots of tattoos and exposed muscles in the room right now. Two women stood off to one side, but they didn't soften the vibe of the room.

"Hey." I leaned closer, drawing her eyes to mine. "You've got this."

Despite the worry still lighting her eyes, a little smile tugged at the corners of her lips. "I've got this."

Eventually, a muscled-out guy who looked like a tatted-up Superman complete with an unruly curl over his forehead led us onto the gym floor. He introduced himself as Owen, and went through his introductory spiel about gym safety and etiquette. I didn't pay a whole lot of attention, since I'd worked in a gym a few years back. Mostly, I just watched Harper.

She listened to every word he said, cataloguing it all away as though this were a life-or-death situation. Then again, he talked as if it could be. She'd opted for the Mixed Martial Arts kickboxing intro instead of the cardio kickboxing one, and Owen laid everything out as though we would be using these skills to protect ourselves in a bar fight in the near future.

Or possibly to start a bar fight—he sort of left the option open.

We threw punches and kicks in the air for a while, practice rounds to get a feel for the method before we actually hit anything. But the class really got into it when half of us held protective pads for our partners to strike, the room suddenly filled with the noise of thumps and slaps as we went to town. The little smile on Harper's face as she jabbed away at the pad I held made my stupid heart sing. Clearly enjoying herself, she put everything she had into her imaginary fight, and I had to brace myself against the blows.

She hadn't lost her ability to throw a punch, that's for sure.

We switched off every few minutes to make sure we'd all have plenty of opportunity to test out the moves. When it came my turn to punch, I didn't like the idea of putting a whole lot into it. I jabbed a few times at the wide pad she held and worked up a couple of half-hearted roundhouses. We weren't really here for me, anyway.

Her frown sank lower and lower with every strike. "Why are you pulling your punches?"

I dragged a forearm across my face. "I'm not."

"You so are. I hit you ten times harder than this."

"You're a tough woman."

Her scowl deepened. "You're not going to hurt me, Sam."

"I'm not worried about that."

Actually, one hundred percent worried about that. She wasn't fragile, but I wasn't eager to test that theory, either.

"Do this for real," she said, "or I'll add another Christmas activity to your list."

I lifted my hands, safely encased in their open-fingered gloves. Couldn't think of one interaction we'd had where I hadn't surrendered to her. "Good to know you still fight dirty."

She returned my teasing grin, and my stomach dove like I'd missed a step.

"Only when I have to."

Under threat of more Christmas-themed punishments, I put enough into my kicks and punches she didn't question it. After a while, we switched off again, and Harper showed no mercy in pummeling the pads I held, like she had to show me up. Which she fully did, staring down at her target as though she might rip the thing apart.

Owen moved through the students, offering advice on style and form the way I sometimes did during yoga classes. When he reached Harper, he watched her go through her routine longer than seemed totally necessary, following her movements. I held the pad handles a little too tight, watching him watch her.

I didn't like this guy. Not at all.

"You want to punch from here." He moved right up close to her, taking her arm in his hands and touching muscles in her shoulder and back. "Use your whole upper body, not just your biceps."

Harper's eyes tracked the way his fingers moved on her arm. Out of breath, her chest heaved, her exposed skin glistening with sweat. Meanwhile, seeing his hands on her made the blood pound in my veins, my jaw clenched so tight it hurt. He had about five seconds before his little demonstration crossed the line from helpfulness over into obnoxiousness.

I counted in my head. I even gave him full Mississippis, just to be generous.

He didn't move on.

Stepping closer to them, I caught his attention. "She's got it."

He blinked hard, pausing his explanation as he looked from me to Harper. He let go of her, hands raised as though I'd threatened him with my mad uppercut skills.

"Just trying to help," he said.

"Doesn't need it. She's good."

He backed away, hands still up in surrender as if he weren't the completely jacked MMA instructor here. Finally turning away, he left us to go 'help' someone else.

My gaze drifted back to Harper, and some of the jealousy

pulsing through me faded. She looked more confused than anything else, her brows drawn down as if I'd just torn off my shirt and beat my chest like Tarzan.

Nope. I'd just run off an overly-handsy instructor. Pretty much the same thing.

I told myself friends would do that for each other. But you know who else acted that way? Jealous ex-boyfriends.

I knew I had no right to be as worked up about that guy as I was. None. But I couldn't stop the image of his hands on her body from flashing in my mind, or the simmering resentment that went along with it.

I stepped back and got the punch pad in position for her again. "What?"

"What, yourself. What was that?"

I shrugged it off and flashed a grin. Nonchalance could work. "You know what you're doing. He should spend his time helping someone who doesn't."

She still looked perplexed, but she went back to punching and kicking, at least.

When Owen wrapped up the intro course with a bunch of stretches and a sales pitch for the gym's roster of classes, I ushered Harper out of there before he could get ideas about stopping to chat with her. Maybe I was being possessive here, but I'd just managed to get her to start talking to me again—I wouldn't let tattooed Superman make me lose that momentum if I could help it.

Out on the sidewalk, she bounced around, still amped up.

"That was pretty great, right?"

Her eyes shone in the glow of the street lamps, and her grin just about knocked me out.

"You were terrific." Seeing all that fiery enthusiasm and energy had affected me more than I wanted to say. "You think you'll sign up?"

She shifted her head to the side, stretching her shoulder and neck. "If I do, I might do one of the cardio classes. I think the guys took the class way more seriously than I did."

"I don't know, you were pretty into it."

She'd been so focused, she'd apparently missed the instructor's flirting. That guy needed to learn some professionalism.

"I was pretty nervous at first, but it wasn't that bad." Her grin returned, lighting up the night. "It's weird, but I'm even more excited to tackle the next thing on my list now."

"How are you going to top this? Learning to ride a motorcycle?"

"Ha. No. That was Eliza's suggestion for conquering a fear."

"I can teach you to ride a motorcycle if you want, but finding someone to let us borrow theirs will be harder."

She glanced over her shoulder toward the gym. "Oh, Owen has a motorcycle."

I stopped in the middle of the sidewalk, my stomach lurching on the ground somewhere behind us. "How do you know that?"

She turned back to face me, a little furrow between her eyebrows. "How do you not know that? He cruises around town on it every day."

I hadn't put the two together, but now that I did...

"It's great you're on a first-name basis with the motorcycle-riding MMA fighting instructor. Cool, cool, cool."

She laughed as if any of that were funny, and started walking again. "Anyway, I don't really want to ride a motorcycle."

I caught up to her in a few strides. "Then what fear are you going to conquer?"

She shot me a sideways look. "I'll tell you once I figure out where to do it."

"Color me intrigued."

Her little smile turned smug. "I won't give anything away."

"So why haven't you done these things on your list before now? You handled that one easily enough."

Her adrenaline high seemed to drop down a notch. "I've just been really caught up with work."

Made sense, I guess. Harper always had been driven, probably even more so now for her career instead of just grades. Didn't seem like the whole story, though. "They work you pretty hard over there."

I'd meant it as a joke, but her laughter sounded forced.

"It's almost like they need two of me."

"Are you doing more work than you should?"

"No."

Her immediate answer didn't convince me of anything. I stared her down in silent question.

"I don't know, maybe? When I started at the Village, it was a Monday to Friday, eight to five thing. But last summer, Olivia decided I should be available evenings and weekends, too, to better suit the residents' schedules. If nobody wants those times, then it's great, I just don't worry about it, but when people do want those times..."

"Then you wind up doing PT Sunday mornings before church." Her strange hours made a little more sense now, even if I didn't think they were okay.

"Now she thinks being on-call is necessary for PT. She wants to get me a special phone line and everything." She shook her head as though it was ridiculous. "But I'm not working all that much over contract."

Not the best defense I'd ever heard.

"You're allowed time off now and then." I shot her a sideways look, my eyes narrowed. "You are, aren't you?"

"Technically. It's kind of fuzzy."

"Harper, that's not right."

"I'll get the week of Christmas off."

"Is that your only vacation?"

She crossed her arms over her chest, but she might as well have stamped her foot. I liked the glimpse of her sassy side, but not how hard she justified the overtime.

"They don't have another PT to fill in for me yet."

"Yet. How long have they been meaning to get around to that?"

The way her mouth twisted, I knew I wouldn't like the answer.

"They just started offering PT when they hired me on. They're still working out the best way to do it."

"You ever think about changing things up?"

Her laughter this time came out a little too sarcastic. "That would be your solution."

I grumbled at her side, knowing I didn't have much to say in my favor. I'd bounced from job to job since high school—meanwhile, she'd become a *doctor*. My suggestion to try something new probably made me sound like an idiot.

"A little change can be good," I said.

"I think my New-Me—um, my *Life* List is change enough."

I smiled at her correction. Wanting to do a few new things didn't mean she needed to reinvent herself. She just needed a little push. Big difference.

"Are you ready to start your end of the bargain?" she asked when we'd nearly reached her car.

"Nah," I said, teasing her. I stretched my arms out wide and faked a big yawn. "I think I'm going to call it a night."

"Oh, no you don't." She linked her arm in mine, tugging me along the sidewalk, laughing the whole way. "You're going to bake Christmas cookies with me, and you're going to like it."

I chuckled at her insistence, but that seemed to flip the switch, as if she'd realized her mistake. For that one, glorious moment, she'd forgotten about our past, her hurt and anger, and just let herself be happy with me. Second-guessing it, she dropped my arm and stepped back, her smile strained.

"If you really don't want to—"

"I do," I said in a rush. "I was just kidding around."

"Okay." She didn't seem relieved.

If anything, she looked more uncomfortable, like she'd been caught between wanting to be with me, and wanting to be as far away from me as possible.

harper

I CHANGED into jeans and a long-sleeve T-shirt, still riding the kickboxing high. Maybe I hadn't loved the idea of learning the basics in a room filled with guys, but I'd forgotten about them pretty quickly once we got into it, and just kicked the crap out of Sam.

Not *Sam,* exactly. He'd been well-protected. But it had felt good to let loose a little bit that way, even if I'd been totally out of my element. Considering my element had become indistinguishable from a retired person's, I needed to get out of it more often.

I set ingredients for cookie dough on the counter while waiting for Sam. Since neither of us had wanted to risk adding sweat to our cookies, we'd agreed to change clothes before meeting up again here at my place. I tried not to think too hard about how Sam would be in my house soon, just the two of us.

Definitely didn't think about how he'd seemed to get jealous when Owen had helped me straighten out my punches. Because *that* would lead me down rabbit-holes I really couldn't explore right now.

I'd told him I needed a friend, and I'd absolutely meant it.

I'd relied on my sisters and cousin to pad out my social life ever since I'd moved back to town, but with their new relationships and Eden's impending motherhood, that wasn't sustainable. I needed to expand my circle a little more, and he'd volunteered.

The question of just why he'd volunteered went straight into the *Do Not Think About* bin, along with the worry this experiment of spending more time with my ex in order to get over him would send me so far in the opposite direction, there would be no going back.

Our list arrangement wasn't exactly sensible. If I wanted to keep my heart safe from completely losing it over Sam again, helping each other tackle a couple of bucket lists wasn't the right move. But I'd agreed to his scheme, and even added more tasks to our to-do lists. I hadn't been completely sober when we shook on it, but I hadn't been drunk, either.

I'd agreed to spend time with him because I wanted to, plain and simple. Even if I didn't think we could recapture what we'd once had, the prospect of seeing him more often proved too tempting. I tried to tell myself none of that meant anything, that it was all in the name of friendship, but I wasn't drunk tonight, and didn't believe my own lies.

On the counter, my phone buzzed.

Eliza: How's the list going? Only 15 days left!

I hesitated a minute, debating. Saturday night after Sam left The Broken Hammer, Eliza had trotted straight over to bat her eyelashes and ask pointed questions. Still processing the conversation, I'd left most of them unanswered. How to say *I'm going to spend time with my ex in a totally platonic way even though chances are slim my heart will come out unscathed?* She'd let me brush her off with one-word answers and vague replies only because Dean provided an excellent distraction.

But I knew well enough my reprieve from her questions wouldn't last long. She'd have no qualms about showing up to my house to demand answers, and I really didn't want her turning up tonight. The thought of her barging in while Sam was here made me pick up the phone.

Harper: I just did the intro MMA class
Eliza: You went alone? I'm kind of mad. I wanted to try the MMA thing, too

I weighed the cost-benefit analysis of lying, but it didn't lean in my favor. She would only ask more questions if I said I'd gone alone. Honestly, she'd ask more questions no matter what I said. More questions were kind of her whole thing.

Harper: Sam went with me

Two seconds after my text switched to *Read*, her incoming call started up. Steeling myself against whatever she would throw at me, I answered.

"Hi."

She made a sound of disgust. "Don't you *Hi* me. *Sam* went to the class with you? What is going on?"

"Nothing's going on."

The more I said it, the less convinced of it I became. That simple friendship I kept holding onto felt a lot like handfuls of sand. I could clutch at it all I liked, but the tighter I squeezed, the more it slipped away.

Just what it would be replaced with—nope. I'd put all that in the *Do Not Think About* bin.

"Why do you lie to me like this? What have I ever done to you? I mean, besides the years of mooching off of you."

I paused, trying to sort out the best explanation that would satisfy her and not completely mortify me. No explanation here left me with the high ground. Not with the way she would quiz me. "We're trying to be friends again."

"Friends." She sounded like I'd said something horrible.

Now that she'd happily coupled up, she seemed to forget the years she'd spent avoiding dating, too. She hadn't even had a guy friend in all that time, let alone a boyfriend. But suddenly I was the strange one for not diving straight into romance with Sam.

"Yes, friends, Eliza. I'm not getting worked up about this, and I don't want you to, either."

And if I did get worked up about it, that would not be open for public scrutiny.

"Maybe you should get worked up about it. Why do you have to be so sensible about everything all the time? Why can't you just let your hair down and say 'I'm getting back with my ex and I love it'?"

Exactly why I hadn't shared anything about Sam with her. She went from zero to heart eyes in three seconds flat.

"We're not getting back together, Eliza. We're just getting to know each other again."

I didn't know what to call our list-swap arrangement. Trying for friendship sounded like the most straightforward description. Trying for more would just leave me disappointed in the end.

Because there *would* be an end. Sam would take off to explore the world again eventually, just a matter of when.

That little reminder made my heart squeeze until it felt wrung out. For the best, though. I needed to go into this list thing with my eyes wide open and my heart firmly shut. Boarded up and out of business.

"Oh. Sure, yeah. I see. You're getting to know each other. Like Eden and Booker got to know each other."

Gah, why did everything have to go there? "No."

"Like June and Ty got to know each other."

"Eliza."

"Like Dean and I got to know each other."

"Absolutely not."

"Because let me tell you, Dean and I know each other *very* well."

Ugh, gross. "I've heard enough, thanks."

Lights flashed outside as a car pulled behind mine in the driveway. "Listen, I have to go, Sam's—"

I shut my mouth on the rest, but too late. Why, mouth, why?

"Sam's what?" She full-on gasped. "Sam's *there*? Oh, my gosh, I knew it—"

"Goodbye, Eliza."

"Call me after—"

I hung up and put the phone on Do Not Disturb for good measure. She'd probably send me sassy cross-examination texts all night.

Throwing the front door wide before he could knock, I let Sam into my living room.

I'd hoped changing out of workout clothes would make the evening feel less intimate, but he hadn't received the memo. Standing there in dark blue sweatpants and a white long-sleeve T-shirt, he might as well have been ready for bed. His damp, tousled hair made him look more relaxed than ever, and that roguish smile? Devastating.

The soft, floating feeling in my stomach didn't bode well for keeping things buddy-buddy.

He stepped over the threshold, looking around. "Nice place."

June said everybody's home decor style could be summed up in a single word. Mine? Comfort. Everything from my plush green couch draped with bulky knitted throw blankets to the thick black and white check rug had been made to be warm and inviting, like a whispered *Welcome home* every time I walked in the door.

"Cozy in here." He moved farther into the living room and paused. "Whoa. Your collection has expanded."

A bit at odds with my cozy kick, shiny snow globes sat on every flat surface of my house: mantelpiece, coffee table, book case. I'd even had to put a couple on the kitchen counter just to give them someplace to go. Hard to find room for twenty-one snow globes in all shapes and sizes.

Strike that. I only had twenty in my collection.

I'd been collecting them since I was a little girl, and they'd become my favorite part of the season. My Grandma Evans gave me my first one when I was seven, and I'd looked at that glittery dome holding two tiny ice skaters and squealed with delight. Ever since, I'd added another each year—some were gifts, some I'd bought, but all held special meaning.

Sam moved slowly through my space, gently picking up each globe, checking out what scene it held, and giving it a shake until it swirled with fake snow. He'd always found my collection amusing. As a kid, I'd hoarded them, keeping them in my room instead of spreading them throughout the house with the rest of the holiday decor. At first, I'd been afraid Eliza's grabby hands might break one, but later on, I'd just wanted to enjoy them for myself.

"This is prime Middle Child Syndrome stuff right here," he'd said once of my refusal to share my collection.

I let him go through all the snow globes now, both wanting and not wanting him to spot the difference. Maybe he'd forgotten that, too.

"Looks like you're missing one." No accusation in his voice, just a simple statement of fact.

"Yeah, it...broke." I chewed my bottom lip rather than say anything more.

The year we'd dated, he'd contributed to my collection in the most Sam way possible. He used to have this T-shirt with a snowboarding Sasquatch in a Santa hat on it he'd worn so often, it had become thin and insanely soft. We used to joke that Sasquatch Santa was the one true Santa, all others were just cheap imitators.

For Christmas, I'd given him a six-pack of obscure brands of root beer and a beanie hat I'd crocheted. And he'd given me a snow globe...with a snowboarding Sasquatch Santa inside. I'd fallen over laughing when I opened it, but that goofy snow globe had immediately risen to the top of my favorite things ever. When I put the rest of them away that January, I'd kept Sasquatch Santa out to sit on my nightstand. I'd fall asleep at night staring at it, thinking about how much I adored the guy who'd given it to me.

I could still feel that intense ache of longing for someone I already spent hours of each day with, that shivery anticipation that coursed through me whenever I so much as thought his name.

After Sam dumped me, I'd seesawed between sad crying and angry crying. When I heard he took Madison Morgan to the prom just weeks later, I'd switched into a full-bore angry cry. I'd double-wrapped Sasquatch Santa in trash bags and smashed him in the driveway, to much applause from Eliza. It'd been cathartic, in a way. Symbolically, I'd eliminated Sam from my life as surely as he'd eliminated me from his.

Years later, I wished I had that Sasquatch back. Not because I missed Sam, necessarily, but because of just how big a part he'd played in my life before the break-up. I wanted a little piece of those memories back, even if I never saw him again.

Plus, the finicky side of me just wanted my collection

complete again. Googling the snow globe, I'd discovered they'd been discontinued and were now considered actual collector's items. Last I checked, I could get one on eBay for a few hundred dollars.

I didn't want to complete my collection that badly.

"That's unfortunate." He sounded as if he knew *exactly* what had happened to that snow globe.

I bit my lip, feeling weirdly exposed even though I'd admitted nothing. Accidents happened all the time. A hundred different things could have happened to that snow globe. Anyway, talking about it wasn't going to bring Sasquatch Santa back from the dead.

"Are you ready to bake some cookies?"

"If I must."

I led him into the kitchen, but he stopped when he spotted the ingredients I'd laid out. "I thought we would do a store-bought dough type thing."

"That's not real Christmas baking, Samuel."

His eyes lit up at how I'd echoed his teasing. Putting on an apron, I told myself not to make anything of it. My heart shimmied away, not listening.

He slipped on an apron, too, and I gave instructions over his shoulder as he mixed the dry and wet ingredients in separate bowls. I'd chosen a simple sugar cookie recipe so we could frost them and add sprinkles when we were done, to get the full Christmas baking effect. It happened to be the same recipe we'd made together several times back in the Before days, whether we acknowledged it now or not.

"I slap it all in the mixer now, right?"

Offended by the very idea, I was about to scold him, but I caught the twist of his lips. "Only if you want me to practice my MMA moves on you some more."

A smile curled along his mouth as he alternated wet and dry

little by little, the mixer spinning between us. Careful not to splash the wet ingredients or dust the dry everywhere, he demonstrated a meticulous streak I didn't really remember from high school. For as much as he'd grumbled about my list for him, he sure gave the cookies his full attention.

Standing so close to him, I devoured him with my eyes. The stubble on the angle of his jaw. The mark on his earlobe from when he'd gotten one ear pierced at fifteen and immediately regretted it. Curls at the back of his head still wet from his shower. Friends probably wouldn't look at each other quite this intently, but I couldn't look away.

Warmth drifted through me like the last of a fire after it's gone out. Or maybe one that'd just rekindled. With only the whir of the mixer to keep us company, my breath sounded weirdly loud. Too breathy. Too excited.

"We're missing something." I grabbed my phone and thumbed around. Calling up my latest playlist, Kelly Clarkson started singing about waiting for her love underneath the tree. I set it back down, giving us a little more space than I had a moment ago. I needed it.

Sam shot me a dirty look.

"It's part of the Christmas cookie-making experience," I told him.

"It's cheating, is what it is. That's two Christmas things at once."

"It's not like you don't hear Christmas music everywhere you go already. It's kind of unavoidable."

"You bend the rules, I'll bend the rules. It's kind of unavoidable."

Naturally, Eliza's saucy suggestion to combine getting out of town with...kissing under the mistletoe sprang to mind. *Not* going to make that suggestion. Not with the way I was already burning up in here.

Once the ingredients were fully incorporated, I switched off the machine and pulled out the paddle. "We need to chill the dough for half an hour before we can roll out the cookies."

"We have to roll them out, too? When will it end?"

I laughed at his put-upon tone. "I think you'll survive a little Christmas cheer."

Slipping the mixing bowl into my fridge, I wiped my hands and pulled off my apron. "Do you want something to drink while we wait? I could make hot cocoa."

He groaned, but it turned into a laugh at the end. "No mulled cider? Wassail? Wait, let me guess—you're going to offer me figgy pudding next."

He could joke around all he liked, but I *had* committed to showing him some holiday spirit. Why not go all in?

"You know, I think I will make hot cocoa. With marsh-mallows."

"You and Georgia should get together. Tag-team to make sure you're really driving the Christmas magic home."

"Is Georgia tormenting you with cocoa, too?" I poured milk into a pan, set it on the stove, and added cocoa powder, sugar, and chocolate chips.

"Wait, are we talking about your mom's special hot cocoa?" Sam asked, his eyes fixed on the mixture as I whisked it. "On second thought, I would like some, please."

His eyes shone like a little boy begging for a toy. I smiled to myself, tallying his desire for hot cocoa as a small win in my quest to un-Grinch his heart.

"With Georgia, it's not always cocoa," he said, returning to my question. "She works at that little bookstore coffee shop on Second, and she's got about a dozen varieties of themed drinks in the house. Spiced this, pumpkin that. Her house is even more festive than yours."

"Well, we still have to get my tree."

He threw his head back and stared at the ceiling. "Of course we do."

"Georgia's been at the bookstore a long time, hasn't she?" She'd been there as long as I'd been back, but I wasn't sure how much before then. She and Eliza were the same age, so she had to have started working at the shop pretty soon after college.

He straightened, his eyes on the mixture in the pan as I whisked the last of the melting chocolate chips smooth.

"She has. She also freelances as a book cover designer. She never really took her graphic design degree anywhere, but she likes doing those."

"She never mentioned that. What kind of covers does she do?"

He hitched a shoulder. "Cartoony covers? I don't know what to call them, but they look good, and she's doing pretty well with it. I guess they're popular for romances right now."

"Good for her." After watching Eliza struggle to get her soap business going, I hadn't been sure she'd made the right choice in veering straight into entrepreneur mode. It'd seemed reckless and irresponsible, and I'd had to stop myself from lecturing her about a hundred times. But now, I had no doubts she'd found where she was meant to be. Happier and more satisfied with work than she'd ever been, she'd made something entirely hers, and I loved that for her. "I'll have to ask Georgia about them next time I'm in the store. Maybe I've seen some of her covers."

"You read a lot of romances, do you?"

Now his eyes seemed stuck on me, as though the answer to this would actually tell him anything about me. Didn't everybody read romances?

"I read a lot of them, yeah." Wouldn't go so far as to say just how many in any given month, but quite a few. Quite. A. Few.

"All except second chance romances."

His voice held a lilt of amusement, but I couldn't bear to face him just yet. I'd probably already gone all pink and blotchy.

"I found out what that means, by the way."

I made a face as though this information were merely interesting instead of mortifying.

"Is it the concept you're against," he asked, "or the execution?"

Kind of wished Jed would materialize in my kitchen to rescue me from the awkwardness of this conversation the way he had in Homegrown. "They just don't seem very realistic."

I stood by that. Who got back together with their ex? I couldn't think of anybody, and yet readers fell over themselves to see how people who had *already broken up* would get back together, desperate to see what would happen next. I'd never been into them.

I especially wasn't into them now, with Sam staring at me from a foot away, heat prickling over my skin as I waited to see what would happen next.

Nope. Not into them.

"I think I'll have to read a few," he said, his voice strangely deep. "Just to judge for myself."

"Maybe you should." Didn't really care, just wanted to move this conversation on to something else. Literally anything else.

I kept my eyes on my work, taking the cocoa off the stove and adding a splash of vanilla as if nothing could be more important than getting the measurement exactly right. Pouring it into two Santa mugs, I topped them off with mini-marshmallows, and presented Sam his mug.

"Ta da!"

"Wow. I guess there are a few good things about Christmas, after all."

We took our mugs into the living room while we waited for the cookie dough to chill. Sitting at the opposite end of the couch from Sam, I watched as he took his first sip of cocoa. When he did, his eyes half-closed, and he made a sinful sound in the back of his throat.

That hungry sound shivered up my spine, waking up long-dormant nerve endings. I had to stare into my cocoa mug, willing the sensation away. Or at the very least, to not be obvious. If I was shooting for friendship here and not trying for a second chance romance, getting excited over him drinking cocoa was not the way to go.

"That's so decadent it's probably illegal in twelve states. I haven't had homemade cocoa in years."

"I guess you wouldn't, on your anti-Christmas kick."

He didn't seem to take issue with my description, just went back for another sip of the scrumptious cocoa. At first, I'd thought he'd just said he disliked Christmas to get a rise out of me. A little everyday, Sam-style teasing. But if it'd been a joke, I really didn't see the point of carrying on this long.

"What happened?" I asked. "To make you not like Christmas anymore?"

He turned his eyes to me as if bracing me for something. Or maybe just debating if he wanted to answer my question. He'd never really held things back in the Before times, but this older version of Sam had grown a little more reticent.

Leaning forward, he set his mug on the coffee table and rested his forearms on his knees. "I'm sure you heard my parents got divorced the summer after senior year."

"I remember."

I'd heard about it second-hand. Sam had already left for goodness-knew-where, and we hadn't spoken in months, but hearing about Teresa and Christopher Donnelly's divorce had still come as a shock. I hadn't been all that close with Christopher, but Teresa had been almost like a second mother to me for all the time I'd spent at their house next door.

"Do you remember our Christmas that year?"

His question made me think of the Sasquatch Santa snow globe, and everything that had come after, but I knew he wasn't referring to us right then.

"We did every last Christmas event they could find. The tree lighting ceremony, wagon rides downtown, they even took us to tell Santa what we wanted in our stockings." He gestured at the quilted red stockings I'd hung over my fireplace. "We baked cookies, and watched movies together. Cut down our own tree and strung it with homemade ornaments."

He shook his head, staring at his hands. "Georgia and I knew it was over the top, but we got into it anyway. They said they were doing it for me, one last big family Christmas before I went off to college and everything shifted in the family.

"Only later, we found out they'd started divorce proceedings that November. Dad's...well, Ava was already pregnant with Finn, and Mom knew it. They'd known all along our big, happy family Christmas was a lie, and they'd fed it to us anyway."

He ran his fingers through his hair, sending blond curls askew. "I haven't felt the same about it since. Everything about it reminds me it's all fake."

I scooted closer to him, just enough to reach him, and took his hand in mine, needing to offer a little comfort. That small contact seemed to crack open a door to an old, familiar place I wanted to sink back into. "I'm sorry they handled things that way."

"I'm sure they thought they were doing something good, giving us a few last months as a family. But I couldn't get past all the lies."

"I had no idea."

He ran his thumb over my fingers, sending shivery echoes up my arm.

"Nobody did. Mom wanted to keep things quiet until it was all over. Dad, on the other hand, didn't care what people thought. He married Ava as soon as the divorce from Mom was final, and Finn came along a few months after that. He went on business as usual, but me, Mom, and Georgia had to figure out how to move forward."

"When did you find out?"

He exhaled bitter laughter. "They told us after graduation. Like, immediately after. We came home, I peeled off my gown, and they told us."

My heart ached as though a cold blade had sunk into it. "Was *that* why you called me that night?"

He met my eyes, softness and maybe a little lingering hurt reflected there. "I didn't have anyone else to turn to."

Guilt and regret poured on top of me like cement until I felt about one inch tall. He'd called me because he'd truly needed me, and I'd turned around and ignored him.

Late in the summer, I'd heard bits of gossip about Christopher Donnelly and his new wife, and how their baby had come along right after their wedding. In my bitterness, I'd focused on the fact that Sam's dad had cheated, but I'd never stopped to think just what that would have meant for Sam. My parents still made moony faces at each other over family dinner every week—I couldn't imagine what it would be like to have that torn apart.

I'd resented Sam a long time for how selfish he'd been in our break-up, but I'd been selfish, too. I'd chosen to hold a grudge over our old friendship, and left him on his own during an emotionally devastating time. The anger I'd clung to for so long didn't seem so righteous anymore.

"Sam, I'm so sorry. I didn't know. I wish I'd understood, I—"

I would have picked up, at least. Would have accepted his

anguished *I need you* as sincerity instead of a ploy. I would have stood by him.

He squeezed my hand tight in his. "I didn't tell you this to make you feel bad. I had no right to expect you to comfort me after the way I'd behaved."

"But you needed me, and I wasn't there for you."

His thumb traced a line along my knuckles. "Did you ever need me when I wasn't there for you?"

I sagged against him, my shoulder resting on his. I'd needed him a lot, especially that first year. Nothing so major as a parents' divorce, but I'd missed him. Wanted to talk to him. Wanted *him*. "I guess I did."

"We were seventeen, Harps. We both screwed up, me way more than you."

I still didn't like the picture of me this painted, knowing now how much he'd been hurting. Knowing I could have offered him even a small amount of comfort if I hadn't been so afraid of losing ground with him.

"Is that why you left town that week?" I asked softly.

He nodded. "I didn't want to be anywhere near my dad for a while."

"I still wish I'd known. I wish I could have—" I wasn't even sure what I would have done, but just now, *anything* sounded better than *nothing*.

Gently squeezing my hand, he laughed again, but it came out more genuine this time. "Harps, that wasn't for you to fix. I needed to deal with that steaming mess in my own way."

"I know. But it might have been nice to have a friend to help you through it."

He watched me a little too long, that one word seeming to put a mile of distance between us on the couch even as we were physically closer than we'd been in years. *Friend*. I needed to cling to that word, hold it tight against my chest so I wouldn't forget what we were doing here.

Because without that reminder? I'd have nothing to stop me from wrapping my arms around him and pressing my mouth to his.

sam

I HELD Harper's hand in mine, so close and yet still so far
away.

That word again. *Friend.*

I had to take it as a good thing. She'd said it herself, so a big
improvement from storming off angry when I'd called her that.
But it wasn't nearly what I wanted. Couldn't very well lay all
that on the line. *FYI, Harper, I came back to Magnolia Ridge
because I realized I want a home and a family, and I don't want any
of that without you. PS, Merry Christmas.*

Would have been true, but way too much. Especially
considering I'd just shared more with her than I'd shared with
anyone. Georgia understood why I couldn't stand Christmas,
but we didn't have to talk about it—she'd lived through it with
me, of course she got it, even if we'd handled it differently. But
I'd needed to let Harper in.

Weirdly, I felt a little bit lighter for having told her just what
had happened that Christmas. It didn't take my dislike away—I
still thought it a massively fake time of year, and had chucked
all but the true meaning behind it onto the pile of made-up

holidays meant to sell more stuff—but sharing the reasons for it had been the right thing to do.

"I didn't know, Sam." Her voice came out so soft and gentle, it twisted something in my chest. "If all this Christmas stuff is too much, we don't have to do it. I won't try to make you like—"

"No." I cut her off before she could finish offering to spend *less* time with me. I'd had enough of that for a lifetime. "I don't love all this like I used to. But I want to experience a little bit of it again. With you."

Would a conversation with Harper ever go by where I didn't have to ask myself *Too much?* at the end? Apparently not. But I couldn't lie to her and say I magically wanted to celebrate Christmas again. The only thing appealing about the season this year was the chance to spend even a small part of it with her.

"Okay."

Her gaze darted between my eyes as if she were trying to sort something out. My sincerity, probably. My intentions, most definitely. Both fully genuine, even if she wasn't convinced of it yet.

I barely moved as the moment dragged out, waiting to see what sort of conclusion she'd come to. I willed her to take the leap and choose me.

"I think it's been half an hour," she whispered.

Right. Cookies.

Her hand slipped away from mine, and she leapt from the couch, beelining for the kitchen. Pushing down my disappointment, I followed. I was supposed to be Patient Sam now, even if my whole body rebelled against it.

Harper pulled the chilled dough from the fridge. "You remember how to roll out dough, right?"

"Let's just pretend I haven't done it since high school."

She made a face. "How about I roll the dough, and you cut out the cookies?"

"Deal."

We worked side by side, the vanilla-sweet smell of her lotion or soap or *something* drifting over me. If I stood a little closer than I had to while she flattened the dough, well, I needed to be sure of her technique. Really, I did it all for Christmas.

"How's your mom?" she asked while I cut out stars and bells.

Took me a minute to drag myself from her maddening scent before I could even think about answering her question. "She's good. Sold the house here and moved to Houston after Georgia graduated high school."

Those two years in town after the divorce had been rough on her, always confronted by my dad and his new wife. Self-ishly, I'd been able to get away, but Mom and Georgia had stayed to face it all. She rarely mentioned him when we talked, but he loomed over conversations anyway, the elephant in every room. I wouldn't have blamed her if she'd moved Georgia to finish out high school somewhere else, but she'd weathered it for my sister's sake.

Harper put the first batch of pale little cookies in the oven. I pressed the cutter into the dough, slicing out more shapes, thinking about how she used to make sure we left as little behind as possible so we wouldn't have to keep rolling it out again. The dough got tougher or something. Or didn't look as nice. I couldn't remember now.

"Georgia didn't want to move to Houston after college?"

I laughed, trying to picture my sister in a city as big as Houston. It wouldn't be pretty. "Georgia is not a fan of cities. Crowds make her cranky."

"Do you visit your mom much?"

"When I can. She remarried a few years ago. Keith. Seems like a good guy."

I honestly didn't know much about my step-dad. We didn't talk a lot when I visited. Big fisherman. Did something in the oil industry. Made my mom happy. I only really cared about the last one.

"That's sweet. I like stories of people finding love again like that. It kind of gives me hope, you know?"

She laughed, but it turned strained at the end, like she'd said more than she'd meant to. Her eyes met mine, so close as we worked together at the kitchen counter. Although, in that moment, I couldn't have told you what I was supposed to be doing.

A hundred questions came to mind. Why wouldn't she have hope for finding love? Was she not over the guy from her list? She'd said they hadn't been serious, but I couldn't expect heartfelt confidences from her yet.

Rather than voice those questions and sound like a jealous madman, I opted for humor. Kind of.

"I don't know about love, but I'm sure if you go back to the MMA classes, you'll wind up with a date."

Okay, a humorous jealous madman.

Her laughter gave me a completely undeserved hope.

"He was *not* into me."

I stared her down, knowing full well he had been. "If I hadn't been there, he would have asked you out."

Still thought that said plenty about his lack of professionalism, but hardly the point.

"Pretty sure he's not my type."

"What is your type?"

Her warm brown eyes stared into mine so long, I started to think I stood half a chance. I tilted closer to her on instinct, but she shifted away to get another handful of flour. She dusted it over the countertop, not looking at me.

"I want stability. A sensible guy with a steady job who knows what he wants out of life. Someone reliable and dependable."

Impossible not to see she'd described my exact opposite. Her answer sounded a little too rehearsed to me, like a thing she told herself rather than something she truly felt. The kind of thing you say to talk yourself out of what you really want.

Or maybe that was still the jealous madman talking.

"Sounds like you're describing a used car."

She made an irritated sound, rolling out the dough so hard, she tore it down the middle. Pressing it back together, she scowled at the mess beneath her fingers. "Reliable cars make more sense than impractical sports cars."

Now we were getting somewhere.

"What about someone who makes you *feel?* Someone who makes your heart race and your breath stall in your chest? Someone who makes everyone else fade away in comparison?"

We stood way too close now, breathing in the same air as my challenge crackled around us. How easy it would be to run my fingers in her hair, draw her close, and convince her with a kiss.

"I had that once," she said softly. "It didn't go so well."

"I had it once, too," I said, my voice low in the stillness. "I've never missed anything more."

Her throat worked as she swallowed, her eyes glued to mine. I'd said too much already, but the fact she still stood here with me had to count for something. Once again, I fought my impulsive default that longed to touch her, hold her, kiss her, and instead forced myself to wait. Forced myself to let her choose me.

The timer buzzed on the oven, and we startled apart, the

moment shattering like her conspicuously missing snow globe. She turned away to pull the cookies from the oven, and I swore under my breath, cursing out the cookies and their terrible timing. Cursing out the years apart that left us uncertain around each other. Mostly, I cursed myself out for not taking the opportunity to be with her when I'd held it in my hands.

She turned back to me with the tray of golden-brown cookies and a strained smile on her lips. "Are you ready to frost them?"

"You know it."

She pulled out sugar and butter, whipping up a quick frosting, but I didn't have much focus for cookies anymore.

Harper thought she needed the reliable sedan-type, some boring, sedate guy instead of me, the impractical sports car? I would prove to her I could be reliable, too. I would prove to her I could be everything she needed, if only she would let me try.

harper

STRAIGHTENING up the PT room after a session, I tried to get my head on straight, but my thoughts were in a permanent tailspin over Sam's low-spoken words: *I've never missed anything more.* Those words had kept me up last night, tormenting me with their hope.

I'd been struggling to squash that hope back down ever since, but I couldn't force that toothpaste back into the tube.

"Wow, it's extra-Christmasy in here!"

I rolled my eyes to the ceiling before spinning to face Eliza. She could have given me at least a day to work through my feelings. Although, at the rate I'd been going, I'd need about a hundred days. My feelings were a box of tangled Christmas lights—tugging at them just made the knots tighter.

"I found a few extra decorations." That I'd done it specifically to get under Sam's skin didn't need to be shared.

She looked around, taking in my handiwork. Then she scrunched up her nose. "Why is that Santa propped up to face the other room?"

"No reason. What are you doing here?"

"Rude." She came closer until we were practically toe to toe, her eyes darting around as if she'd missed a gray-haired resident hidden in a corner somewhere. Dropping her voice, she said, "I think you know."

"Don't you have soaps to make or something?"

"I just dropped off a delivery to Bluebird Lodge and I thought, why not visit my beautiful sister, Harper, and see how she's doing today? Since her night was so very surprising."

She had no idea. And really, I should probably keep it that way.

"I only have about fifteen minutes before my next appointment."

"Then get to spilling your guts."

I shot her my best look of reproach, but she'd grown impervious to them when it came to Sam. If they'd ever bothered her at all.

Clasping her hands in front of her, she bobbed on the balls of her feet. "I need to know what happened, Harper! Please?" She dragged out the word like she used to when we were kids, the sound just as irritating now as it had been then. "Sam was at your place, wasn't he?"

I sank onto one of the yoga balls, bouncing for a second as I settled. "Yes. We made cookies."

She sat on a ball next to me, letting loose a witchy cackle. "Is that what you kids are calling it these days?"

I narrowed my eyes on her. "You've got twelve minutes. Do you want to waste them?"

Sitting bolt upright, she schooled her expression. "No, ma'am, I do not." Leaning closer on the ball, she still acted as if someone were in the room with us ready to eavesdrop. "What is going on there, though?"

If only I knew.

"Sam found out about my New-Me List at The Broken

Hammer Saturday night. He offered to help me with some of the things on there."

Eliza's slow smile was the equivalent of a hundred *I told you sos*. "I like where this is headed. But what's with the cookies? That's not on your list. Unless it's still a euphemism for Twister, which I endorse."

"Eliza, no, geez. I said I'd only let him help if he let *me* help him find the spirit of Christmas again. Or something like that."

So far, my counteroffer seemed sort of silly. I'd had an exhilarating time in the kickboxing class, and he'd...baked cookies. But considering the small glimpse he'd given me into his reasons for disliking Christmas, the night hadn't been entirely pointless. Maybe I could help him see that even though his parents had used the holiday to deceive him and his sister, it still held genuine goodness, too. Even though it had hurt him once, he could still enjoy it again now.

I willfully ignored how the same sentiment could be applied to me and him.

"I'm so happy!" Eliza shimmied on her yoga ball, her fists pumping in the air.

"Nothing is happening."

She came to a dead stop and stared me down, her eyes gone hard. "You're still on that kick? I tell you things, you know that? When I realized I was feeling stuff about Dean, I told you first. I shared with you, even though it was scary. And you give me this *Nothing is happening* garbage?"

It reminded me of my conversation with Jed. The denial here was strong, going on about how nothing was happening with Sam, even though I'd tossed and turned all night thinking over every last word he'd said to me. And she *had* been up front about her own romantic feelings, even when they'd confused and frightened her.

If Eliza could be brave about her feelings, I guess I could, too. To a point.

I edged closer to her, deciding to pony up. "The other day, Sam apologized for dumping me the way he did back in high school. When we agreed to help each other with our lists, I told him I just wanted to be friends, nothing more. But last night...I don't know, it made me think maybe he does want more than to just get to know me again."

Her little grin returned, even though she fought it.

"But," I added, before she could get swept away, "think about how astronomically dumb this would be. Would you ever get back together with an ex?"

"You're trying to be nice, but I know you mean Carter. And I'll just say what you told me once about Dean: Sam is nothing like Carter. You were best friends forever before you dated, this wasn't a guy manipulating you for a few months so he could steal a promotion out from under you. It's not remotely the same."

It wasn't, I knew that. But it still felt like a strange scenario to be in.

"Why are you so all-in for us to get back together, though? You wouldn't talk this way if Teddy had come back for Eden, or if Bret tried to waltz back into June's life."

Eliza laughed. "You're crazy if you think Teddy or Bret would risk the beatings they'd get from Booker or Ty if they turned up again."

"Fair, but not really my point."

Her teasing smile disappeared. "Okay, I know. The thing is, you and Sam were awesome together. You were the perfect team. He was the extrovert to your introvert, the sunshine to your grump, the adventurer to your homebody."

"Wait," I said, tossing up a hand before she could add any

more opposites into the mix. "I'm the grump in your description?"

"I mean, kinda."

I sagged a little more on the yoga ball. "Kind of a rude awakening there."

"All I'm saying is, you and Sam fit. And I know you don't want me to illustrate my point by mentioning all the other loved-up couples around you, but you worked together in the same way we do, your strengths lining up with each other's weaknesses."

Great. Second chance *and* opposites attract. Not that I'd ever been unsure about that one.

"And I don't know why he dumped you the way he did, but…" She laid a hand on my arm as though preparing me for hard news. "It was a really long time ago. Maybe you guys didn't work then, but wouldn't it be worth it to find out if you work now?"

I sighed, the walls I'd built to protect my heart from Sam fracturing. Soon, that break would become critical, and he would find his way in. His teasing flirtation and eager enthusiasm, his soft confessions and earnest apologies—he would burst through and zap my heart to life again.

But then, I'd wind up even more shattered when he left the next time.

Because as much as I liked the idea of him staying, I still wasn't convinced Magnolia Ridge had anything he'd stick around long-term for. Including me.

"I don't know. I think being friends is the safest option right now."

Her little frown came out again. "Safest, yeah. But I thought the whole point of your list was to try things that aren't always safe."

Wasn't that what I'd told Eliza during her crisis a couple of months ago? Real living is in the mess. Didn't mean I was ready to let that play out in my own life, though. I'd get *really* messy if I let him back into my heart only for him to walk right out again.

"Hey." A voice at the doorway nearly sent Eliza and me backward off our yoga balls.

Sam stood just inside the PT room, ready to teach his class. My stomach lurched, my brain reeling over all the embarrassing things he might have overheard. How long had he been standing there? His expression gave nothing away. Was that an *I know you want me* smile? Or his regular *I'm having the best day* smile? No way to tell.

Eliza popped up off her ball. "Hey, Sam. I was just on my way out."

"You don't have to leave because of me."

"Oh, no, Harper's got an appointment in like, four minutes. I just stopped in to say hello."

They exchanged quick goodbyes, but the moment Eliza passed Sam, she turned around, eyes wide, flashing two thumbs-up. Way to be subtle. I gave her a thin smile and then she marched off to scheme up all kinds of conclusions she'd leap at head-first.

At this point, I couldn't be sure they'd be all that wrong, despite my constant insistence Sam and I needed to stay just friends.

"If you've got an appointment, I won't keep you." Contradicting his offer to leave, Sam shuffled farther into the PT room, hands stuffed in the pockets of his gray sweatpants.

As the weather became cooler, his yoga outfit had moved from shorts to sweatpants, but the change hadn't served to make him any less exposed. This look made him seem even more casual, as if he were just about to cuddle up with someone on a couch in those sweatpants.

I pulled my eyes away from his sweatpants and reminded myself to focus. Friends didn't ogle each other in their workout clothes. "I've got a little time. What's up?"

"I found a place to go rock climbing in Austin. Depending on your last appointment here, we could go Friday afternoon."

I nodded, thinking the plan over. "That should work. Doesn't leave a lot of time afterwards for decorating a tree, though."

His mouth squeezed the tiniest fraction at the reminder of his part of our bargain. I wouldn't have even noticed it if my eyes hadn't been glued to his lips.

Focus.

"Are you up for cutting one down?" I asked. "I normally do, but if you think it's too much, I can do that on my own, and we can just decorate later."

"A tree farm, Harps? You're really pushing your luck."

I grinned back at him, well aware my suggestion went above and beyond simply putting ornaments on a tree, but fairly confident his teasing response meant he was okay with it.

"Don't tell me you were never a lumberjack in all your travels."

He put his knuckles together, flexing his arms in a body-builder pose. "I think I can handle it."

Even as I laughed at his silliness, a tingly little something started up in my stomach, urging me to move closer to touch those muscles. Just run my hands all over his biceps and see for myself if he had what it takes to chop down a tree. I resisted, but barely.

"Maybe we could get the tree Saturday? I have a couple of appointments in the morning, but then I'm free."

His grin faded, his expression suddenly uncomfortable. "I can't do Saturday. I've got a...thing."

A thing. Right. Sure. My Christmas tree farm tingly excitement washed out, replaced by a greasy agitation squirming around in my stomach like a hungry tapeworm. Of course he had other things going on. Probably for the best—I'd needed the reminder we weren't doing...whatever it had seemed like we were doing.

Friends, and friends only.

"Okay." I tried to copy Eliza's patented *No big deal* attitude, grinning wider than usual even if it had zero joy behind it. "We can decorate the tree another time."

"Unless you want to come with me."

I drew in a breath and held it, trying to sort out his offer. "Come with you where?"

"Georgia and I are taking Finn and Willa—our half-siblings —to see Santa on Saturday. That seems like it would be right in line with your Christmas obsession."

I blew out the breath, shaking wisps of hair around my face. "It's not a Christmas obsession, Samuel, it's a normal celebration of the holiday season."

"Sure." His little smile proved he still considered it abnormal. Or maybe he just liked me using his full name. "Does that mean you'll join us for the Santa glorification?"

"You think it will be okay if I go? It's not a family-only thing?"

He jabbed a finger my direction. "You're coming. I'm not taking no for an answer." He paused, then dropped his hand. "Unless you don't actually want to come, then I will absolutely accept your no."

I fought the little smile that wanted to burst out. Shouldn't love a confident man second-guessing his behavior, but it kind of worked for me. "I want to come."

That grin reappeared, lighting me up like the Christmas tree in town square.

"Good. I'll drive us Friday, if that's okay. We don't need to take two cars to Austin."

"Sounds good. Should I—I mean, should I look anything up about rock climbing? Watch some videos or something?"

Would not confess the number of beginner videos I'd watched already.

"You'll be fine, Harps. You've got me."

Maxine walked in for her appointment, catching us grinning at each other like fools. Sam ducked out right after, heading for the exercise room and his class later. I tried to get the goofy expression off my face, but from the way Maxine watched me, I couldn't be sure I'd succeeded.

I started our session, guiding her through her exercises, Sam's little comment etched in my brain: *You've got me.*

But how long could I keep him?

sam

CONTORTED AWKWARDLY IN THE CAR, I pushed the shop-vac's nozzle deeper into the crevice between the driver's seat and center console. I'd already filled a garbage bag with debris from beneath the seats and the sad no-man's-land behind them, and now vacuumed up all the little bits I'd missed. This station wagon had held innumerable tiny treasures from my travels: sand from California and North Carolina; obsidian from Oregon; granite from Montana. And now, I was sucking it all up to chuck in the trash.

A sad day for dirtbag climbers everywhere.

I felt a tap on my shoulder and turned to see Georgia staring at me. Flipping off the vac, I eased back out of the car as she leaned past me, craning her neck to examine my progress.

"Are you selling your wagon?" she asked, sarcasm twisting her question.

I knew I should have finished cleaning while she was still at work. "No."

Her hand flew to my forehead. "Oh my gosh, are you sick? Are you feverish?"

I brushed her hand away. "Ha ha."

"Seriously, what pushed you over the edge? Was it the smell?"

I frowned down at her. "There was no smell. It was just time."

"Um, *way* past time. When you gave me a ride in this thing last week, I found a receipt from five years ago."

"And you already gave me crap about it, so we can skip that part."

She nodded, looking me over. "What are you really doing? Are you interviewing for a place where you need to impress somebody with your clean car?"

I shifted, rubbing my finger over the vac's on/off switch, debating just how much I wanted to confess to Georgia. Telling her any of this would be about as bad as confessing it to one of the gossips at Fiesta Village. "Not exactly. I'm driving somebody to Austin tonight, and I figured they wouldn't want to sit in an archeological dig of old receipts and climbing ropes."

She smiled slowly, her satisfied expression reminiscent of teenage inquisitions where she would grill me mercilessly about my dates with Harper. So. Things were pretty much the same between us after eleven years.

"Who is the somebody?"

I shook my head, my lips pressed together, battling my own smile. "Not sure we should do this."

She grabbed my shoulder, her short nails digging against my muscles. "Now you have to tell me. Are you seeing someone? When did I miss that?"

"You didn't miss anything." I pulled her hand off my shoulder, rubbing at the spots she'd jabbed. "And we're not seeing each other."

My brain went straight to the conversation I'd accidentally overheard between Harper and her sister at the Village on Wednesday.

"Being friends is the safest option right now."

She'd said as much to me in The Broken Hammer, and several times since. Harper had slotted me into the Friend category, and took every opportunity to remind me. The idea of only ever being friends with her felt a little like a slow torture, keeping what I really wanted perpetually out of reach. But if renewing our friendship was the most I could have with her this time around, I would still take it.

I'd take anything she'd give me.

"I heard a silent *yet* in there," Georgia said.

Not going to spill all that to my sister. "A guy can hope."

"Thank the Lord. I was afraid I'd have to do some matchmaking, and you are *not* right for any of my friends."

"I want to say thank you, but also ouch."

"I just mean, you're way too *you* for anybody I know."

"Did you think that would reassure me?"

She waved away my insulted face. "So? Who?"

I moved my hands to my hips, staring her down. "I'm taking Harper Webb rock climbing."

Georgia moved back a little, her thoughts whirring behind her eyes. I hadn't told her anything about Harper because I hadn't had all that much to tell. Then again, I hadn't told Grandpa much of anything, either, and he'd come to his own conclusions without any help.

"That's *interesting.*" Her salacious tone made it sound like I'd confessed to a whole lot more than just intending to drive Harper to Austin.

I coiled the shop-vac's hose around the canister and looped up the cord while she figured out just how she wanted to gloat about this. Georgia didn't play things cool. Putting the vac away in the car port cupboard, I turned to face her.

"I also invited her to the Santa thing tomorrow with the littles." Best to get that shock out of her system right now.

Her comically wide eyes made me chuckle. Probably had mere seconds before she lost her ever-loving mind.

"Holy crap, this is huge! I guess I should have known you weren't just volunteering over at the retirement community because of Grandpa."

"Way to make me sound like a mercenary."

Coloring my volunteer work as purely selfish didn't sit right. I'd wanted to be closer to Harper, yes, but I also enjoyed working with the seniors. They weren't my typical yoga clientele, and they certainly kept things interesting over there. I looked forward to my time in the Village, and not just for the chance of running into their resident physical therapist.

"But are you two, you know...?" She lifted her eyebrows as though that finished her question.

"We're just friends right now." Probably needed to tattoo that somewhere on my body so I wouldn't forget it.

"*Right now.*" She clasped her hands together. "Oh, this is so romantic. High school sweethearts reunited. I'm going to make a whole second chance romance display at the bookstore in your honor."

"Not necessary."

"With giant paper hearts everywhere."

"Tell me you're going to be normal tomorrow and not do that thing with your face."

She drew in a playful little gasp. "What thing with my face?"

I traced a circle in the air in front of her. "The thing you're doing now. Grinning so wide, it's like you're getting paid by the tooth."

"I'm going to be perfectly normal tomorrow. It's the littles you should be worried about."

My enthusiasm for sharing the Christmas activity with Harper stalled a bit. I'd assumed the littles would take right to her; I hadn't really thought about how they would react to *us*. "What are they going to do?"

She shrugged, but from her devious look, a fair bet she liked the possibilities. "Who knows. Ask questions. Make assumptions. Sing the *K-I-S-S-I-N-G* song."

Yeah, had not considered that. I didn't know that much about kids, but I assumed telling a six-year-old to play it cool would have the opposite effect. Finn would probably be indifferent to the whole situation, but Willa? I could see her making up rhymes featuring me and Harper.

Georgia's laugh wasn't all that reassuring, either. "Now you're the one who needs to get their face in control."

I tried to wipe away the distraught look and shift into a more neutral facial gear. "They'll be too dazzled by Santa to worry about anything else."

"Keep telling yourself that."

She moved to head up the stairs to her apartment but stopped. "Sam? In all seriousness, I'm happy for you. But don't mess this up. There's no such thing as a *third*-chance romance."

Her teasing warning unsnapped something in my chest, and my heart dropped as if its lead rope had been cut. I already knew I couldn't ruin things again, but her confirmation cranked up the pressure to get it right this time.

* * *

Harper's nervous energy had her practically dancing in the passenger seat as I drove us to Austin, her excitement spelled out in every cute little wiggle.

"Is this a pretty good climbing gym?"

"I'm hurt." I grinned, proving the wound only superficial. "You think I'd take you to the worst one in the city?"

"I wouldn't know the difference."

She ran her hands over her black yoga pants, tracing her thighs down to her knees and back. I knew it was just a nervous habit, but I wished she wouldn't. The emphasis on her thighs distracted me from the road.

Eyes forward, pal.

"It's a great gym. Plenty of courses at different difficulty levels. They have a beginner's wall, which is where you'll start before we move on to top-roping."

"You mean you want me to start without a harness or anything?"

"You'll do great." I patted her leg twice, but my stomach plunged at the contact, so I put my hand back on the steering wheel. *No touchy.* I needed lots of new rules today if I wanted to keep this Just Friends thing front and center. "It's a shorter wall, just to get you familiar with the hand-holds."

"When did you become certified as an instructor?"

"A few years ago."

She nodded. "And your certification...is there an expiration date on that?"

I threw my head back and laughed. "So confident in me."

"My life is literally going to be in your hands. It's fair I would have a few questions."

"I can see that. Yes, the certification has to be renewed. It's good for another year, and then I'll take a recert course. I've taught dozens of people on indoor and outdoor climbs, and last I checked, my Google review score was pretty high."

"You have Google reviews? I guess I'll trust you."

Even though she meant it as a joke, her decision to trust me felt significant, like I'd earned something important I wanted to lock away and treasure. This time around, I wouldn't take that trust for granted.

"What else do you want to know? Since your life is going to be in my hands, and all."

"I don't know. I don't have a clear picture of what you've been doing all this time. The parts I've heard don't really add up."

"You mean the town gossips have been failing you?"

"I'm serious. You had plans to go to Texas State and study mechanical engineering, but the next thing I knew, you were in Vermont learning how to be a ski bum."

"There's a lot to learn about being a ski bum."

A faint smile flickered across her face, and I knew my joke hadn't landed. This wasn't really the way I'd wanted to spend our drive to Austin. I didn't love revisiting those times, and I struggled to put my feelings into words on the best days. Why had I left?

Her.

It wasn't her fault, and I could never blame her for what had happened. I bore all the responsibility, no question. Finding out about Dad's betrayal had moved up my decision to leave, but I'd known from the moment I decided to break up with her that I couldn't just stick around. Leaving her had been the last thing I wanted to do, and somehow, I'd let that convince me it was the only thing I *could* do. But I couldn't very well force that to make sense sitting in my station wagon, weaving through evening traffic.

"I know you said you had to get away from your dad, but you could have done that at college."

"I didn't want to go to college." True, if only part of the truth.

"But you'd been accepted. You had a major decided."

She seemed unable to reconcile that I'd abandoned something written on a calendar somewhere.

"My college plans had never really been for me. My parents wanted me to go, but it wasn't something I wanted for myself. When everyone else was taking their SAT tests and writing up four-year college plans, I was throwing darts at a map of the U.S., daydreaming about our big road trip."

"Oh, right. Our trip."

Her soft little voice curled around me, soothing and wounding all at once. She sounded like she'd found something precious she'd lost, but also wasn't sure she wanted to unearth again.

Once upon a time, we'd planned to cash in all our somedays and set off on the road the summer after graduation. I'd derailed a lot of our study sessions senior year with *What ifs* and *Would you rathers*, trying to piece together the ideal trip for both of us. I would have been content flipping a coin at every crossroads, but she'd needed a plan. So I'd planned. I'd wanted to see mountains, whether the Smokies or the Tetons, and her heart had been set on seeing the Atlantic and Pacific oceans. It should have been the trip of a lifetime, exploring the country with the girl I loved.

Instead, I'd headed to Stowe after graduation, where I got a job as a waiter at an upscale resort, telling myself the bridges I'd burned back home had been the best for everyone. And Harper...

"Did you ever go? On any part of the trip?"

She released a sad sort of laugh. "No. At first, I didn't really want to."

She didn't have to explain. I'd ruined the whole idea of the trip for her. I'd always hoped she'd gone anyway, living it up in all the places we'd meant to see together. I'd liked the idea of her on a beach somewhere, her toes in the sand, defiantly staring out at the horizon. Hating me, maybe, but still out there living her best life.

"Then came college and the PT program, and I just never had the time. I haven't been the best at taking vacations."

"Do I want to ask if you've even taken *one* vacation?"

She shrugged as if to say not to bother. "I've been maybe a little too focused on work."

In Harper-speak, that meant she'd made way too many sacrifices for her job. Suggesting she consider looking elsewhere again would probably earn me a dirty look, but all work and no play wasn't tenable for anybody. I'd meant it the other day when I'd called her selfless, but this seemed to cross the line into being taken advantage of. Definitely taken for granted, if Olivia could just change her schedule as she pleased based on residents' whims.

"You've been this focused on work since you started?"

Her lips tugged into a cringey smile. "More like graduate school."

Should have called it. What did I say about her being wicked smart and competitive?

"In my defense, the DPT program was intense. I kept my head down, focused on my coursework and practical experience. I had to—I mean, if I got three bad grades, they'd kick me out of the program."

"What was a bad grade?"

"B-minus."

Yeah, that sounded intense. "Makes sense, I guess. They want to be sure you're doing good doctoring."

"Good doctoring is key," she said with a laugh.

She slid her hands together, massaging them. After a minute, it looked more like wringing them.

"The thing is...I got two B-minuses."

She hated to admit defeat—I could imagine how much those grades must have eaten away at her, and just how much it meant that she'd even confide it in me.

"I was terrified I would get one more bad grade and lose everything. I didn't want all my big plans to fall apart again."

Again. Guilt settled a heavy hand over me, squeezing my

lungs. She'd had our next few years after high school planned out, and I'd ripped up the roadmap.

"I stopped going out with my friends because I always needed to study just a little bit more. I didn't come home for weekend visits the way I had been, and I stayed in my apartment through a few holidays, too. I didn't mean to shut myself off from everyone, but that's kind of what I did. I didn't want to let anybody down, you know?"

I'd already used up my platonic touch allowance for this drive, but I reached over and took her hand in mine, anyway. She didn't brush me off or pull her hand away, but held on tight.

"Harper. You could never." I knew her family almost as well as I knew mine. Even if she'd had to quit that PT program and switch gears, her family would have rallied around her and provided a soft landing so she could bounce back.

Her thin little smile didn't look convinced. "Anyway. I *did* graduate, and I passed the exams on the first try. I came back to Magnolia Ridge, got the job at Fiesta Village, and just...haven't figured out how to turn it off, I guess."

"Looks to me like you're figuring it out."

She turned fully to me, her eyes squinting their skepticism. She wanted me to spell it out? No problem.

"First, you absolutely crushed yoga night. Easy peasy."

She laughed at the silly phrase, her shoulders loosening as the tension that had wound through her a minute ago slipped away.

"Then you kicked my butt at the MMA studio. Excellent work there, by the way."

Her mouth twisted, fighting more laughter, but she nodded, accepting my praise.

"Now you're going to kick this rock wall's butt. Honestly,

you don't kick butt often enough, Harps. You should give your-self more opportunities to dominate."

"Well. I'll see what I can do, Samuel."

She grinned in spite of her haughty tone. Then, like some-thing out of a dream, her hand shifted in mine so our fingers interlaced. Driving down the highway at sixty miles an hour, the moment seemed to catch and freeze. My days mostly zoomed by so fast, I could barely pay attention to everything that sped past me, conversations and experiences blurring together, but *this moment* slowed down so I could savor it. I tried not to let myself smile, because I knew it would give my fool heart away, but I couldn't help it.

The rest of the way to the climbing gym, I looked like I'd just summited my personal best mountain and could only sit back and take in the glorious views.

harper

PEOPLE SCALED the wall in front of me, their little hands and feet scrambling over holds, screeching with glee when they got to the top, and screeching just as loudly when they leapt off halfway up and tumbled onto the thick mat below.

To be clear, nobody climbing looked over twelve years old.

Sure, a bunch of parents stood around helping or coaching, but all the figures on the wall here or on the giant wall in the next room were hobbit-sized.

"Better or worse than the MMA crowd?" Sam asked at my side.

I bit my lip, watching as one kid hung by a single hand, his toes dangling several feet above the ground, until he finally dropped to the mat and somersaulted, giggling the whole time. "Draw."

"When they told me it was beginner's night, I figured there would be a few more adults in the mix. The upside is, no shortage of climbing shoes in your size."

He held out a pair of blue shoes that looked more like heavy-duty ballet slippers than anything else. As soon as we got here, he'd done a quick demo for the gym manager to prove he knew what he was doing on the big climbing wall. I guess the gym had to make sure Sam wasn't going to do anything dangerous, but seeing him belay the volunteer climber had fired up skittery nerves in my stomach.

Really, they'd been there ever since he'd held my hand on the drive down. He'd soothed me the way I'd soothed him a few nights ago—a simple touch, really. But not simple at all. My stomach had swooped so low, I wasn't sure it would ever go back to its regular position.

And then, I'd gone and laced my fingers with his. I couldn't tell you why.

Okay, total lie. I'd known exactly why. My stomach had been full of swoops, my heart all fluttery like it was trying to grow wings, and my brain scrubbed of everything except Sam's voice. *"Harper. You could never."* How was I supposed to resist that kind of sweet support?

We'd stayed like that straight up until he had to maneuver through Austin traffic. I'd relinquished his hand for safety's sake, but it'd been a hard call: make it to the climbing gym in one piece, or keep learning every last callus on his palm?

But now, I faced learning to rock climb with kids who obviously had zero fear of falling, and no sense that anyone around them might think leaping six feet down from the bouldering wall could be a bad idea.

I slipped on the super-tight shoes and joined Sam where he'd claimed a small section of wall. Thankfully, this part only reached about ten feet high and didn't have any overhangs or tricky gaps between hand holds. It did, however, have a huge sign blaring *Beginner* pasted across the top.

I gazed at the wall, trying to plot a course up the knobby plastic holds.

"This wall is pretty basic, but it will give you a good idea of what the beginner top-rope climb will be like." Sam toed one foot onto a hold and boosted himself up before grabbing two hand holds just above his eye level. "You want your legs to do most of the work. Always lead with your feet."

He demonstrated by finding another foothold and extending his leg before moving his hands to their next holds.

"Keep your core engaged, and try to keep your center of gravity close to the wall."

I nodded, mentally logging his tips and filing them away as he climbed another foot higher. Focusing extra hard, I tried not to also log the fact his butt was now eye-level, or just how fabulous that butt looked. Friends definitely didn't stare at each other's butts.

Didn't mean I stopped right away.

"If you get tired, or if anything doesn't feel right, come on back down. This is supposed to be fun."

To prove how fun it was, he pulled himself into a chin-up position against the wall, his feet hovering in the air. The muscles in his arms and shoulders popped out, his T-shirt suddenly two sizes too small like Captain America trying to keep that helicopter from flying away. Those nerves coiling around my stomach warmed and hummed at the sight.

He pushed himself off the wall, letting go to drop the three feet to the mat.

"Show off." Not that I minded.

His little wink made that swooping start up again. As if I needed one more thing to be nervous about right now.

He gestured at our section of kid-free wall. "When you're ready, give it a try."

I stepped up to the wall, wobbling a little as I moved across the extra-thick mat. Finding two hand holds just above my head, I grabbed on lightly. I toed my foot onto a hold about eighteen inches above the mat, taking deep breaths as I psyched myself up to climb a wall even six-year-olds had mastered. I could do this, too.

I found a second foot hold and hitched myself up, letting my legs do the work like he'd said. Good thing, because if I'd tried to pull myself up by my noodle arms, I wouldn't get very far tonight.

"That's the way," Sam said at my side.

I inched up the wall, Sam offering encouragement and advice from below. Not so much I wanted him to shut up, but enough to keep me going. Even though I hadn't done anything like this since I was a kid, a little shot of exhilaration rang through me with every foot I gained on that wall. I didn't scramble up at top speed the way the children around me did, but my slow ascent would get me to the same place eventually. Alternating smiles and grimaces as I searched for holds, I worked higher, my sense of accomplishment bursting at the seams.

When I reached the top of the wall, I turned my head and spotted a girl who must have been around ten hanging out a few feet away from me. She gripped the wall, flashing me her giant, gap-toothed grin. I grinned back. Kind of fun to have a buddy up here.

"Good job, lady!"

Hmm. I appreciated the praise but could have done without the *lady*.

I looked down for Sam, only to realize his head was roughly level with my feet. So. Not that high of a climb, after all. Still, a start, and a big win for my Life List.

"What do I do now?"

His grin looked about as wide as the little girl's. "You climb back down."

I blew out a breath, noting the details of the faux rock in

front of me. "Of course I climb back down," I muttered to myself.

Climbing down took longer than climbing up. The footholds were harder to find since they were below me, and I danced my feet around, searching for purchase as Sam coached me along. Worked a different muscle set, too, and by the time I reached the cushy mat, I'd thoroughly warmed up for the big climb.

Stepping away from the wall, I slicked a hand over my hair, smoothing tendrils that had come loose from my braid. "I think I'm sweating more than I did after kickboxing."

"Mm hmm." Sam nodded, seeming weirdly pleased by this. His leisurely once-over cranked up the heat inside me. "How do you feel?"

"I'm ready to try the big wall."

He grinned, definitely pleased now. "That's my girl."

We paused a beat, both of us seeming to snag on that phrase. He looked almost embarrassed by the slip-up, a Sam rarity—nothing ever fazed him. But the awkward little tug around his eyes and his crooked, frozen smile showed a hint of self-consciousness. Maybe I should have called him out on it... but I didn't quite want to.

"Where do we start?" I said, letting the remark slide. Or letting it stand, I hadn't quite decided.

His easy smile shone out again. "I'll show you."

I followed him to the base of what I could only describe as a ginormous climbing wall. Probably fifty feet tall and twice as long in total, it bent and curved like an origami swan someone had stopped making halfway through. Some sections had overhangs at bizarre angles and oddly-shaped holds for what I assumed were the more advanced courses, but Sam led me to a more or less vertical part of the wall covered in uniform green holds. The bottom of the wall here read *Beginner Zero*.

Level zero sounded perfect to me.

He'd already rented harnesses for us, and talked me through putting mine on. Stepping into the leg loops like pants, I shimmied them up into place, got the belt around my waist and pulled the straps snug, then slid the adjustors on the leg loops around my upper thighs.

Basically the weirdest piece of apparel I'd ever worn.

"I'm going to make sure it fits right, okay?" he asked.

When I nodded, he tugged on my straps, checking everything was secure but still reasonably comfortable. He stood close, his expression dead serious as he inspected the loops and clips on my harness. I'd been prepared for it when his hands brushed my waist as he pulled on the safety belt, but when his fingers ghosted over my thighs to check the leg loops, a shiver rocked through me.

This was for *safety*. No different from when they tug on your seat belt at the carnival to make sure you don't slip out of the ride. I had no business getting all fluttery over safety checks, but here we were.

"Sorry." He didn't sound especially sorry. Smug would have been a better descriptor. "I have to be sure everything's stable."

Everything was stable but me.

"It's fine," I said, counting the brightly colored hand holds that dotted the wall in front of me. I told my body in no uncertain terms it would absolutely not shiver again.

"Okay, you're good to go. I'll go through my checks, and you'll be ready to rock 'n' roll."

He went through the same meticulous inspection on his own harness, double-checking straps and loops with equal care. This responsible side of him made me stop and take notice, as though seeing him for the first time. For so many years, I'd painted him as a careless, carefree nomad—seeing just how seriously he took this did something weird to me. It brought out admiration, sure, but something else, too.

Heat. Another shiver worked up my spine, as though I was actually getting turned on by his responsibility.

If Eliza could have seen me now, she would have laughed her head off.

Safety checks were totally normal protocol for him. He had to make sure we were both secure. But that didn't stop the next shiver from shuddering through me. That made three too many shivers just from watching a man make sure I wouldn't tumble down a rock climbing wall. Anyway, if I did fall, I'd probably land on him, and *that* would just be...

Yeah, no. Get it together, Harper.

He checked the ropes that snaked down from the ceiling before creating complicated knots to secure them into both of our harnesses. Last, he clipped a chalk bag onto my belt, explaining why to use it, and how.

"Okay," he said, giving me a huge smile that made his dimples pop. He leaned closer, practically humming with boyish mischief. "Are you ready to absolutely destroy these kids?"

I laughed at his teasing. All around the loudly echoing room, kids darted up the walls, tethered to their parents in similar harnesses. A few feet down from us, one had made it to the top and waved like mad while what had to be his mother took pictures from below, his father belaying him at the other end of their rope. From all the excited shouts and giggles bouncing around the space, the kids were clearly having a blast. Wasn't sure I could match their exuberance, but I'd give it a try.

"I'm ready."

"Only go as high as you feel like. I can bring you down safely any time. It's not a race, and there's no competition."

He put enough emphasis on the last two words to give me pause. "Why'd you say it like some kind of ominous warning?"

"Because I know you like to win."

I frowned even though it was completely true.

He pulled most of the slack through the belay contraption on his harness. "Climb on, then."

I moved to the wall and started climbing, relieved to find this section actually had more holds than the shorter wall. All the beginner green over here meant it should be an easy route to the top, assuming my muscles held out that far. The short bouldering climb had already made me aware of my glutes, shoulders, and fingers, but I didn't want to give up before trying my whole reason for coming out here.

Sam's advice running through my mind on repeat, I found footholds first before straightening up to reach the next handholds. The noisy gym hummed in the background, his encouraging words drifting up from somewhere beneath me as I worked my way higher.

"That's the way."

"Nice."

"You're a natural."

His spirited cheerleading came out maybe a little overzealous, but it helped me get in the zone. As I climbed, my body adjusted to the mechanics of pushing myself up each small section, my focus zeroed in on the wall and finding the next place to put my hands or feet. Even the yelling kids all around us couldn't distract me as I worked closer to my goal. Sam had said I didn't have to reach it, but I wanted to make it to the top. I couldn't cross rock climbing off my list if I stopped halfway.

I got into a rhythm, foot-hand foot-hand, my eyes never straying far from the next hold. Stress and worries vanished— nothing mattered more than my hands wrapped around the holds and my toes finding purchase as I moved up the wall. I needed to get to that red line at the top.

An ear-rattling shriek broke my concentration. Turning, I saw a little boy about ten feet away, laughing as he was let down on his rope. My gaze followed the rope all the way down to the floor, a seemingly endless distance that made my stomach lurch and bottom out, somehow cramping and rolling at the same time.

Puking while thirty feet in the air would be the worst way to celebrate this Life List win.

Sucking in a breath, I drew closer to the wall, my hands clinging tight to the plastic grips. My heart thundered in my chest, my fight or flight instinct left with no good options up here. A cold sweat broke out on my forehead, my mouth as dry as if I'd coated it in chalk.

Why had I wanted to do this again?

"Harps?" Sam called up. "You okay?"

I shook my head, my nose scraping against the wall. "No!"

Should have been a blood-curdling scream, but I'd only worked up a half-hearted shout. He probably couldn't even hear me down there.

Oh, Lord. I didn't have to look down again to sense that yawning space between me and the ground, and my head spun with the vivid image of my body falling to the bottom of that chasm.

"Talk to me, Harper. What's going on?"

I couldn't look at him, couldn't look at anything but the wall. In my peripheral vision, the kid on my other side continued down and out of view, making my stomach turn over again.

"Is it the height?"

The tender concern in his voice would have kick-started

flutters if my heart weren't already thrashing around in my chest like a caged animal trying to break free.

I nodded, squeezing my fingers tighter over the hand grips. My palms had started sweating now, but I couldn't do anything about it. If I reached down for the chalk, I could fall. The noise of the gym seemed to thin, and a clammy sensation crawled over me as though I might actually faint right off the wall.

"Harps, I've got you no matter what."

Sam's steady voice, so calm and confident in the middle of my panic, pierced that fear, deflating some of it. Not all of it, not by a long shot, but enough for the clammy feeling to pass.

"Breathe slow and deep. You're okay."

I tried to do as he said, but pretty sure my breath was coming too fast to qualify as deep. Hyperventilating up here wouldn't do me any good, either, but I couldn't seem to control my lungs. Methods of slowing my breath completely escaped me as I gulped in air.

"I'll bring you down," he called. "Just let go when I take up the slack."

"No!" That did come out a scream. Climbing down felt impossible, but dropping down in the harness would be plummeting into exactly what I feared. "I can't."

"Harper, I've got you. You're safe."

"I can't," I said again. Let go of the wall? No way. The rope tied to my harness wasn't all that thick. Why hadn't I noticed that before? I should have asked for the biggest, thickest rope available.

"You can wait where you are until the feeling passes," he said, his voice echoing weirdly up here. Maybe the echoing was just in my head. "Or I can bring you down right away. It's up to you."

I didn't like either option—I just wanted to be down on the mat with my head between my knees until this panicky queasiness disappeared. My body shook, my hands and feet wobbling on their grips as terror jolted through me all over again. Clinging to the wall would only last so long. I'd eventually go down one way or another.

"You're safe, Harper. I've got you."

But did he? I'd seen a bunch of kids lowered to the ground by a parent, but I probably weighed twice what they did. What if Sam couldn't handle me? What if something went wrong with the ropes?

"Harper, honey, you're okay. I'm here. But I need you to trust me."

I squeezed my eyes shut, those words echoing in my mind. *Trust me. Trust me.*

Did I trust him? I hadn't, not for a long time. But I wasn't sure that guy I'd imagined as the villain of my past existed anymore. If he ever really had.

"Don't let me go!"

"I won't let you go," he called back. "I won't ever let you go again."

The rope connected to my harness went taut, and my eyes shot open. My heart rate ratcheted up, and my lungs ached like that rope had looped around them, too, squeezing my rib cage.

"I've got you," Sam called. "Just let go."

I couldn't swallow as cold fear gripped me tight.

What if I fall?

What if something goes wrong?

So high up. This had been a terrible choice for my Life List. More like Near-Death List.

Trust me.

Trust me.

Trust me.

I let go of the holds.

He didn't even let me drop as he took my weight, but slowly

began lowering me down the wall, fast enough I knew this would all be over soon, but not so fast it spiked my panic any worse. My waist and thighs didn't love the makeshift chair the harness made, but the straps held strong.

My feet touched the mat, and I steadied myself against the wall. Turning, I saw Sam coming toward me, and I launched myself at him. Our harnesses clattered between us, the rope hanging to one side as I burrowed against him, burying my face in his neck.

"I've got you," he soothed, his mouth at my ear. "You're safe."

I crushed myself to him, needing to shut out the rest of the gym and put my panic far behind me. Every stroke of his hands along my head and back seemed to melt my fears away, grounding me again, reassuring me. My heart rate came down to almost normal levels, my breathing finally evening out as I relaxed against him.

Safe.

I sighed, savoring the warmth of his embrace, how perfect it felt to be nestled this way.

I couldn't remember the last time I'd been held like this. I touched people all day at work, but right then in his arms, I realized I'd been longing for a more personal kind of touch. Sam held me with a tenderness and familiarity I wanted to cling tight to. I could stand here cocooned in his arms smelling the minty spice of the soap on his skin for days.

But...we were in the middle of a crowded gym, after all. Probably some climbing etiquette against prolonged snuggling, especially when surrounded by children.

I pulled back just enough to look Sam in the eye. "I crushed it, right?"

His smile banished the worst of my panic, soothing the last

of that frantic fear. He moved his hands from my back and over my shoulders to cup my cheeks.

"Never been prouder."

My breathing stilled as he leaned in to press a kiss to my forehead, his mouth soft and warm on my skin for barely a second before he drew back. I thought he might kiss me for real, but he just held me that way, watching me. Making sure I was okay.

One hand slid to my neck, lightly hovering over my racing pulse point. Again, weird to find his care and responsibility so attractive, but knowing he was checking on me stoked a fire deep in my chest. A fire I'd once thought long-gone but knew now had never truly died out.

A child ran by, drawing my eyes to the people around us, the adults belaying and cheering from the mats, the children on the walls.

"Did everyone just see me have a panic attack up there?" I asked.

"Nope." His hands moved lower to squeeze my biceps. "They don't have a clue. Everyone's too busy doing their own thing and making sure their kids are safe."

"So, just *you* saw me have a panic attack up there."

"Just me."

He slowly released me, stepping back to give us space I wasn't sure I wanted anymore.

"We should probably get you out of this. Unless you want to try again?"

His voice held no hint of teasing, as though it were a perfectly serious offer. As though I really might head back up and see if I'd have a different outcome this time. My impulse was to laugh in his face and get the heck out of the building, stat, but I hesitated. I'd been having fun climbing that wall—

right until the actual height hit me. I wasn't sure I wanted to write it off forever.

I didn't want to get back up there anytime *soon*, but that didn't have to mean never.

"Maybe next time."

He nodded. "That's my girl."

sam

SO. Rock climbing had *not* gone as well as I'd hoped.

Should have been my time to shine. Show Harper a little bit of what I could do and connect with her over a sport I loved.

Instead, she'd had a panic attack on the wall. Not her fault, but at least partially mine.

I'd let her climb as high as she liked on her first try, thinking she'd stop when she felt ready. Truthfully, I'd figured her competitive streak would send her straight to the top, even if her muscles had revolted. Hadn't even considered the possibility she'd have trouble with the height. She hadn't been in danger—I'd had her the whole time—but that she'd *felt* she'd been in danger still left me sick inside.

It'd bothered her, too, even if she hadn't mentioned it. But from how she'd worried her bottom lip the whole drive back, easy to guess she saw what happened back there as a failure.

After going through a drive-through on our way out of Austin to give her the salty shot of starch she'd needed to physically recover, I'd brought her back to her place, where she'd taken a quick shower, laid out some of the sugar cookies we'd made a few days ago, and tucked herself beneath one of her soft blankets on her couch.

She might have recovered from her shock on the wall, but now, I needed a few minutes to pull myself together. She'd taken her hair out of its braid and changed into pajamas printed with Christmas elves. The pajamas I could handle. Well, barely. Her cozy T-shirt and lounge pants sent my pulse into overdrive, but I would manage it.

But the hair? I hadn't seen her hair down since I'd been back in Magnolia Ridge. She'd always kept it in braids or buns, up and out of the way for work or for exercise classes. But now, seeing that golden-red glory sweep over her shoulders, wisps of it trailing along her jaw, I was like a man dying of thirst catching sight of a cool glass of water. My mouth went dry, my attention caught, my hands flexing with the need to feel her hair run through my fingers.

Yeah, way to be normal at her house, dude.

"Can we skip ahead to Christmas movies?" she asked. "I just want to veg for a while."

"Sounds good to me." I sat in the middle of the couch and patted my thighs.

Funny how a long-gone habit could come back so easily. But Harper didn't hesitate, just twisted in her seat and stretched her legs out so her calves laid across my lap. I covered them with her blanket and worked them a little with my hands, loosening her up from her shins to her socked feet.

"Were you a massage therapist, too?"

I chuckled, squeezing her toes through the blanket. "Nope. Haven't tried that one yet."

She clicked around on the remote until a movie pulled up on the TV screen. A couple gazed lovingly at each other in front of a snow-covered house.

"Am I about to find out what a ghost romance is?"

She laughed, pressing Play. "You're going to love it."

We watched for a while, my hands moving aimlessly over Harper's calves and feet. I tried to pay attention to the story, but my brain was shorting out over this much contact with her. I didn't feel too bad about not following the movie's plot, since she seemed as distracted as I was. After a while, she turned to watch me instead of the television.

"You're thinking awfully loudly," I said, finally shifting to face her.

She shrugged, her fingers playing over the plush blanket covering her lap. "I'm just wondering."

Pretty sure I could guess what she was wondering, but I still had to ask. "What?"

"Have you ever had something like that happen to you? On the wall?"

I kicked myself all over again. I could have at least warned her. A little heads-up might have helped her be aware of her feelings about the height before they had a chance to overwhelm her. She'd climbed too far without looking, and the change had shocked her.

"It's more common than you think. Plenty of people get thirty or forty feet up before their brain's self-preservation instinct kicks in, demanding they return to the ground. A lot of seasoned climbers deal with it, too. You're in good company."

Her irritated look told me she hadn't missed how I'd avoided the question.

"But are *you* in that company?"

I shook my head, even though it wasn't the reassurance she'd been after. "Heights have never bothered me."

Her mouth twisted into a little frown. "I never thought they bothered me, either, but I guess I'd never been high enough to know it. I'm strictly a sea-level kind of gal."

I curled my fingers around her feet, working the arches. "There's a lot of good stuff to see at sea-level, too."

She squinted at me as if she didn't agree. "How high have you climbed?"

Wasn't sure if my answer would make her feel better or worse. "I've done some fourteen-thousand footers."

"You said that like it was no big deal. That's really impressive."

"It's not all lead climbing and belays. Most are just hikes with some handholds to get through the tricky parts." Downplaying it a little, but it wasn't all climbing straight up a mountain face on a rope, either.

"And you never get nervous? Never freak out a little bit?"

I squeezed one of her heels between my palms, rubbing in circles until I reached the top of her foot. Her soft little sound of satisfaction made my stomach dip, but I tried to focus. "Not on a mountain. I've had a panic attack, though. Pretty recently."

"Will you tell me?" she asked gently.

I hadn't talked much with anyone about what had really been behind my decision to come back to Magnolia Ridge. Partially out of respect for Ian, but also because I didn't love how much it said about me. For all their prodding, not even Grandpa or Georgia knew what had finally driven me to come home.

But I needed to tell Harper. Not just to reassure her about her feelings on the climbing wall, but because at this point, I wasn't sure there was much about my life I wouldn't tell her. I wanted her to know it all. I wanted her to know *me*.

"In Durango, I worked for a mountain guide company run by three brothers: Pierce, Steven, and Ian. They became my mentors in the business, especially Ian. I don't know if you've ever read any climbing magazines, but he was pretty famous for what he does."

"I think I let my climbing magazine subscription expire."

I smiled at her dry delivery.

"I was a fan of his before I started there, I'll put it that way. He'd built a career out of climbing and guiding, and had a pretty good amount of fame in that part of the world. The greatest guy, too, always quick with a joke, made everyone around him feel like a friend. But he knew his stuff. Skilled like you wouldn't believe. Watching Ian Vaughn climb was like seeing a master at work. I can only hope to ever be that good."

Pierce and Steven were skilled, too, but I'd spent most of my time with Ian, first shadowing him and later working side by side. We got along well, with our similar dispositions and mutual inability to sit still. He was only about ten years older than me, but that's who I'd wanted to be when I finally got myself together and grew up.

Right until I saw just what a future as Ian Vaughn could be like.

"What happened?" she whispered.

She sounded like she expected me to whip out Ian's obituary.

"It's not as bad as I'm making it sound, just so you know. He's okay. Kind of. But he had an accident in June."

Her face contorted as though all kinds of grisly images swirled in her mind. "He fell on a climb?"

"Not climbing. He crashed his motorcycle."

Her concern shifted gears. "Oh. Is he okay?"

"He lost a leg. I visited him in the rehabilitation center he was in about two months after the accident. I'll never forget seeing the man I'd looked up to so broken. I knew right then I needed to make a change. I never wanted to be like that."

She shifted, pulling her feet out of my hands. "Sam, losing his leg does not make him a different person or less capable. I've worked with tons of people who have lost limbs, and let me tell you, they're not any less people just because they have prosthetics."

She tucked her legs beneath her, punishing me for being so superficial.

"No, that's not it," I said, huffing a breath. "I'm not explaining this right. I don't care about his leg. Ian wasn't the same man *inside*. As far as he was concerned, he'd lost his career, and maybe he has, I don't know. But when he needed people to rally around him, he pushed everyone away."

He hadn't acknowledged me during my visit. I'd said a few empty phrases of reassurance, but he hadn't so much as looked at me. According to Pierce, he'd been the same with his brothers. Whatever comfort anyone tried to offer, he'd rejected it all.

"He almost died after the crash, but I don't think it was pain in his leg that hurt him, it was that he'd never have that life back again. He'd sacrificed everything for his career in guiding and climbing, and when he lost that, what did he have left?"

I paused, fighting off the image of the fearless Ian Vaughn lying in that rehab bed as if his life was over. I'd never lost a leg, so my opinion might not mean much, but it looked to me like he'd given up. If he couldn't have the life in the mountains he'd created, he didn't want anything. I wouldn't even say he'd looked miserable—that would be a strong emotion. He'd just laid there, staring at the wall, shutting everyone out and waiting for the world to end.

He'd looked like *nothing*, and that emptiness was so much worse.

"When I left his room, I went outside and sat in my car. My heart was racing, I couldn't get my breathing to even out, my hands shook. I panicked."

Harper put her legs back across my lap, scooting closer to loop one hand around my elbow as though she could soothe those old memories away.

"I'm sorry. It must have been hard to see him like that."

"It was, but I admit, I wasn't thinking of him right then. I was thinking of me. I was scared."

"Scared of what?"

"How alike we were."

I took her hand in mine, stroking her fingers, trying to find the right words. "I'd been living from one experience to another, always looking for my next personal best. No plans, no long-term goals. No long-term relationships, either. I was living my best life, but I was living it alone. That day, everything shifted. I sat in my car imagining myself brought down by an injury in ten or twenty years—what would I have left then? My achievements? The mountains I'd climbed? The places I'd seen?"

I turned her hand over, lacing our fingers together. "None of that would matter if I didn't have anyone to share it with."

"That's why you came home."

She sounded like she'd finally put the last piece in a puzzle after a long search.

"I didn't want to be alone anymore. I'd developed friendships through the years, but they were short-lived. I wanted more. I wanted a relationship again with everyone I cared about here. Georgia. Grandpa. Dad and the littles." I shifted so I could face her fully. "You."

Her soft little intake of breath made my stomach flip. I'd said too much this time for sure, but I couldn't keep pretending like seeing her again had only been a happy coincidence. I might not have had a plan for winning her back, but the hope that I *could* had been my main reason for coming home to Magnolia Ridge.

It didn't line up with her plans for keeping me in the friend zone, but if I wanted to avoid Ian's lonely fate, I'd need to take a few risks.

Her gaze seemed stuck on mine, her lips parted as if searching for something to say. I stared into her caramel eyes, waiting for her to decide. Back in high school, we'd made a game of staring at each other this way. Sometimes, this much charged eye contact would make one of us burst into laughter. Other times...

Harper crashed into me, her mouth on mine. No hesitation, no tester kisses, just a comet lighting up the night sky. Her hand came to the back of my neck, urging me even closer as though I might slip away. I shifted her until she was almost in my lap, her legs across mine, our arms circling each other to block everything else out.

I groaned like a desperate man, the years and miles between us erased with every touch. Kissing Harper felt more like coming home than crossing into Magnolia Ridge's town limits ever had. The sliver of my mind still capable of stringing together words wanted to know why I'd left in the first place, but the rest of me just rejoiced in the moment.

Her silky hair sliding beneath my fingers on her shoulder. The sweet taste of sugar cookies on her mouth. The tiny, glorious sounds she made with each breath. My chaotic brain paused its frantic hop-scotch, devoting itself fully to every last detail.

I traced the line of her jaw, my hand splaying to span her neck. How could skin be this soft? Her pulse jumped beneath my fingers, her heart rate zooming as fast as mine. I bent down so I could press my mouth there, nipping lightly at her neck, that heady vanilla scent imprinting on my synapses.

She drew in a long breath like she'd just come up from a deep-dive. I shifted, opening my eyes to find uncertainty in hers. A fire of desire shone there, too, but the thread of indecision sobered me like a shot of caffeine, jolting me out of my daze. I didn't want her to second-guess or regret any part of this.

Right now, I needed to be the reliable sedan, not the sports car ready to hit one hundred miles per hour.

Loosening my hold on her, I gave her a little more space, trailing my fingers along her hairline even as I pulled back. "Okay there, Harps?"

"Maybe we should…" She swallowed hard, her gaze dropping to my mouth for the barest second before darting back up again. "Maybe we should watch the movie. It won't count for your list otherwise."

Her mouth curved, but the hesitation in that smile slayed me.

"Whatever you want."

She watched me a full minute, like she was still deciding something. I meant exactly what I'd said—I'd give her anything she wanted. An excuse? Time? Pull her back into my arms and kiss her until she had no questions left about what either of us was feeling? She could take her pick.

Although, my vote would be a solid yes for that last one.

"Okay," she breathed. She shifted her legs off my lap, but tucked herself up against my side, her head on my shoulder.

I'd take it.

harper

SATURDAY AFTERNOON, I scurried up Center Street looking for Sam. We'd originally planned to meet at four to see some of the Christmas decorations downtown and take his little siblings to visit Santa. Instead, his texts had started up just after two.

Sam: Bad news. Georgia's coworker is sick, so she had to go into the bookstore today. That means I'm on full-time kid duty

Harper: You'll do fine

Sam: I've lost Finn twice

Harper: I'm sure it's not that bad

Sam: Maybe I shouldn't have bought them banana splits

Sam: Can you meet us early?

Harper: Are you asking me to help you babysit?

Sam: I'm asking you to enjoy these precious moments with my younger siblings before time steals their childhoods in the blink of an eye

Harper: It's going to cost you

Sam: Ugggggh. What fresh Christmas horrors do you have in mind?

Harper: I heard they're doing wagon rides downtown

Sam: ...

Harper: And the wagon's lit up with Christmas lights

Harper: And it plays Christmas songs

Harper: And the driver dresses up like one of Santa's elves

Sam: Googling how to slip into a coma

Harper: I could let you struggle with two little kids all night

Sam: Wagon rides for everyone

I found him wandering down First Street, a little girl tugging him along by one hand and a little boy several feet in front of them wildly waving at a store window. Just before I caught up, Sam noticed me. His smile switched on, lighting me up with flickering, buzzing flames.

After our kiss last night, I'd feigned amnesia. Didn't mention it again, didn't come close to doing it again. Hadn't I already said platonic friendship was the only solution for us? I'd snuggled him a little, sure, but no further. After the movie, he'd said goodnight in my doorway, and if I'd secretly hoped for another kiss, I hadn't let on. Following my lead, I guess, he hadn't tried for one. I'd gone to bed wound up and disappointed, trying to decide if I'd rather have the stability of Sam's friendship, or the shaky ground of his kisses.

Too late to do anything about it, I'd cast my vote for those earth-shattering kisses.

Seeing him now, my heart rate skyrocketed while my stomach plummeted, making room in my ribcage for all the butterflies his smile unleashed. Pretty sure this was not how buddies reacted when they saw each other.

"Harper." He said my name like reaching for a lifeline. *Thank you,* he mouthed.

Now *that* made the butterflies go wild. He'd unwittingly keyed into my need to be needed, the thrill of rescuing him setting my ridiculous heart on fire.

"Guys," he said, catching the attention of his siblings. "This is Harper. She's going to see Santa with us. This is Willa."

The little girl turned her big brown eyes up to me. Her black hair had been set into two braids that looped in on themselves like hard candy curls, and the tiniest chocolate smudge graced one corner of her mouth.

Kind of thought he'd been joking about the banana splits.

"Hi, Willa. That's a very pretty dress you're wearing." She wore a red smocked dress that reminded me of Clara's nightgown in the Nutcracker, only about ten times fancier. "I like your shiny shoes."

"The skirt twirls." She did a few quick spins to demonstrate, never quite letting go of Sam's hand.

I clapped in appreciation, making her grin.

"And this is Finn," Sam said, indicating the little boy who had joined us.

"Hi, Finn. You look ready to meet Santa."

Finn wore a red plaid suit complete with green tie covered in Christmas trees, his dark hair slicked back making him look like a little banker. Well—a festive little banker, who also sported remnants of his banana split on his face.

He smiled but went back to ogling the board game store's window and all the video games laid out front and center.

I leaned closer to Sam. "I feel seriously underdressed."

His gaze raked over me, taking in my old jeans and blush sherpa hoodie. Nothing very nice or remotely revealing, but his eyes heated in approval anyway.

"Not underdressed," he said, his voice gravelly. Then he

seemed to snap out of it. "They're over the top. My stepmom gets a little extra over the holidays. Like some people."

"It's normal Christmas spirit, Samuel."

Willa's head whipped around. "Is your name *Samuel?*"

He shot me a stern look before turning his attention to her. "Don't sound so horrified. It's a good name."

She laughed, clutching her stomach with one hand and rocking back and forth in perfect mime of a belly laugh. "*Samuel.* That's so funny."

"Off to a great start, Harps," he muttered.

His eyes still sparkled, though, so it couldn't have been all that bad.

"So when are we going to see Santa?" I asked, hoping to right the ship a little bit.

"Maybe we should do that first and then look at decorations. If we do the reverse, they might get dirty before their Santa pictures."

"Yeah, we wouldn't want to do anything risky like give them ice cream first."

His mouth thinned, his eyes narrowed on me in a way that made my stomach dip low. Getting easy-going Sam irritated should not give me a perverse thrill, and yet...

Oh, no. I was becoming as bad as Eliza.

That knowledge did not stop the stomach-swooping going on at the moment.

"In my defense," he said, "I didn't know the banana splits would be so big."

A high-pitched cackle bubbled out of Willa. "They were super big, Samuel."

He stared at me, his eyes flat, before cocking one eyebrow in silent *Are you happy now?*

I really was.

"Georgia said Santa is set up in the pavilion in town square," Sam said. "Let's head that way."

"You know, the night market is just another block away."

His wide-eyed look of warning made me bite back the rest of what I'd been about to suggest. The kids might enjoy looking at everything the market had to offer. Then again, they might expect presents, too.

"There's no telling exactly where Dad and Ava are," he said.

Right. His dad and stepmom were Christmas shopping. Probably would ruin a bit of the magic for Finn and Willa if we stumbled across them checking off Santa's list.

Willa kept her hand locked in Sam's, swinging it as we wandered along the sidewalk. Finn darted to store windows anytime something inside looked interesting, dodging people in a blur of red and green. I snuggled deeper into my hoodie, soaking up the sights.

I loved downtown Magnolia Ridge at Christmastime. Most shops decorated their windows and storefronts until everything sparkled with the colors of the season. Could hardly move five feet down the street without passing a miniature tree or faux-snowman, and one store even had a whole herd of light-up animatronic reindeer out front. Doors chimed as they swung open, Christmas music drifting around us as we passed. I felt as cozy and snug as if I were walking through one of my snow globes.

Minus the snow.

Sam whistled as we neared the pavilion. "Line's longer than I expected."

"Everybody wants to see Santa," Willa piped up.

Sam's eyes met mine. After everything he'd told me, I knew one person who didn't want to see Santa. Yet here he was, stepping up to take his little siblings to participate in a tradition that brought back bad memories for him, and doing it with a smile.

His responsible streak at the climbing gym had made my little heart flutter, but seeing him in line to greet Saint Nick with his younger brother and sister had it spinning like a top. His obvious affection for them—and their adoration of him—proved hard to resist.

"This isn't the real Santa." Finn looked down his little nose at his sister. "There are lots of Santas, and none of them are real. Everybody knows that."

Willa turned big eyes up to Sam, her lower lip wobbling at that shocking news. He frowned at her for a second, and I held my breath, afraid he truly might burst that bubble. He bent down to get his face close to hers.

"There are lots of Santas, that's true. But they all work together, and report kids' Christmas lists back to the North Pole." He leaned even closer, ready to share a secret. "And if you're really lucky, you get to see the *real* Santa."

Her face shone out her joy at his perfect response, her grin hitting me smack in the tender spot behind my ribs. That spot was getting a workout around Sam lately.

"I hope we get to see the real one," she whispered.

"I hope so, too," he whispered back.

I hadn't had Sam reassuring a little girl about Santa on my bingo card, but he'd thoroughly checked that box. Those walls I kept trying to rebuild to keep him out? He'd just bulldozed them courtesy a tender interaction with his tiny sister. Affection flooded in, drowning out my resolve to keep my feet firmly planted in the friend zone.

He straightened up and caught me goggling at him. A trademark Sam smile crept over his mouth, his lips dipping and tugging until his dimples popped out.

Oh, those dimples.

I used to trace them, running my fingertips lightly over the divot, testing their depth. I used to kiss them, too, feeling the little hollows beneath my lips. They were never covered with this much scruff back then, but I could probably still find them beneath a soft kiss.

His smile grew wider as though I'd said all that out loud. I wasn't doing a very good job of playing it cool tonight. Erasing the glazed expression from my face, I snapped out of my dimple-contemplation.

Platonic friends, I reminded myself. Sounded weak even in my head.

"Do you know what you're going to ask Santa for?" I asked generally. Anything to take my mind off dimples, scruff, and kisses.

Finn rattled off a video game console name. "It comes with thirty-six games."

No surprise that the kid who didn't believe in Santa anymore still expected to get expensive goodies from him on Christmas morning.

"I want a dolly that looks just like me," Willa said from Sam's other side as we moved forward in line. "With black hair and brown eyes, and we'll have matching dresses and everything."

"Ooh, I love that idea."

Willa tilted her head up to look at Sam. "What about you, Samuel?"

Kind of loved she'd latched on to that so quickly.

He turned to me, silently telegraphing...*what* exactly, I had no idea, and didn't really want to speculate.

Such a bad liar. I did want to speculate. I could speculate for days.

Shifting back to her, he flashed a benevolent smile. "I want a doll that looks like me. Although I don't know if this town can handle two such gorgeous men."

He wiggled his eyebrows at her until she giggled.

"*Samuel.* What do you really want?"

He hesitated a second before answering, seeming to really think about the question this time. "I want to get a good job in town so I can stick around a while."

That hit me even harder than his sweetness with his siblings had. He really wanted to stay this time. My insides went gooey, all warm and soft and tender. But the rest of his comment sank in right after. He wanted to stay, but he probably couldn't do that living off of volunteer work and part-time pay.

And if he couldn't find something in town?

I tried not to let my mind flood with possibilities. Really, there was just the one. If he couldn't find work in town, he would leave again.

Suddenly, I felt as frosty as though a cold snap had swept in.

Willa scowled. "Santa can't bring you a job."

"Dad says you need to take work seriously for a change." Finn didn't seem to realize the rudeness of his remark. "You've been couch sailing too long."

"It's couch surfing," Sam corrected.

"Are you staying with your dad?" I hadn't thought much about where he lived since he'd been back. Sort of just assumed he'd found a place of his own, but it had never come up. Naturally, if he didn't have a solid job, he couldn't get a place of his own, either.

"No, I'm staying with Georgia. She's been more generous than I deserve."

We shifted forward a few more feet in line, slowly getting closer to the pavilion and the waiting Santa, my thoughts tripping up over this seemingly innocent conversation.

"It's just temporary though, right?" I said. "I'm sure you'll get a full-time job soon."

Unless that wasn't his intention. Sleeping on his sister's couch and working part-time jobs meant he could leave Magnolia Ridge again pretty easily. He still had a lot left to see out in the wide world. He'd only said he wanted to stick around *a while*.

"Here, or wherever," I added, just in case my reassurance had sounded too much like criticism. Or wishful thinking.

He shot me a stern look. "Here."

His firm response made a smile spring onto my face.

"Samuel!" Willa tugged hard on his hand, breaking him away from me. "A job is not a present from Santa."

"Right, a present. Well, what I want this year won't fit in a stocking."

His eyes darted to mine, his meaning whipping up the embers in my chest into a little bonfire cozy enough to roast marshmallows over.

This was exactly what I'd said I wanted to avoid, all his sassy flirting that left me thinking he really wanted me and would really stick around. The sensible thing to do would be to slow down and definitely not let his teasing go to my head.

But Eliza's admonition rang through my mind again: *Why do you have to be so sensible about everything?* Maybe, as an addendum to my list, I could do the non-Harper thing for a change. Flirt with the guy. Brazenly kiss someone. Take an actual risk.

"I think I'll ask for mistletoe," he added.

"Urgh." Finn sounded like he'd just been offered a bite of moldy cheese.

"What do you want from Santa, Harper?" Willa asked.

Despite my resolve to be less Harper-like, I couldn't very well copy Sam's answer—Finn might lose his banana split.

Much safer to choose a non-flirty option, at least in front of the kids.

"I'm going to ask for a snow globe," I told her.

"Good idea, you're running low on those," Sam said.

"I know what I like."

And for good or bad, I still liked spending time with Sam more than I liked anything else.

sam

HARPER AND I had managed to scrub the last specks of chocolate sauce off of Finn and Willa's faces before their turn came to sit on Santa's lap. Following Ava's instructions, I'd had them go together, and thankfully, they'd behaved like little angels in their effort to impress the big guy. We snapped pictures from different angles, capturing more than enough candids and posed shots to please my dad's wife. Hopefully, anyway.

"I can't wait to see my doll." Willa walked between Harper and me, holding our hands and swinging our arms.

"What will you name her?" Harper asked.

"Hallelujah."

Harper's eyes darted to mine, a smile twisting her lips. "Good name."

"What time are Mom and Dad getting us?" Finn asked.

"Are you sick of me already? We're not done yet." More importantly, Dad and Ava weren't done yet. Georgia had agreed to get the littles out of their hair and away from the toy store for a couple of hours. We still had a while yet to go before it would be time to meet up with them at Dogeared.

"Don't you want to see the decorations?" Willa said, the middle R pronounced like a W. *Decowations*. "Look at that tree!"

She pointed across town square at a ten-foot-tall Christmas tree lit up in front of a realtor's office. Her enthusiasm seemed limitless—we'd seen about a dozen Christmas trees so far tonight, and she'd been impressed by every last one.

"Trees are boring."

Finn sighed loudly after that downer proclamation, and I suspected I didn't have long before the evening went fully sideways. Sure wasn't prepared to deal with an unhappy kid when I couldn't hand him off to his parents for another hour.

"Are wagon rides boring?" I asked.

All three of my companions gave little squeals of delight, Harper the loudest of all. Her pure joy curled through me like an endless spiral staircase, my own happiness climbing up, up, up. We herded our little group to the other side of town square where a line waited. More standing around wasn't anybody's top pick for the evening, but thankfully, the line was short.

"After wagon rides, we'll visit Georgia in the bookstore."

"Georgia's my big sister," Willa said, craning her neck to look up at Harper.

"She knows," Finn said from my other side.

"She gives me toenail parties and cupcakes."

Harper glanced at me, but I was about as baffled as she looked by that info.

"What are toenail parties?" Harper asked.

"It's when she paints my toes." Willa kicked a foot in front of her to demonstrate.

"My big sister used to paint my toenails, too."

Harper's sweet smile made my chest contract and swell at the same time. I'd known she'd be good with the kids, but I hadn't counted on what seeing that would do to me. Crazy longings took root deep in my chest, painting visions of the future I'd come home to find.

"She's a good big sister," Willa said, more to herself than us. "And now, I have two big brothers."

"You always had two big brothers," I said, shaking her hand in mine.

She hitched a shoulder in disagreement, the little move a silent, stinging rebuke. I'd come home once or twice a year at most, maybe even less since she'd been born. Never stayed more than a few days. Couldn't be surprised she didn't think much of the memories of me she'd had so far. Why not consider me a new brother? I sure hadn't acted like one before now.

"Maybe when you're a little bigger," Harper said, "Sam will teach you how to rock climb."

"Will you?" Willa asked.

"Really?" Finn joined in.

"If you want to." I hadn't thought to offer, but Harper's suggestion sounded like an even bigger hit than the wagon ride idea had been.

"We do!" they chorused.

"I'm big enough now, aren't I, Samuel?" Willa asked.

"You're too small," Finn told her. "But I can go, right, Sam?"

"You're both big enough for the beginner wall if you really want to try."

They whooped and cheered, talking over each other in their enthusiasm. I got a weird sense of brotherly satisfaction to know they'd be that excited to spend time with me. They'd been game enough so far, but not this overjoyed. And yeah, a fair bit of that was for the rock climbing, but it still warmed me up inside.

I glanced at Harper, whose soft, subtle smile made my heart kick against my ribs. *Thank you*, I mouthed to her for the second time tonight.

You owe me, she mouthed back.

I sure wouldn't mind paying that debt in full.

Not ten minutes later, Finn and Willa had lost the camaraderie they'd briefly displayed, and had taken to lightly shoving each other and tossing out mild insults as we waited in line. Wasn't really sure how to handle the situation, but I probably needed to do something. I only had minimal memories of those years of Georgia and me calling each other names behind our parents' backs, but a spontaneous cease-fire didn't seem likely.

"If I hear the word 'booger' one more time, I'm going to march you two over to Dogeared and we'll skip the wagon ride."

I'd never thought I had a dad voice, but they'd brought it out of me.

Harper stifled a laugh, her eyes sparkling at my stern façade. She could laugh all she liked—if it made the kids get along, I'd whip out my dad voice all night. They straightened up, so a solid point for me.

Finally, the Christmas-spangled wagon came back into view. Pulled by two draft horses and led by a man who indeed wore an extra-large elf costume complete with pointy shoes, the wagon had been decked out in red and green garlands and loops of string lights. Not nearly so fancy as the carriages and sleighs that popped up in Durango or Stowe at Christmastime, but it had its magic.

A good percentage of that magic was the Nat King Cole song drifting through hidden speakers, crooning about the wonders of Christmas.

Willa gasped and clapped, practically coming unglued from excitement. Finn looked excited, too, but the crowd around us seemed to put a damper on his urge to jump up and down like his sister was doing. Kid was only eleven—what everyone else thought should have been the least of his concerns.

I whooped and clapped my hands right along with Willa, proving Finn didn't need to keep a straight face just because he'd reached double-digit age. A few of the waiting families around us joined in, cheering as the last passengers stepped down out of the wagon bed. At last, Finn rolled his eyes but clapped along, giving a self-conscious little whoop of his own.

We climbed aboard, claiming blanket-covered hay bales on one side of the wagon. Wasn't sure the kids should sit together after all the name-calling just now, but they seemed to have made up for the ride. Harper took her spot next to me, smiling almost as wide as Willa.

Everyone got settled, the driver elf closed up the wagon gate, and we set off. Every last kid *oohed* and *aahed* like we were on a ride at Disneyland. Wasn't any more than tooling around Magnolia Ridge streets in an old wooden wagon, but with the Christmas music playing and so many shops lit up for the season, it had a certain appeal.

Most appealing of all was Harper sitting next to me. The outside of our legs pressed together, her shoulder against mine as we jostled along the road. If I'd known we'd be so cozy, I would have figured out a way to get two wagon rides tonight.

The wagon jolted over a pothole, bouncing Harper almost into my lap. I snaked my arm around her shoulders, tucking her up against me to keep her steady. In the glow of the string lights, I caught the wash of color on her cheeks and the way she pulled her lower lip between her teeth.

"Okay there, Harps?" I asked softly.

She nodded, her eyes drifting to my mouth before they clocked the dozen or so other people in the wagon with us. For a second, I thought she might push away and wiggle free of my arm, but she relaxed against me, resting one hand on my knee as she turned her attention back to the decorations we passed.

Maybe I'd spent a little too much time enjoying her nearness, because a small voice knocked me right out of my reverie.

"Is Harper your girlfriend, Samuel?"

Willa no longer watched the Christmas goodies on either side of us, but leaned toward the middle of the wagon, angling her body to get the best view of Harper and me. Georgia's warnings about the *K-I-S-S-I-N-G* song crossed my mind, but those fears weren't enough to make me let Harper go now.

"We've known each other a long time." There. Diplomatic and concise.

Willa's gaze narrowed until she looked far older than her six years. "Do you kiss? That's how you know if you're boyfriend and girlfriend."

A couple of the parents closest to us in the crowded wagon looked away, trying to hide their sniggers. I'd had a pretty good run with the kids tonight—only fitting that Willa would smash it all with some public inquisition.

Harper shifted, putting the tiniest space between us, but I told myself she was just trying to get more comfortable on the hay bale. She didn't step up to say we *weren't* boyfriend and girlfriend, so I marked that up as an overall win.

And yeah, fully aware I was a twenty-eight-year-old man wondering if the woman I cared about and had kissed senseless the night before could be called my girlfriend yet.

"You can't just ask people if they kiss," I told Willa. "It's not appropriate."

Maybe a plea for decorum mixed with the dad voice would get me out of this. Considering who I was making my plea to... probably not.

Willa's eyebrows tugged together. "You're not people, you're my brother."

"He means you're embarrassing him," Finn said from her other side. "You're an embarrassment."

"You're not an embarrassment," I told her, shooting Finn a hard look. "And I'm not embarrassed. But kissing isn't really wagon-talk."

"That means they kiss," Finn said, and they both giggled.

Okay, so much for decorum.

Willa got up on her knees and leaned in until her face hit my ear as we went over another bump. "I like her," she whispered.

"I like her, too," I whispered back.

She sat down again, grinning like mad at Harper before finally focusing her goldfish-like attention back on the Christmas decorations on Center Street.

I risked a glance at the woman still snuggled against my side. Her smile hit like Christmas crackers *pop-pop-popping* in my chest. Only the threat of more interrogation from Willa kept me from kissing Harper again right then and there, and setting everyone straight about whether or not she was my girlfriend.

sam

THE CHIMES over Dogeared's doors rang as our little group barreled through. We'd managed to survive the rest of the wagon ride with no further talk of kisses or girlfriends, and the kids didn't even mention boogers once. Dad and Ava would be here soon, and the kids' clothes had come through the night unscathed. Might as well start doing my victory dance in the end zone now.

First thing I noticed in the store was Dogeared's owner, Miles, standing at the register. His thick-framed glasses and red cardigan gave off Mr. Rogers vibes, but he appeared one hundred percent healthy. Next came my sister's defiant look, one hip jutting out as if to demonstrate how unapologetic she was. Finally, the realization I'd been set up.

Scheming sisters everywhere could learn a thing or two from mine.

"Georgia!" Both kids ran up to tackle her in a hug.

She laughed, holding them hard for a second. "Did you have fun seeing Santa?"

"Samuel said he was the really real Santa," Willa told her.

Georgia shot a look of shock my way, her face comically contorted. "Did Samuel say that?"

From her surprise, she must have figured I'd blab about the true nature of Santa. Didn't love she thought I'd ruin their childhoods that way.

"I can't wait to see my doll," Willa said dreamily.

"What did you think, Finn? Was he the real Santa?"

Finn shrugged. "His beard was real."

For thinking only his beard was real, the kid had been pretty sincere when he explained exactly the type of video game system he wanted to find under the tree.

"Let's get you two set up with hot cocoas while you wait for Dad and Ava." Georgia took two ceramic mugs from Miles and led them to an empty table.

Most of the store held aisles of books new and old, but the front corner morphed from bookstore into café, with a few tables and chairs set up in the picture windows. They served coffee and tea, along with a small selection of pastries Miles made every morning. Apparently, he was a writer, too, which went pretty perfectly with Georgia making book covers.

From the way he watched her, I suspected he thought they went pretty perfectly together, too. Given Georgia's total ignorance of his admiration, the guy didn't stand a chance.

Finn eyed the tiny scones and cinnamon rolls as he passed the glass case. "Can we have something to eat?"

"Aren't you still full from your banana split?" I asked.

Georgia raised her eyebrows at me. "Banana splits? In these outfits? Do you want Ava to rum-pum-pum you right in the face?"

In hindsight, the banana splits hadn't been one of my brighter ideas, but since things had worked out, I figured we could let it go.

"They did okay."

She got them situated with plenty of napkins for any cocoa drips, and Miles set a little plate with two scones on it between them. So glad it wasn't just me ruining their appetites tonight.

Georgia returned to Harper and me. "Thanks for helping Sam out today, Harper. I hope he wasn't too much trouble."

She just laughed. "He wasn't too bad. The kids were great, though."

"Surprised to see Miles has made a miracle recovery." I nodded at her boss who had returned behind the counter. "From your call this afternoon, I would have thought he'd be hospitalized by now."

Georgia tilted her head. "Might have exaggerated a tiny bit." She flashed a *Too bad* look before turning to Harper. "I'm starting a romance book group in January—would you be interested? The plan is to choose books from a different trope every month. Kind of mix it up with all the flavors of romance through the year."

"I would love that," Harper said, a genuine smile breaking across her face. "I've never been in a book club before, though."

"It's going to be really casual, just a bunch of romance readers getting together to talk about the latest swoony hero. If you don't have time to read the book, just come and chat with us. No big deal."

"Okay. I'll plan on it."

"Great." Georgia turned an overly-satisfied smile to me. "Maybe we can get Sam to join in sometime and give us the male perspective."

"You joke, but I'd do it." Didn't need to say I was already reading one of Georgia's romances, or why.

The guy in this one had been paid off by the woman's evil mother to skip town, and had come back five years later ready to grovel. Seemed convoluted to me, but I could relate to the need to grovel. I hadn't done nearly enough of that yet.

The chimes over the door rang as Dad and Ava walked through. I felt my smile slip and my back stiffen reflexively. I could hope that in time, seeing them together wouldn't give me the sudden urge to be airlifted out of the vicinity, but so far, it wasn't my favorite.

"There's my babies!" Ava buzzed over to Finn and Willa, taking each of their little faces in her hands and kissing their cheeks as though they'd been apart for months. "Did you have a good time with Georgia and Sam?"

"Georgia had to work," Finn said, licking the last of his scone from his lips.

"But Samuel and Harper took us to see Santa and on a wagon ride," Willa added.

Ava turned to us, but Dad had already crossed the room, his hand extended.

"Harper Webb. It's been too long." He shook her hand hard. "How have you been?"

"Things are good."

Ava joined Dad, who made introductions. "Harper here is a doctor over at the retirement community."

He sounded as proud as if he were bragging on one of his own kids. Not me, of course, but the others. I appreciated the support he showed her, even if it burned a little he'd never talked that way about me. I'd never really given him a reason to, but still. You wanted your parents to be proud of you.

"That's impressive," Ava said with an appropriate level of awe.

"I'm a physical therapist," Harper said as if the clarification made her less extraordinary.

"Still," Dad said. "A doctor's a doctor. Your parents must be proud."

And there it was. If I resented him for his choices, he resented me just as much for mine. No degree, no career to speak of—I hadn't done much he could brag about. And Christopher Donnelly loved to brag.

"I think they're just happy I live in town."

"Sam and Georgia live in town, too, but I think I'd be happier if they were doctors." He laughed as though he'd said anything remotely funny.

"Georgia's doing some pretty awesome freelance work." Unfair of him to lump her in with me. I'd seen the covers she'd done. They looked really good, even if they weren't for some big-name corporation the way Dad hoped. Sounded like the work already matched her income at the bookstore, too. "Doesn't even have to wear a stethoscope."

"Are you still doing that?"

That he didn't know ticked me right off. Georgia nodded but didn't seem nearly as irritated as I was. Maybe she'd grown numb to his casual indifference, but that just made me madder. Me, I'd been gone for years—his ignorance about me or what I'd done made sense. But she'd at least been here, he should know what was going on in her life.

"Sam was invaluable at Vaughn Mountain Views." God bless my sister, fighting my losing battle for me. "The owners call him every few weeks, begging him to come back."

Harper's eyes found mine, a clear question written there. I ticked my head to the side in subtle confirmation. Pierce had called a few times to find out how serious I was about staying in Texas. At first, I hadn't committed to anything for sure—wanting to stay, and finding a way to make that work weren't the same thing. But the last time we'd talked, I'd told him flat-out I intended to stay in Magnolia Ridge. He'd wished me well, and asked me to keep them in mind if I ever made it back to Colorado.

"Any potential for advancement there?"

Right. The only climbing Dad cared about was the corporate kind.

"Not likely." Pierce, Steven, and Ian Vaughn had the executive positions pretty well covered. If Ian really didn't come back to the company, they might have to bring someone else in, but none of that meant anything to me if I wasn't going back, either.

"Too bad. My offer still stands."

"I'll keep that in mind." Read: I would forget it immediately.

He flicked his wrist to check his watch. "Well. It's time I get my kids to bed."

That little remark shouldn't sting. It was accurate. He probably didn't mean anything by it. But it still felt like he'd drawn a circle around Finn and Willa as his kids, shutting Georgia and me out.

"Say thank you to Sam and Harper." Ava guided the littles over, dusting their faces with a napkin for every last trace of cocoa stains.

Finn waved and muttered a thank you, but Willa wrapped her arms around my waist in an exuberant hug.

"Thank you, Samuel." She turned those big brown eyes up to me, and my heart just about overflowed with affection. Dad might be hard to love right now, but his kids sure weren't.

I lightly squeezed her shoulders. "No problem, Willalujah."

She laughed, her cheeks rosy at how I'd merged her name with that of her future look-alike doll.

She let go of me and moved to Harper, flinging her arms around her just as easily. "Thank you, Harps."

Huh. Didn't think she'd heard that. Then again, she'd picked up on plenty between Harper and me the last couple of hours.

Dad scooped her up into his arms, nuzzling against her. "Did you ask Santa for what you want?"

She nodded, that huge, hopeful smile on her face.

"I think you've been a good girl this year. I bet you'll get it."

She tossed her arms around his neck and snuggled him, probably dreaming up exactly how perfect her doll would look come Christmas morning. Dad just grinned away, his late-in-life babies somehow making him look younger than I remembered him when I was growing up. The whole little tableau made my chest squeeze, but I couldn't tell if affection or jealousy had the upper hand.

Ava pulled Finn away. "Thanks again. You're coming to Christmas breakfast, right, Sam?"

"Well—"

"Great, we'll see you then!"

I suspected she disappeared out the door in a flash so I wouldn't have a chance to say no. I hadn't refused all that many invitations since I'd been back, but she seemed to know I'd been on the fence about the Christmas one.

Dad patted Willa's back, but her eyes were already drooping closed. "See you, Sam. Georgia. Harper, don't be a stranger."

They left, the door swinging shut behind them. I'd already needed to decompress after a day with the littles, but spending any time with Dad warranted a beer, at least. He had a way of dredging up my worst insecurities until I felt seventeen again, needing to escape. Seeing him dote on his new family only added an extra layer of awkwardness into the mix.

Georgia faced me, hands on her hips. "What offer did Dad make you?"

"Some admin thing in the office." Being a financial planner had never appealed, and I couldn't imagine being an underling for one would be any better. To be fair, I didn't have any other offers on the table at the moment.

"Probably the same job he's suggested for me. He'll get over it." She turned to Harper as if putting our dad behind her. "So, you got this Christmas Grinch to do the wagon ride? How'd you manage that?"

Harper's little grin made me forget all about Dad.

"He's surprisingly un-grinchy when he's desperate."

"Desperation's a good look on him."

"I'm discovering that, yes."

"Okay, okay, we're leaving." I grabbed Harper's hand and headed for the door. "Thanks for the push, Georgia."

"Anytime," she called. "I'll text you about the book club, Harper."

Harper turned and waved over her shoulder. "Definitely. See you later."

Finally, we made it onto the sidewalk, free of interfering sisters.

"Where did you park?"

"On Center," she said. "In front of the pharmacy."

I headed in that direction, hoping the cool evening air would focus my thoughts. Unlikely, since every last brain cell lasered in on the feel of Harper's hand in mine and the nudge of her shoulder on my arm. We had a little time before I needed to get to Lotus Flower for tonight's gentle yoga class. I would invite her to dinner—drinks, bare minimum. The wagon ride hadn't nearly paid her back for helping me out with my little brother and sister.

"The company in Colorado is trying to get you to come back?"

My hopes for the evening shattered like glass. She'd focused on the one thing I wished Georgia hadn't brought up.

"They are. I didn't leave at the best time. I still feel guilty about that."

Cutting out while Ian was still in the hospital and they were already running around trying to replace him had been a dick move on my part. Pierce and Steven had been good about it, but I still shouldn't have done it. In the moment, though, driven by the fear of following too closely in Ian's footsteps, I'd had to get back to Magnolia Ridge as quickly as I could.

"It sounds like a good opportunity."

"It is. It's a great business."

"You said it was your favorite job. And they really want you back. It sounds better than stringing together a few yoga sessions here and there."

I stopped beneath a lamp post and tugged her hand so she faced me. "Harps, hear me. I'm not going back there."

"I know," she said, even though she obviously didn't. "But if you ever change your mind, if you realize Colorado is where you're meant to be, it's okay if you—"

I tugged her the rest of the way to me. She hit my chest with a soft *oomph*, her eyes wide. I ran my hands into her hair, cupping the back of her head as I drew closer inch by inch. My eyes drifted over the little furrow in her forehead, the freckles dusting her nose and cheeks, her soft, full mouth.

"Harper," I said so close, my lips brushed hers. "I'm exactly where I want to be."

She made a little sound in her throat as I erased the last breath between us.

My mouth traced hers from one corner to the other, gentle caresses that lit me up with a slow-moving fire. Last night's fervent kisses had been like a hurricane, powerful and all-consuming, but tonight was a gentle breeze. My mind whispered we were in public on a sidewalk in the middle of Magnolia Ridge, with no privacy and nothing between us and the grind of the gossip mill. But my lips on hers outweighed those concerns, and I pressed on, showing her in every touch what she wouldn't hear in words.

I'm here.

I'm staying.

I'm yours.

Her hands splayed against my chest, her body yielding as she relaxed into the kiss. I'd never been much for planning, but in that kiss, I saw what I wanted next week, next month, for years and years in the future. She was my forever, right here in my arms.

"She *is* your girlfriend!"

Willa's delighted little voice broke us apart. We turned to see my dad's car paused on Center Street, the windows down so everyone inside could get a good look at us. My little sister sat in the back, up high in her booster seat, grinning like no tomorrow. Next to her, Finn looked fairly disgusted but still goggled at us. In the front, Ava wore a wry expression.

Dad leaned across Ava so we could see his face in her open window. "You two might want to take it somewhere else," he said, gesturing around.

As though Christopher Donnelly were the model of public decency and morals.

Still, I'd needed the reminder of our surroundings. Downtown bustled with shoppers going in and out of stores and workers taking off from their late-night office jobs. Wasn't quite the same as kissing Harper among the crowds beneath the tree downtown would have been, but a close second. Being exposed didn't bother me. I didn't care who saw us together.

Probably didn't mean I should display it for the whole town, though.

Their car started rolling forward, but Ava leaned out her window. "Invite Harper to Christmas breakfast!"

They drove off, leaving Harper and me standing in the chill beneath a Christmas bedazzled awning. She'd shifted out of my arms during the awkward conversation with my family, and the faint smile she wore now unsettled me. Relaxed, in-the-moment Harper was long gone.

"Sorry. Anybody else would have just driven past, but you know my dad."

"It's okay."

We set off again, no hand-holding or snuggling this time around. Definitely no pausing for tender kisses. I was not a fan of the new arrangement.

Two blocks later, we'd reached her car, and the silence was killing me. Had my family scared her off? Or was it all the hinting we were together? Didn't love either explanation for her distance.

"Are we—" I started, but she spoke at the same time.

"Do you want to get a tree with me tomorrow?"

I paused, probably looking like I didn't have two brain cells to rub together. Not what I'd expected her to say after our mini-walk of shame. "Sure."

"The farm opens at ten, but it's pretty late in the season so it shouldn't be too crowded."

"Okay."

"It's been dry lately, so we should be able to bring it in and decorate it as soon as we get home. Maybe get lunch and watch another Christmas movie after?"

"Definitely." She'd get nothing but *Yes* from me when her plans sounded this much like a date. Except... "I have a yoga class in the evening. But we have plenty of time before then."

"Okay. Good."

She stepped forward and kissed me square on the mouth. Brief, but intentional. I'd hardly registered she'd done it before she pulled away again and headed around the side of her car. What a time for my brain to stop and play catch up.

"I'll see you tomorrow at ten, then," she said as she opened the driver's side door.

"See you, Harps."

She got in, started up her car, and pulled away into the night. Kind of loved that she'd taken me by surprise. I headed toward my station wagon, grinning as I considered all the ways she might surprise me tomorrow.

harper

"THIS IS a lot more than just a Christmas tree farm, Harps."

Sam and I crunched through the gravel lot toward Vanderpool Farm's main buildings Sunday morning, the rich smell of pine needles drawing us closer. The day had turned out perfect for tree-hunting—crisp enough to see our breath but dry enough we wouldn't have to walk through mud. I'd bundled up in an old college sweatshirt, jeans, and big green rubber boots, with a scarf and hat I'd crocheted. Warm enough to keep me cozy, but nothing I'd be sad to get dirty.

Ignore what everyone's Christmas cards try to tell you—cutting down your own tree is a messy, sap-covered business.

My eyes skated over Sam, and my stomach nose-dived for the fourth time this morning. Seeing him in work boots, old jeans, and layers of thick flannel did something visceral to my insides, like my ovaries had started an interpretive dance in his honor. He looked ready to chop down every last tree on the farm, and I was here for it.

"We don't have to do everything they offer." Maybe I should have warned him. For someone Christmas-averse, Vanderpool's might have been a bad option.

They had an ornate sleigh tucked away in the heart of the cluster of buildings, with Jolly Old St. Nick listening to kids' wish lists as parents snapped pictures. The line snaked past the bonfire where sticky-fingered families roasted marshmallows, past the gift shop crammed top to bottom with handmade ornaments, all the way to the little building with an order window in the side where they served up coffees, caramel apples, and the ubiquitous cocoa. They had a bouncy castle shaped like a gingerbread house, a rustic shack full of hand-made wreaths, and topping it all off, two snow machines worked overtime pumping out short-lived ice crystals.

He shot me a sideways look. "Like you're not going to want a s'more."

"I wouldn't say no."

We headed that way first and popped marshmallows onto skewers, quickly roasting them over the blazing fire. Reaching past the little kids crowding the s'mores assembly table, we grabbed a few graham crackers and chocolate sections for our own gooey confections. I immediately took a bite of mine and was grateful I'd dressed appropriately, since the marshmallow and chocolate oozed onto my fingers.

"You said this place wouldn't be too crowded."

Sam ate a quarter of his s'more in a single bite, which should *not* have been sexy but absolutely was. Chewing? Totally not a sexy activity, either, but weirdly did it for me today.

"The other weekends, we wouldn't have even been able to find a spot around the fire." I nodded toward the lean-to where the tree farm attendants passed out hand saws. "Let's grab one of those and go find our tree."

Sam took one of the old metal bow saws and followed me away from the central crowd. Leaving the noise of the snow machines and the tree baler behind, I marched toward the massive fields of Virginia Pines. I loved the smell of pine tree and dirt out here. This late in the season, the acreage had been pretty well picked over, with mostly smallish trees, too-tall trees, and awkwardly shaped ones left behind, but we would find a good one eventually.

"How big a tree are we looking for here?" Beside me, Sam popped the last of his s'more into his mouth.

"Six or seven feet is enough for my house." I finished up my last bite of s'more and tried to clean up my chocolatey hands. I should have grabbed wet wipes at the assembly table or something, but the single napkin I'd stuffed in my pocket would have to do.

"Some of these are looking pretty sad." He gestured at a tree that must have been hit by one of the four-wheelers the farm attendants used. It had a big bare patch where lower branches had been broken off, and some of the remaining ones were skewed at weird angles.

"That's the peril of getting a tree late in the season."

"When do you usually get yours?"

"The weekend after Thanksgiving." I walked around a tree that looked promising, but its needles were turning orange. Must have had some kind of disease. Even getting it this late, that thing would be bald by Christmas Day.

"Should have called it."

"It's when they have the best selection."

He grinned at me over a three-foot tall tree. "Yeah, because normal people don't rush out to buy their Christmas tree the minute they clear Thanksgiving dinner off the table."

"Those are fighting words, Samuel."

He maneuvered closer until we stood toe to toe. I rested my hands on my hips so I wouldn't put them on his chest the way I had last night, hoping like heck the expression on my face said *defiant* and not *completely smitten*.

Even if completely smitten was accurate.

"I don't want to fight you, Harps."

His low voice snaked through me, warming me up from my toes to the top of my head. He raised one hand, his fingertips skating along my jaw, his thumb stroking at the edge of my mouth.

"You've got chocolate...right here."

Chilly embarrassment fought with the heat that wanted to burst to life on my cheeks and neck. Of course I'd got chocolate everywhere. I probably had strings of marshmallow hanging from my chin.

But Sam didn't look too concerned. In fact, his eyes hadn't left the spot where his thumb grazed the skin by my mouth. Those tiny touches shifted, and he rubbed his thumb over my bottom lip in a move that I'd only read about in romance novels. My stomach flipped, and I shuddered in a way that would have been embarrassing if his eyes hadn't been so full of heat. Mine traced his full mouth, registering the tiny gap between his stubble and the line of his lips.

Lips I couldn't stop thinking about kissing.

Somewhere, a child's shrill shriek of joy broke the moment. Why did we keep going places where we'd be surrounded by little kids?

"Got it."

His ragged voice undid me. I would have flung my arms around him and kissed him senseless in front of a thousand children, I didn't care. But he took a step back, swallowing hard, his eyes searing me until I wouldn't have been surprised if the whole tree farm went up in flames.

"So, we're looking for a six or seven-footer?" he confirmed.

"Yeah." My breathy voice was the best I could do under the circumstances.

We went back to wandering through the trees as I waited for my heart rate to come back down to everyday levels. Really, probably a good thing those meddling kids kept turning up to interrupt our moments. Just because I'd decided I wanted to try again with Sam didn't mean I needed to jump straight into the deep end of the pool.

But I did want to try again. Between his sweetness with Finn and Willa, the demonstration of his secret responsible streak at the gym, and the levelheaded way he'd handled my freak out on the climbing wall, he'd pretty well demolished the last shreds of my resistance. My Sam inoculations hadn't taken, after all, and I'd come down with a full-blown crush.

Maybe worse.

"Why didn't you get your tree early this year?" he asked, frowning at a particularly misshapen specimen.

"I thought I'd go with the girls the Saturday after Thanksgiving, but that didn't happen."

He looked over, catching way more than I'd said. "Because of the whole happy couple thing?"

"Pretty much. But I get it. Of course they want to pick out their tree with the guy they're nuts for."

"Oh." His expression turned naughty again. "So that's why you invited me."

I rolled my eyes, but my cheeks burned in an instant. "I can't talk to you right now."

"Because you're so nuts for me."

I said nothing so I wouldn't prove myself a horrible liar.

We passed a cluster of too-tall trees, but I spied one that looked the right size and shape in the distance, and headed that way. As long as the small family also wandering in that direction didn't get there first, we'd have a shot.

"What have you been doing for Christmas all this time?" I asked. "Do you participate against your will, or do you just skip as much as you can?"

"Bit of both. At Mom's, it's pretty easy. Keith likes to fish on

Christmas, so things stay relaxed there. I haven't been back here for Christmas since high school, but I doubt Christmas with the littles will be as calm."

"No, I'd imagine they get pretty wild on Christmas Day over there." With fancy clothes and gelled hair but still wild. "Have you always spent Christmas with your mom, then?"

"Maybe half and half. The rest of the time, I've been on my own."

I tried to imagine waking up Christmas morning knowing I wouldn't see my family. No dinner around their big table, no stockings in front of the fireplace, no family togetherness. Sounded awful, but I wouldn't say that out loud.

At my side, Sam chuckled.

"What?" I asked.

"Your face. You're lost in a daydream of me sad and alone on Christmas morning."

I pursed my lips at him and tried to relax the rest of my expression. Must have been pretty incriminating for him to guess so accurately.

"Did you picture me in my underwear eating gruel in front of the TV?"

I'd need to see a doctor about all this eye-rolling. Couldn't be healthy.

"That's how I picture you every day."

"You picture me in my underwear every day?"

Oh, sweet merciful Lord. He'd switched his flirting back on full blast, and I could barely stay upright in its wake.

"Ignoring that."

The sparkle in his eyes proved he knew I hadn't.

"Don't feel too sorry for me. A few years ago, I spent Christmas Day surfing in New Zealand. And last year might have been my best yet—hiking the Colorado Trail with Vance Vickers."

Whipping my head around, I almost tripped over a stump. Vance Vickers was only the biggest action movie star in the country. I didn't actually go to his movies, preferring shows with more romance and fewer gunshot wounds, but the guy had starred in summer blockbusters for at least twenty years.

Sam bobbed his eyebrows at me. "Who's sad and pathetic in their underwear now?"

I really needed him to stop saying *underwear*, please and thank you.

"But how did this happen? How do you know Vance Vickers?"

"I don't actually know Vance Vickers. But Ian had guided him through some trails in preparation for a movie a couple of years ago, and Vance started sending him celebrity clientele for private tours. Last year, he and a few of his friends wanted to spend a few days around Christmas on a hike, so that's what we did."

Couldn't really process the idea of having celebrity clientele in any capacity. Some of my Village patients were pretty well known for their gossip, but that was about it. "Wow. And you walked away from that job?"

Sam shrugged. "Ian was the one they wanted. No movie stars are breaking down my door. I just helped him on the trip because I was the only one of us on the crew without a wife who'd be pissed I wasn't home Christmas morning."

"Oh, I definitely would have been pissed."

Sam's wide smile made me realize my mistake. My stomach seized up, embarrassment squeezing me tight. If I could somehow *not* say stupid things around him, that'd be neat.

"Not that I would have been your wife. I would have been more like a neighbor. But not a next-door neighbor. A concerned acquaintance on the other side of town."

"A concerned acquaintance?"

"Yup. On the other side of town." Exactly where I wished I was now.

He shifted closer, his naughty boy grin on full display. "You're adorable when you're embarrassed, Harps."

"Noted."

The family reached the tree I'd been eyeing before we could get there, so I veered off in a different direction. Twigs snapped beneath our boots as we climbed a small rise. Nothing to see but pines for at least a half-mile. One of them would be right for us.

"You do realize we passed two perfectly good tree lots on the drive out here, right?"

"Pre-cut trees are for emergency situations only. Like cocoa packets and store-bought sugar cookies."

He chuckled. "No sense doing things halfway."

"Darn right."

I paused near a tree that looked about the right height, and circled around it. A little bit shorter than I liked, but it had a good shape. No broken branches or crooked trunk. Needles pure green.

"Is this the one?"

Sam had come closer than I realized as I inspected the tree, his arm brushing mine. Even through layers of flannel and fleece, the touch made my stomach dip.

"It looks pretty good. What do you think?"

He angled his head down, eyebrows furrowed as if seriously assessing the tree. "I like it."

"You're just ready to be done with the search."

"That, too."

I nodded at the bow saw he'd hooked his arm through. "You ready to use that thing?"

"Let's get to lumberjackin'."

Laughing at his silliness, I grabbed the trunk near the top as

Sam got down on his knees. The steady whish-whish of the saw started up, the smell of pine overpowering this close up. The one thing I'd forgotten on my way out the door this morning was work gloves. This one wasn't too pitchy, but my hands would still smell like fresh-cut tree the rest of the day.

The trunk started to give way, but I held it upright as Sam finished the cut. It rolled off its stump, and I lurched forward to make sure our prize tree didn't fall and damage any branches. He popped back up again, success sparkling in his eyes.

"That's how it's done."

I laughed. "You never doubted yourself for a minute."

"I suppose we have to lug this thing back to the other side of the farm now."

"We could always flag down one of the ATVs and have them tow it back in a trailer."

His eyes narrowed on me, taking my teasing as a challenge. Without a word, he bent down, grabbed the trunk, and hefted the tree onto his shoulder.

Once again, Sam had me all twisted up from doing something that by all rights shouldn't be attractive. Carrying a pine tree? When had that become so stinking hot? But warmth curled through me like a red Christmas ribbon, confirming I'd been charmed by his secret lumberjack side.

My brain kept saying I needed to wade into this new thing with him slowly, but my body was ready to push me right off the edge.

sam

"HOW DID YOU DO THAT?" I asked. "How did you know this tree would fit perfectly in your living room?"

Harper smiled as we stood back, admiring the bare tree we'd set up in its stand. It'd taken a little bit of maneuvering to get it standing just right, but looking at it now, the thing fit like a puzzle piece in front of her picture window.

"What can I say, I'm an expert at picking out trees."

Made sense she'd know exactly the right dimensions. She hadn't half-assed anything about Christmas so far.

"And now, we chuck a bunch of ornaments at it and see what sticks?"

She twisted her mouth at me. "There's a method to it, Samuel."

Man, I loved it when she called me by my full name. Not too proud to admit I provoked her in the hopes she'd scold me with it.

She crooked a finger at me and—oh, yeah. From the way my stomach dove, that ranked right up there with calling me by my full name.

I followed her into what must have been her guest

bedroom. Not nearly enough personality in here to be Harper's actual room. Her bed would have double the throw pillows and a soft blanket folded up at the foot.

I shook my head like I was trying to wake myself out of a daze. Really shouldn't be imagining Harper's bed right now.

She indicated a couple of plastic tubs, and we carted them back into the living room. Popping mine open, I found ornaments that might have been handmade. Fabric stars, burlap snowmen, and flannel birds sat on top of the soft collection.

I grabbed one of the birds and moved to hook it on the tree. Before I could get it there, Harper grabbed my hand. I would have relished the zing of awareness her touch carried through me if she hadn't looked so horrified.

"We have to put the lights up first." She sounded like I should have known better. Maybe I should have, but it'd been a lot of years since I'd put a tree up, and I didn't really remember all the particulars.

"Right. There's a method to all the madness."

She pulled two spools of white lights from her plastic bin, and we got to work looping them through the tree. Turned out there was a lot more to Harper's method than just running lights around the outside—she strung them along branches toward the trunk so the whole thing would look like it glowed from within. And she didn't go around and around the way I remembered, but she worked up and down, gradually moving on to the next section of tree.

"This is a lot of work," I said as she poked and prodded the lights into place in the center of the tree.

"It looks more natural this way."

"I'm going to let you think about that for a minute."

She laughed. "You know what I mean."

I fed the lights out to her and tried to pretend I was being useful. Mostly, I watched her face as she focused on getting the lights where she wanted them. How she pulled her bottom lip between her teeth whenever she reached an especially tricky bit. How she double-checked her work and smiled to herself every time she was pleased with the look.

I liked those secret smiles most of all. They weren't meant for me, they were just a natural reaction, but somehow, I was lucky enough to see them, anyway. I should always be so lucky.

"We've only got about a week until your birthday," I said, plugging the second string of lights into the first. "What are you knocking out next?"

"I have an idea for Wednesday night. Are you free?"

"For you? Absolutely."

She smiled at that. "I've accepted that I'm not going to get everything done in time. Getting out of Magnolia Ridge was always kind of a long shot."

"Not necessarily." I hadn't been sure I wanted to suggest my idea to her, mostly out of self-preservation. Asking her to go out of town with me was still probably a one-way ticket to getting shot down, but after the last couple of days, I was ready to push the big red *Do it!* button. "Do you have a night you could get away?"

She paused, the lights hanging loose in her hands. "Away, like overnight?"

"Overnight," I confirmed, bracing myself for the emotional firing squad. "It's a couple of hours outside Magnolia Ridge, and it's at its best advantage at night."

"You mean you want to go somewhere for stargazing?"

Her soft voice uncurled something in me. Maybe she'd thought we'd just go out in her backyard and look up at the stars for a few minutes one night, but that would never do.

"This is a list of adventures, we've got to do it right. I have a place in mind, but only if it works for you."

"Where?"

I grinned. "That part's a surprise."

This woman didn't get thrown nearly enough curveballs in her life. The thought I might be the man to do it made my fool heart soar.

She tilted her head, apparently debating whether or not she wanted to agree to an overnighter with me to an undisclosed location. Fair enough.

"No expectations," I said, hands raised. "There are two beds, I already checked. We're not going to get stuck in one of your tropes."

She laughed. "You've been reading up?"

Would neither confirm nor deny.

"Let's see...we're facing my fear Wednesday night, and I thought we'd do the Christmas market Saturday night if you don't have a yoga class."

My heart lost a little altitude. I'd never given a lot of thought to my odd hours before, but just now, I wished for a regular nine-to-five. Something where I could count on spending evenings with my—well. Too soon to get carried away with labels here. But I'd like to know my evenings were free for Harper, whenever she'd have me.

As much as I hated to say it, Dad's job offer was starting to sound...if not tempting, at least like a possibility.

"I do have a class. How late does the market go?"

"Until nine."

"We can catch it after my six o'clock class, if that's okay?"

Her smile told me everything I wanted to know.

"I could do an overnight Thursday as long as I'm back in time for my eleven o'clock appointment at the Village on Friday."

"Won't be a problem."

"Then it's a d—" She seemed to choke on the word and went back to stuffing lights in the tree. "That's settled, then."

"You can call it a date, Harps," I said low. "I'd like it to be one."

She met my eyes again and, to my delight, some of her sauciness had returned, along with a sheer wash of color on her cheeks.

"Seems a little quick, going on an overnight for our first date."

The fact that she hadn't argued about semantics set off a whirlwind in my chest, excitement and a spike of nervousness buffeting around in there. Plus, every time she said *overnight*, my stomach tightened as I pictured our accommodations.

"We had that dinner where I saved you from a waitress whose only crime was wanting to bless your heart. Does that count as a first date?"

Her laughter wrapped around me like a perfect hug.

"I guess it does."

She finished arranging the lights and plugged them in. Stepping back from her work, I had to admit her efforts had been worth it.

"You're right, this does look more natural."

Nudging me with her shoulder, she grinned and knelt down to rifle through the bins. "Now we put the ornaments up."

She hummed along to the Christmas songs that streamed through her phone as she carefully selected and placed each ornament. I helped, but I loved watching her. Like the way she'd strung up the lights, I just enjoyed seeing her doing some-thing that made her happy.

A couple of weeks ago, I hadn't thought I'd actually have a good time decorating a tree again. For so long, the activity had called to mind Mom and Dad's huge, fake smiles when we decorated our last Christmas tree, playing make believe at family togetherness they knew wouldn't last. I hadn't wanted to be near a tree, real or fake, since then.

But here I was, smiling to myself as I arranged a string of burlap stars on the branches of a tree I'd cut down myself. I'd resented the falseness and deception of Christmas for years, but there was nothing insincere about this moment with Harper. It was perfect and pure, and more than anything, I wanted to stay like this as long as I could.

Maybe I'd caught a little bit of her Christmas spirit, after all.

sam

WEDNESDAY NIGHT, I'd followed Harper's instructions, and wore my most comfortable shoes, jeans, and a button-down. Hadn't figured out yet how my clothing choices had anything to do with her facing a fear, but I was up for whatever.

"In a quarter mile, turn left."

I did as the GPS instructed, having zero clue where I was headed in the darkness. Harper sat beside me in the passenger seat, similarly attired, but she'd kept mum about our destination.

"Why are you keeping it a secret? I'm going to find out soon enough."

She hitched a saucy shoulder. "It's more fun this way."

Couldn't deny that. To tell the truth, driving to locales unknown had always given me a certain thrill. Several of our dates in high school had involved her feeding me directions while I drove, waiting to see where we'd wind up. Still, the question of just what fear she wanted to face had me racking my brain. It couldn't be far outside of Magnolia Ridge, and we'd put on western wear for the occasion.

Yeah, no, I had nothing. Seemed like a helmet or a parachute would make more sense for facing a fear.

"No hints?"

She grinned at me. "We're almost there."

"In one thousand feet, your destination will be on the left."

I squinted in front of us in the dark, trying to spot anything that could make sense as where we'd face Harper's fear. But there was nothing out here except dirt roads and a fairly crowded—

"Harper." Couldn't keep the dread out of my voice. "This?"

I slowed and pulled into the roadside honky tonk's massive lot beneath a blazing neon sign that read Fool Hearted Memory. Two neon blue cowboy boots flickered back and forth, clicking their heels next to the bar's name. Even at this distance, the twang of a country song barreled through the doors to invade my car.

"You have reached your destination."

"Seriously?"

She looked way too pleased with herself. "Yup. This is one of my biggest fears."

"Line dancing is your biggest fear?"

I mean, it made sense. Line dancing was the worst.

"Not line dancing—doing something embarrassing in a public place."

I found a spot in the gravel lot but made no move to leave the car. In the light of the dash, I caught the way her smile strained just a bit in admitting this. Without thinking, I grabbed her hand.

"I don't like people watching me when I don't know what I'm doing," she said. "I don't like feeling like I look stupid."

"Harper, you never look stupid."

She shot me an unimpressed look. "Doesn't change how I

feel about doing it. Out of all the scary things I could think of, the idea of coming here and dancing freaked me out most."

I gave her hand a squeeze. "You know, you already conquered a fear on the climbing wall."

"That was an accident, though. I didn't know I'd be afraid of heights. And I wouldn't say I conquered anything that day."

"You conquered me." No such thing as too much anymore.

She squeezed my hand right back. "But I'm not afraid of you."

Wasn't too sure about that, but I liked how confident she sounded. I glanced in the rearview toward the loud honky tonk and neon lights. Several beer logos flashed in the windows, and I could just make out movement inside. Born and raised in Texas, I'd managed to have a pretty good streak without line dancing. Looked like that record was about to end.

I sighed. "All right, Harps. Let's do some boot-scootin'."

* * *

If I hadn't been convinced line dancing was really Harper's fear when we were in the car, I had no doubt as we stood at the fringes of the crowd in Fool Hearted Memory. She scanned the place as though expecting to find someone filming her, and we hadn't even stepped onto the dance floor yet. When she wasn't checking for critical observers, her attention zeroed in on the dancers moving in unison on the huge dance floor, looking both intrigued and repulsed.

Pretty clear all skill levels had representation in the mix. A lot of the dancers looked like they came here every night, exuding confidence as they progressed through the choreography. Others, though, were just as green as Harper and I, laughing as they stumbled over the steps and turning at the wrong time. I even spotted a group of gray-haired women who might have been right at home at Fiesta Village kicking up their cowboy boots along with the rest.

I could understand her concerns, though. The sheer number of people watching the dancers from the bar and the tables around the dance floor made me hesitate to put a toe on those wooden boards, too, and I wasn't a guy who normally cared what strangers thought.

"You ready to give it a try?" I asked, my mouth right up against her ear so she'd hear me over the loud music. We'd already watched through several songs, and I figured she'd had all the learning by watching she could realistically get for the night.

Her mouth curled down as she tried to follow an especially complicated move. "There's no beginner wall here."

"You're going to have to dive in sometime, Harps."

Maybe I was being pushy, but pretty sure that was part of the reason she'd let me come. Encouraging her along used to be a skill of mine, but I typically encouraged her to do things I actually liked. Tonight was purely for her.

"Fine. Next song, we're getting in there."

I held my hand out to shake on it. "Next song."

She laughed but shook my hand, her eyes darting back to the dancers as though she could memorize every last step before the upbeat song ended.

The song died out, but was replaced by a slower melody. The line dancers dispersed and coalesced again, some retreating to tables to sit the song out, others returning with partners to sway under the dimmed lights.

I leaned closer to her. "We did agree to dance to the next song."

A smile curled along her mouth, her sauciness back.

"We'd probably better follow through on that."

She slipped her hand in mine, and nothing had ever felt so right.

I led her onto the dance floor, taking her right hand in my left, my other hand at her back just below her arm. I moved us around the space in a slow two-step, mesmerized by the way the light played across her face and hair, making her look other-worldly.

"I thought you didn't dance."

"I don't line dance," I clarified. "Two-step is easy."

To prove it, I encouraged her into a twirl before pulling her back into my arms. She laughed against my chest, her hand on my shoulder holding me tight.

"I've missed this." She sounded as though the confession surprised her.

"I don't remember us ever dancing." Would say nothing of the jackass way I'd thwarted our prom back in high school.

"Then I guess I mean I've missed you."

Her voice came out so soft, I couldn't be completely sure I'd heard her right. My heart swelled anyway, her words soothing even as they thrilled.

"I've missed you, too, Harper. So much."

"I wasn't sure you ever thought about me when you were out there traveling the world."

I pulled her closer, my two-step slowing to a back-and-forth sway.

"All the time, Harps. The first time I saw the Atlantic Ocean, I wished I'd had you with me. When I stood on top of Arthur's Pass in New Zealand, I thought of you. Every time I looked out across the never-ending bright blue sky in Wyoming, you were on my mind."

We moved together beneath the lights, the rest of the dancers forgotten.

"You were always with me, Harper." Pouring all my sincerity

into a few short words, my voice broke. "I never stopped thinking about you."

She leaned closer until our breath mingled, her hand moving to the back of my neck, her gaze stuck on my mouth. Finally, she pressed her lips to mine in a kiss so gentle and sweet, something in my heart seemed to snap in place like I'd found what I'd been missing all these years.

Like I'd found my home.

Her soft, lingering kiss laid all my former fears to rest, confirming with every touch I was where I was meant to be. I still didn't have everything sorted out, but this—this wasn't in question.

"You two are sweet and all, but y'all have to clear the floor."

We broke apart, turning to find one of the gray-haired women smiling up at us. In our enthusiasm, we'd missed the song change, and now stood surrounded by line dancers trying to keep time in spite of us blocking their path.

"I'm so sorry," Harper said, pulling out of my arms. "We just got a little..."

"Oh, I know," the woman said with an impish smile. "It's easy to get carried away. Save some for the next slow dance, though."

Harper nodded and offered another apology, but the woman had already started up her line dance routine, her friends circling around to join in.

We moved to a secluded spot along one wall, ignoring the knowing looks that followed us. Harper put her face in her hands, but I wrapped her in my arms anyway.

"After that, line dancing in front of them will be a piece of cake."

She laughed, relaxing into my embrace. "This wasn't part of the plan."

"That's what makes it so perfect. Not everything has to be planned out and written on a list somewhere."

She glared, twisting her lips into a scowl. Too bad her mouth was so distracting, or I might have felt the weight of her silent reprimand.

"Okay, then," she said, grabbing my hand. "Let's not plan."

Before either of us could think too hard about it, she tugged me to an empty space on the dance floor and started kicking up her heels, mimicking the other dancers. I went along, my heart ricocheting around in my chest at the way she'd taken me by surprise. I loved it.

I loved her.

Not just the Harper I'd known when we were teens, but the woman she'd become. The Harper who gave everything she had to her patients at the retirement community. The one who showed up when I needed her without question. The one who tackled adventures, faced her fears, and loved Christmas with all her might. I adored this woman.

The time apart, the distance, the mistakes—none of that mattered now. We had each other again, and I intended to hold onto her for as much and as long as she'd let me.

Line dance, chop down a tree, take a job in my dad's firm— I'd do whatever it took to make a life with her happen.

harper

OKAY, so it turns out line dancing is a lot harder than it looks. And it looks really dang hard.

"Maybe this is expert night." I had to shout at Sam to be heard over the upbeat music. He just raised his shoulders, flailing along about as well as I was. At least he looked cute in his button-down and jeans.

I'd never thought of myself as all that uncoordinated, but like my fear of heights on the climbing wall, my inner klutz had shown up without an invitation. Although, to be honest, it wasn't just my two left feet tripping me up, it was the whole night with Sam.

"I never stopped thinking about you."

Would have been more poetic if my overflowing heart had turned me into a graceful swan, but the big, unwieldy emotions swirling around inside me made it hard to focus on the moves. After a line like that, I should have pulled Sam out the honky tonk's doors and kissed his face off.

But instead, here I was shimmying around on the dance floor, moving a second too slow on every step. But at least I had a big smile on my face while doing it.

I shifted the wrong way and collided into the woman next to me, who laughed as we steadied each other.

"I don't know if that was you or me," she said with a wide grin.

"Pretty sure it was me. I have no idea what I'm doing."

"This your first time here?"

I nodded, still kind of trying to follow along with the steps even though we'd stopped moving in our little section of dance floor.

"My first time here, I broke a guy's toe." She laughed but gave me a *seriously* look.

She looked younger than a lot of people here, maybe even younger than Eliza, but she'd clearly done her time on the dance floor. Wearing red cowboy boots, jeans with a red plaid hem, and a matching red plaid flannel button-down, she fit right in with the themed bar. Maybe best of all, she wore a miniature Christmas light necklace that created a sparkling little glow as it switched colors.

"I don't feel so bad, then."

"You want a few pointers? I hardly injure anybody anymore."

Now I laughed at her easy-going attitude. "I'd love pointers."

She clapped her hands. "Great. Let me show you a few basic steps."

She moved through a dance number I'd been struggling to master. Keeping the footwork slow, she walked me through the steps, and my stiff legs followed along like Frankenstein's monster figuring out how to walk. When I finally got the maneuver down without kicking my own feet in the process, I felt like I'd just mastered an essential life skill. She led me through a few more steps, patiently explaining the moves as she demonstrated them. Folks around us spread out to give us room, and I almost forgot my little tutorial was happening in view of the whole bar.

Nerves still threaded through me, and my stomach churned over how foolish I must have looked, but I reminded myself I'd come here to face a fear. I would get through it, even if I needed Sam beside me and this guardian angel to show me how.

"You're doing great," she said when I'd successfully completed another step. "Now you can do any of the dances."

I laughed at her optimism. "I don't think I'm there yet."

The songs switched, and as the opening strains of the new tune started, the woman's eyes lit up. "This is the perfect song for you. Very beginner-friendly."

If a beginner zero song existed for line dancing, I would welcome it. Although, I hadn't exactly aced the beginner rock climbing wall.

She started dancing along with everyone else, nodding and encouraging me to follow. I wouldn't say I rocked line dancing, but that song was decidedly less awful than the others had been. Grinning the whole time, I managed most of the steps I knew and fudged my way through the ones I didn't.

Looking to my other side, Sam gave me a thumbs up. "You're on fire."

I was no such thing, but by the time the song ended, I was sweating like I was. My dancing coach cheered the end of the song and gave me a double high five.

"I need a break. Do you want to come to our table?"

"Sure." I beckoned to Sam, and we followed her to the far end of the bar.

Chairs had been piled with purses and jackets, and pitchers of beer littered the table tops. The woman sank onto a bench seat, exhaling loudly. She pushed her dark, sweaty hair out of her face and grinned.

"Do you want a beer? There's water here, too, if you want."

"I don't think beer will help my coordination."

"Probably a good call."

She poured waters and passed them around. After stumbling my way through several songs, cool water had never tasted so good.

"I'm Callie," she said. "I probably should have said that before."

She held out a hand, and Sam and I made our own introductions.

"Thank you for helping me out there," I said. "I would never have caught on without you."

She waved a hand in the air. "Now that you have the basic steps, you'll pick it up, easy. It took me a couple of visits before I got the hang of things."

"Have you been coming here for a while?"

"About a year." She gestured to the cluster of gray-haired women shaking their stuff. "My granny and her friends come every week, but I can't keep up with them, so I just come every month or two. How sad is that? I'm twenty-four, and I can't keep up with my grandma on the dance floor."

Callie broke into nervous laughter that dissolved into a cringe. I looked over at Sam, who raised an eyebrow. Honestly hadn't expected to find a kindred spirit tonight in the honky tonk.

"Granny blames it on my job as a kindergarten teacher," Callie went on. "She thinks I've forgotten what it's like to socialize with people who aren't five years old, so she drags me out to places like this to show me what it's like to really live or something. She's always signing us up for new classes and springing crazy activities on me. Last month, we learned how to macramé. The month before that, it was a class on how to maintain a vehicle. It's like she's afraid I'm going to miss out on a social life if she doesn't hold my hand through it."

She took a breath, paused, then a big smile broke over her face. "Sorry, I'm babbling."

"Not at all. I work at a retirement community, and I think I've forgotten what it's like to socialize with people who aren't *seventy*-five years old."

"Hazards of our jobs, I guess. The other day, I was in the grocery store, and I knelt down and tied a man's shoelaces for him. Mind you, I didn't know the man, and his wife looked like she wanted to take the can of beans she was holding upside my head."

"Last week, I thought to myself that yoga might be too hard on my joints."

"Your joints were safe with me," Sam teased.

"Doesn't mean the thought was normal."

"If you're trying to avoid socializing with people over seventy-five, better stay away from my granny and her friends." Callie nodded past me to the dance floor.

Laughing, I turned to watch the group of women shake their stuff. They did the grapevine and slid their boots, stepping and kicking right in time with everyone else. Their laughter and joy in the moment was obvious, four friends living it up and enjoying each other's company. I hadn't been that way with a group of girls since college. I loved my sisters, but it'd be nice to have a friend group, too.

I turned back to Callie, who watched her grandma's antics with affection in her eyes.

"Would you like to have lunch with me sometime?" I asked.

Her mouth dropped open in surprise. Maybe I'd jumped the gun. I suddenly felt like a little kid on a playground, trying to strike up a friendship based on mutual love of the swing set.

"I know it's kind of weird, but I don't have a ton of girl-friends, and—"

"I'd love to have lunch sometime!"

Her enthusiasm relieved my fears I'd come across too needy or strange.

"Sorry, that came out a little much. I'd like that, though. Hanging out with my grandma and her friends is great, but I kind of need to be around people my own age again."

"So do I."

* * *

A couple of hours later, I got out of Sam's car in my driveway, my feet aching with every step. We'd danced to way too many songs at Fool Hearted Memory, and the best I could say was I hadn't broken anybody's toes. But it'd been fun, despite my fears of embarrassing myself in a public place.

And no chance I hadn't embarrassed myself. Between my missteps on the dance floor and kissing Sam in the middle of a crowd, I'd gone all-in on making a public spectacle of myself. But I'd enjoyed myself, too, and needed to focus on that as the bigger takeaway.

Sam walked me to my door, but I grabbed his arm to stop him halfway up the path.

"Wait."

I paused to admire the glowing white tree in my front window, the multi-colored lights along the house's eaves, and the evergreen wreath on the door. Slipping my hand into his, we stood there a full minute in silence, just appreciating the view. Nights like this, I really wished I lived someplace that got snow in December. I didn't need it all winter, but a nice flurry around Christmas would be perfect. Just a few flakes to fully set the scene.

"Thanks for going tonight." I kept my voice low as though my holiday-bedecked house were worthy of reverence.

"Thanks for the dance."

I turned to him, and his hands found my waist at the same time mine went to his shoulders. He swayed us slowly back and forth, tiny movements in the stillness.

"You're a surprisingly good dancer."

He made a sound of mock indignation. "Surprisingly? I'm graceful as hell."

I laughed as he tugged me closer. "I admit it. It's probably all that yoga."

"Yoga helps with so many things."

His voice came out a low purr, stirring my insides like stoking a fire. I made an embarrassing sound in my throat, a half-sigh, half-moan. He tightened his grip on my waist, his hands an inferno against the thin fabric of my button-down.

"Like what?" I breathed out, blatantly provoking him.

The heat in his eyes singed. I should have burnt up on the spot, leaving nothing but a curl of smoke behind. Thank goodness he held me so close or I might have swooned, too. I wasn't prepared for this kind of all-consuming longing.

"Relaxation," he said, his voice low and deep. "Flexibility. Stamina."

Nope, not prepared at all.

"You're making this difficult."

His lips quirked up. "I really am."

No denying now I wanted more than just friendship with him, not after what we'd confessed tonight. But I also knew I wasn't ready for more. Maybe physically, but emotionally, my heart was still a big junk drawer, everything tangled in messy layers. I couldn't tell if the time we spent together helped me sort through it or only made everything more confusing.

I hugged him closer, sliding my nose against the skin of his neck, breathing him in. He pressed a kiss to my temple, and we held each other a moment. Sighing against him, I tried to prepare myself for our eventual goodnight.

Keep the goodnight kiss PG-13.

Do not make that sighing, strangled sound again.

No inviting him in.

Leaning back, he smiled at me in the semi-darkness. "Your thoughts are deafening."

"I'm thinking about our overnight tomorrow."

"So am I."

Oh, that voice. He fought dirty.

"No expectations, right?"

"No expectations," he confirmed with a stout little nod. "Just stargazing."

We finally broke apart, and he walked me the rest of the way to my door. I shouldn't have worried about keeping the goodnight kiss PG-13, since the sweet brush of his lips against mine stayed firmly G-rated.

And yet, my body buzzed and fizzed as though his simple kiss meant so much more.

"Goodnight, Harps," he said, pressing his forehead to mine. "See you tomorrow."

Reluctantly, I let myself inside and shut him out. I stood in the front window as he drove away, my heart still pounding with possibilities I'd just closed the door on. I reminded it we had no expectations for tomorrow.

But I had a whole lot of hope.

TWENTY-SEVEN

sam

"YOU'RE LUCKY I TRUST YOU," Harper said. "This is looking like a real Cabin in the Woods type situation."

"You've watched that?"

"Heck no, but I know enough to reference it."

Could have done without the horror movie reference, frankly. We'd turned off the highway over an hour ago, and the last headlights we saw were probably fifteen miles back. When this rental listing billed itself as remote, it hadn't been kidding. Totally off the grid, they provided drinking water from barrels they filled in town, solar power for lights, and a single-burner propane stove for a kitchen. But its benefits should far outweigh a few inconveniences.

Provided we got there in one piece.

I snaked the car through the darkness more on edge than I'd been since I climbed my last fourteen thousand-footer. Nerves didn't usually bother me, but tonight, they ate me up whole and spat me out again so they could go back for seconds. Georgia's reminder about no third-chance romances kept spinning through my mind. I didn't want to mess any part of this up.

"Are we staying in an abandoned summer camp, by any

chance?" Harper asked.

"Please. It's an abandoned gas station."

"Whew. That's a relief."

I glanced at my phone, but we were still several miles from the turnout to the rental. Hopefully, in less than an hour, we'd be settled in, tucked under blankets, and watching the stars.

"As long as we don't go near any rivers, I think we'll be okay."

That teasing remark uncoiled some of my nerves.

"Got stuck in the mud one time, and I can never live it down."

"My dad was so mad at you."

"Yet you can laugh about it." Didn't matter. I loved her laugh.

She only laughed harder. "He had to drive out in the middle of nowhere to tow us out. It was kind of funny, even if he didn't see it that way at the time."

"Neither did I. I was afraid he was going to string me up."

We hadn't been hurt, we'd just gotten stuck after a trip down to the Oxtail River. We'd taken a picnic and waded in between sultry afternoon kisses. It'd been a perfect day. Right up until I realized my back tires had sunk deep in mud and I couldn't get us out.

Calling her dad to the rescue had been a low spot in my dating life, and a personal high for anxiety. Not a panic attack exactly, but I'd certainly been panicking I might get attacked.

"He always liked you."

She hesitated, and she might as well have said *Until* out loud.

"Am I going to have to watch my back when he finds out we're dating again?"

"Are we? Dating again?"

Didn't love the question. She trusted me enough to go into

the middle of nowhere with me, but not enough to believe I wanted something more with her.

"Thought we'd cleared all that up when we specified this is our second date. You think I'd take someone I'm not dating on an overnight trip?"

Actually, strike that joke from the record. Wasn't sure I wanted to know just what she'd imagined of my dating life in the years we'd been apart. Didn't really want to hear that she'd seen me as some heartless Lothario with a woman in every town I'd visited. I hadn't been a monk, but I hadn't loved them and left them, either.

"Well," she paused, and my heart twisted right in my ribcage. "You did take Vance Vickers on an overnight trip."

I barked out a laugh, relief flooding my system. "World famous celebrities don't count."

"Speaking of Vance Vickers, do you have any leads on something more for work?"

All that relief turned cold. Did not relish telling Dr. Harper Webb the truth. "Not yet."

I'd called a few more places, but hadn't found anything hopeful. I was quickly running out of options.

"There's that guiding place out of Georgetown. They look like a pretty big deal. Have you tried them?"

My hands tightened around the steering wheel, unease worming through my stomach. "You're looking up jobs for me?"

"I was just curious what's out there."

I shook my head, my eyes fixed on the road. "An outfit like that probably wants someone mountain certified."

"I thought you were."

"I'm an indoor rock climbing instructor. That course is just a small part of getting mountain certified. I was working my way toward that in Colorado, but..."

But I'd decided to leave my mentors to come here.

Certification was only part of the problem. I'd seen the kinds of trips they offered. I'd hardly ever be home if I took a job like that. No matter how much I liked rock climbing, I couldn't build a life and family with Harper that way. As much as it pained me, Dad was right. It was time for me to settle down and get a real job.

"Dad's firm has an opening in the new year. I was thinking about trying that."

"Financial planning?"

She sounded as horrified as Willa had been about my full name.

"It's a good opportunity. Good pay. Eight to five, no travel."

I'd thought she would have appreciated those benefits, but her silence didn't feel like approval. She turned to look at me, leaning her cheek on the headrest. I couldn't make out her expression in the darkness—hopefully, she couldn't see mine.

Getting mountain certified and becoming a full-fledged mountain guide had been a great dream once but was no longer my top priority. I couldn't leave on three- or four-day guides every week and also have something lasting with Harper. Couldn't expect my relationships with everyone here not to suffer if I wasn't around. I needed to be in Magnolia Ridge if I wanted my dreams of a home and family to come true.

"Is that what you want to do?"

Her question seemed to hang in the air, a word bubble I'd rather pop than answer.

"Might be worth a shot."

Thankfully, the beam of the headlights caught a small sign reading *Hideaway*.

"This is it." I turned down the dirt road lined with scrub brush. Not much to see out here even in the daylight, but at night, this amounted to a lot of nothing. The whole point, but still.

A small building came into view in the darkness. "I think we're here."

"That's an outhouse."

"Past that."

She turned to me, her expression unreadable in the near-total darkness. "You didn't say anything about an outhouse."

"Is that a dealbreaker?" On a lot of my trips, an outhouse would have been a luxury, so it hadn't occurred to me to warn her.

"No, I just...you know...snakes."

She whispered the last word as though speaking it out loud would summon them to her.

"Now that would have been a good fear to face for your list."

She made a sound of disgust. "No, thank you. That's a normal, God-given fear."

"I'll keep an eye out for you."

A tiny house sat about seventy-five feet away from the outhouse, and I pulled up in front.

"Oh," Harper breathed a sound of delight as we drew nearer. "Is this it?"

Luckily, she sounded enthusiastic. This night would have busted up real fast if she'd been as disgusted by the thought of staying here as she was by the thought of running across snakes on her way to the outhouse.

The small house wasn't much bigger than my dad's lawn-mower shed but stood twice as tall, with a steeply sloped roof like half an A-frame. A fire pit sat somewhere close by, along with Adirondack chairs and a picnic table, but I hadn't planned to put those to use. From the pictures on the rental's listing, we'd be completely secluded out here, with nothing but trees for miles.

Trees and stars.

"You ready?" I asked.

"Let's see it."

We grabbed our things and climbed the three steps to the tiny house's door. I punched in the code the owner had given me and helped Harper inside. Cold in here—I'd have to get a fire going before we did anything else. Flipping on a switch by the door to get the solar generator up, I turned on the lights.

"Oh," Harper breathed again.

I'd become a real fan of her breathy sighs.

The main living area was maybe six feet by ten feet, with a tiny kitchen by the door, a fold-down table and chairs on the opposite wall, and the high wall nothing but windows. Harper took a few steps across the glossy hardwood floor, soaking it in.

"Oh, wow."

A queen-sized bed sat in a nook facing the windows, beneath the sloping ceiling. The chill in the air made its plush pillows and soft blankets especially inviting. The small space had been hung with thick tapestries, making it feel like its namesake: a hideaway.

"This is beautiful." Harper spun in a slow circle, her hands clasped together in front of her chest as she examined the tiny house. "But—"

She ducked past me and looked around, her brow furrowed. Not much to see over here except for a single-burner camp stove that barely qualified as a kitchenette and a small wood stove.

"Where's the second bed?"

My stomach bottomed out. "There should be two."

"Pretty sure I just had the grand tour, and there's no other bed."

I looked around, too, as though a hallway might have materialized with another cozy bed tucked away. Even a cot would have been something. But she was right, no other beds here.

"The listing specified two beds." I pulled out my phone but

remembered another of the tiny house's charms: no cell service or WiFi.

I searched all around the queen bed, my fingers scrambling for a secret latch to a trundle bed, an air mattress, anything. Stargazing had been my prime motivation for booking this house, but the listing had said two beds. Or...had it? Sometimes with my concentration issues, I couldn't be sure of myself. But I'd wanted two to make sure Harper would be comfortable, and now—

"Sam?" she said, rattling something. "I think this is the other bed."

I turned around, patting down the raised bed frame as though a second might still turn up. She'd swung a net out on a chain set in one wall and locked it into place on the other by the door, revealing...

"A hammock," we both said at the same time.

Not my first choice, but I'd slept in worse. "I can make that work."

She frowned hard at me, unlocking the hammock chain and swinging it back into place on the opposite wall. "You're not going to sleep in a string hammock like some castaway."

"I promised you two beds."

"We're both adults. I think we can control ourselves in one bed."

So optimistic. She had no idea the scenes already running through my mind. That cozy little bed nook would be a whole lot cozier with two.

"Anyway, the main attraction is outside, right?"

"Wow. You went straight for the jugular."

She shot me a stern little look.

"You know what I mean. Are there chairs outside?" She turned to the collapsed hammock. "Are we supposed to use that?"

"Definitely not. Climb into bed."

Her eyebrows jumped. "We just said no Twister."

"Harps. Trust me. Climb into bed."

"Okay." She dragged out the word as she slipped off her ankle boots. Crawling onto the plush bed, she made herself cozy.

"Don't move."

"Not excellent pillow talk, Samuel."

I chuckled, not letting myself imagine real pillow talk with her. "Just stay there."

She looked at me like I was nuts as I slipped away to the light switch. Flicking it off, the tiny house plunged into total darkness.

"This is not as awesome as you think it is," she trilled.

"You have no faith in me." I patted down the tapestries on one wall of the bed nook until I found a pull cord. I tugged hard and the tapestry covering the sloped angle above the bed drew upward, revealing a six-foot-long window. We'd have a front-row seat to hundreds of stars.

"Oh my gosh," she breathed out. "This is incredible."

I crawled onto the bed beside her. The view was pretty fantastic. Not a cloud in the sky, no light interference for miles, just bright constellations above us.

"Is this a good way to check it off your list, or what?"

She rolled over and kissed me on the mouth. "It's perfect."

Rolling back into place, we stared up at the glorious scenery.

"There's just one problem," she said after a minute.

I figured she'd rethought the whole hammock thing, after all. We were awfully close in here. My back would hate me in the morning, but I'd sleep in that monstrosity for her.

"What's that?" I asked.

"I have to pee."

TWENTY-EIGHT

harper

PERFECT GENTLEMAN THAT HE WAS, Sam escorted me to the outhouse with a flashlight and thoroughly checked for snakes before I dared use it. The tiny building had soft lighting inside so I didn't have to do everything in total darkness, but I was grateful for the once-over before I made myself completely vulnerable out there.

"Is that a shower?" I asked.

He turned the flashlight on the side of the outhouse and, sure enough, a shower head and fixture gleamed at us. Seemed awfully exposed, with no screens or shelters in sight.

"What are people supposed to do in the winter?" I asked.

"Get frost bite."

We each took a turn in the rustic bathroom before scrambling back to the tiny house. Sam grabbed the cooler he'd brought out of the car and set it inside the so-called kitchen before he started up a fire in the wood stove. For now, we'd switched the lights back on, but after seeing the view waiting for us, I was itching to turn them off again.

And spend the night in our lone bed.

I'd be fine as long as I remembered the rules I'd made for myself back in the outhouse.

Only touch when necessary.

Keep the kissing at a minimum.

Absolutely no Twister.

"What's in the cooler?"

"Eggs, bacon, and milk. There's no continental breakfast out here, so I thought I should bring our own."

"That's really sweet of you."

He winked at me over his shoulder. "I do like to keep us alive."

"I'm going to change into pajamas."

He swiveled his head around to face the fire he had going and gave a little nod, his Adam's apple working as he swallowed. "Sounds good."

His voice sounded strained, but I would just ignore it. I'd need to if I wanted my *We're all adults here* crap to work.

Crawling into the nook, I pulled the tapestries shut at the foot of the bed. I liked a plush bed, but I didn't like maneuvering around on one on my knees while I stripped down. Pulling off my jeans and changing into lounge pants on my back? Mortifying. But the wiggle room on either side of the bed was barely enough to stand in, I couldn't comfortably change there. Finally switching into my red plaid pajamas on top of the bed, I tugged the curtain open.

The swish of the drapes revealed Sam facing the wall of windows as he pulled off his shirt just a few feet away.

I was a medical professional. I'd seen naked backs a hundred times before. But no other naked back had ever made my stomach dip and heat until I got dizzy from just looking at it.

Artists could have done charcoal rubbings on the ridges of his muscles. He could have been a model for any one of my anatomy and physiology books. Trapezius and deltoids, rhomboids and latissimus, all beautifully defined. God bless his years of rock climbing.

He spun around, revealing a light dusting of chest hair, impressive pecs, and six-pack abs. Wasn't sure which view left me more flustered. Probably should check them both again just to be sure.

His lips quirked up into a smirk.

No. I definitely did not need to check them again.

"I wasn't staring," I said, ducking back into the bed nook.

"Sounds like something a starer would say."

He moved toward the door.

"What are you doing?" My voice went all squeaky as if he'd brandished a snake at me.

He shifted back into view. I darted my eyes to the nook's ceiling, examining my reflection in the window so I wouldn't stare at his abs.

But holy moly, those abs.

"I'm turning the lights out."

He sounded amused. Made sense, considering how weird I was acting. Still. I had good reason.

I pointed in his general direction. "You can't come to bed wearing just that."

He'd changed into thin, heather gray lounge pants that were even worse than his sweatpants for the way they hugged his butt and thighs. At the moment, he had nothing else on. Even his bare feet on the hardwood floor did something for me, one more sign I'd completely lost my mind.

"What happened to both of us being adults here?"

"That doesn't mean you can get into bed half-naked."

"Harps, normally I sleep all-the-way naked."

"Don't tell me that!" I chucked one of the bed's throw pillows at him. Busying myself with turning down the covers, I slipped between the sheets, keeping my eyes anywhere but on him. "Put a shirt on, please."

Okay, fine. I peeked. He was *right there*. And—oh, should not have looked.

He slid his hands down his chest, grinning wickedly. "Does all of this bother you?"

I rolled my eyes, clamping down on my laughter. Among other things. "How would you feel if I was wearing nothing but a tiny camisole and booty shorts in bed next to you?"

Dropping his hands, his teasing smirk disappeared. I made the mistake of meeting his eyes. The heat there started up an answering fire in me, shuddering its way out to my fingers and toes. Probably safest to make him sleep in the hammock, after all.

"Fair enough," he finally said, his voice gone low. He found a T-shirt in his bag and pulled it on. "Better?"

Not really, no. Now that I knew what was under it, the thin fabric couldn't hide anything.

Best be grateful, though. "Thank you."

He switched out the light, and I blinked hard in the darkness. Settling down into the soft bed, I looked through the skylight at the stars while Sam crawled up next to me and tucked himself beneath the sheets. He laid down in mirror image of me, staring through the window above, motionless.

Minutes ticked by. Pretty view, but good Lord, the awkwardness.

Was this really how we were going to be? Lying side by side without touching? Clothing had seemed like a pretty big necessity, but I hadn't meant to rule out *everything* just now.

"Do adults cuddle while they look at stars?" he asked.

"Yes, please."

He looped one arm around my shoulders, and I snuggled right up to him. My stand against him coming to bed shirtless had been for nothing. He could have worn a snow suit and I'd still thrill to be held by him.

Kissing my temple, he ran a hand over my arm. "This is better."

After a minute, I had to ask. "Do you really sleep naked on your sister's couch?"

He laughed, the sound tingling through me everywhere we touched. "Nah. I wanted to see if it got a reaction. And I got my answer." He tickled my side. "Try to keep your desires under control."

I laughed, tickling him back, and doing my best to ignore the firm muscles beneath my fingers. "Control yourself."

"Oh, Harps. I am."

Tucked safe in our hideaway, I just might forget stars even existed.

Looking up at the sight above us, I tried to focus on our reason for coming out here. This really was the perfect night. Constellations shone like a diamond blanket over us, the only sound the fire crackling in the stove. The moment brought more peace than I'd felt in a long, long time.

"Thank you for bringing me here."

His fingers pressed against my waist, not quite exploring but not quite still. "I wasn't sure you'd want to come."

"All you had to say was stargazing." I tucked my chin, pressing my nose against his shoulder. "And maybe abs of steel."

A chuckle had never sounded so self-satisfied. "I see how it is."

"Were the views this good when you were up on moun-taintops?"

"Better. But the company was never so ideal."

I smiled to myself, drinking in the stars. Maybe we were both feeling a little smug tonight.

"A few summers ago, I was climbing in the Tetons during the Perseid meteor shower. Perfect viewing conditions up there. Everywhere I looked, another streak lit the sky. That used to hold the top spot in my stargazing vault. Until right now."

My heart pitter-pattered in my chest. How could I have ever forgotten this man's romantic side? He was adventurous and fearless, and could be a flirt-and-a-half, but even as a teen, he knew how to sweep a girl off her feet when he wanted to. As an adult? I'd never stood a chance.

"You're really laying on the charm."

"Maybe. I've got a lot to make up for."

A few weeks ago, I would have relished reminding him, but now, enjoying the present seemed a lot better than punishing him for the past.

Except for one question I hadn't figured out yet.

"Why did you break up with me a month before graduation? You don't have to apologize again, I'm just trying to understand what went wrong."

He sighed, his arms tightening around me. "Nothing went wrong, Harps."

Half a minute went by, and I could almost feel him trying to piece his thoughts together.

"When we spent those months planning our big road trip, I realized I didn't want to be a mechanical engineer. I didn't want to go to college, I didn't want to be tied down to a desk job—I wanted to travel and see all the places on the map."

"You never told me that."

He'd loved coming up with ideas for our road trip, but I'd never thought he enjoyed it so much he'd sacrifice college for it.

"I didn't think you'd be a fan of that plan."

I stilled, shutting my eyes to block out the stars shining overhead. Guessing at his reasons for eleven years hadn't prepared me to hear them. He thought I wouldn't have supported him in his dreams?

"I wanted you to come and see it all with me, Harps. But I was convinced you never would. You had all these plans for yourself that didn't line up with mine. I was afraid you wouldn't change them for me."

My breath sounded loud in the stillness as I fought the tightening in my chest, my lungs squeezed from all sides as I processed his confession. "You could have asked."

"And if I had? If I'd asked you to give up your college plans and come live the nomad life with me, would you have done it?"

I wanted to tell him I obviously would have, that I would have gone anywhere with him...but I had to face the truth. I opened my eyes as the hurt trying to take hold in my heart again gave way to acceptance. It stung a little, but that didn't make it less true.

"You're right. I wouldn't have given up college for you."

I would have wanted to be with him, and maybe I would have considered it for a little while, but I wouldn't have skipped college and chosen the same path he had. I'd had goals. I knew what I wanted. If he'd told me exactly what he'd intended to do, I still would have gone to Texas State in the end. Even if that meant *I* had to break up with *him*.

That realization brought a strange sort of comfort.

"I'm not trying to put this on you," he said. "This was all my fault. I wanted to leave, and having no ties back home seemed like the easiest way. It was selfish and short-sighted, I know that."

"And prom?" If we were going to air the last of our dirty laundry, better throw that one up on the line, too.

"I thought if I dated someone else, I'd get over you faster."

His breath fanned the hair around my face as my fingers traced lines on his bicep.

"Did it work?"

"Nope."

My heart might have been the brightest thing in the night right then, shining like a little fireball. "I told myself spending time with you for our lists would help me finally get over you."

"Yeah? Did it work?"

"Nope. How pathetic are we? Never got over our high school relationship."

His hand splayed on my back, his fingertips touching the line of skin exposed between pajama top and pants, little radiant points of heat. "So pathetic."

"We're probably only fit for each other."

He turned his head, nuzzling against the side of my face. His breath on my ear made me shudder as I tried to get even closer to him.

"I'm good with that," he said.

Tangled up with him, safe to say I'd forgotten about our stargazing mission.

"I'm still sorry, though, Harps. If I'd just told you what I wanted from the beginning—"

"Things wouldn't have been any different. I would have stayed, and you would have gone off exploring."

The truth of that both hurt and healed, somehow. Understanding I couldn't have changed our fate, but I also wouldn't have wanted to soothed those old wounds like nothing else ever had. I'd clung to my plans ever since he took off, thinking knowing the end from the beginning was the only way to avoid more heartache. But that hadn't worked, and Sam had popped back into my life, upending it in a way I couldn't have predicted, and now wouldn't want to give up for anything.

"We could have kept in touch," he said. "Maybe I would have found my way back home sooner."

"Maybe. But maybe this is the timing we needed."

He pressed his forehead to my temple. "I hope so, Harps. I want that."

"But from now on, you'll tell me what you're thinking, right? Even if you think I won't like it?"

He rolled us so he hovered over me, his fingers in my hair, his thumbs stroking my cheeks. The soft glow of the stars left him in outlines and shadow, but I knew every inch of his face whether I saw it or not.

"I promise, Harper."

His mouth found mine, echoing that promise with a soft kiss. The give and take set off endless fireworks across my skin, my thoughts tangling and drifting even as I tried to memorize every moment. His fingers trailed over my neck, tracing my collarbone until I shuddered. Those tender touches turned me upside down and inside out, his gentle kisses growing wild as I squirmed against him, wanting more.

He finally drew back with a groan, tipping his forehead to meet mine again. "I think we're breaking all our rules."

My ragged breath sounded unbearably loud in the darkness. "There's still one rule left."

He brushed the backs of his fingers over my cheek. "We said no expectations."

"Is that set in stone?"

He laughed but shifted away, tucking me back up by his side again. "No. But it might be good to step back a little."

"Hmm." Being wrapped up in his arms was good, but I could imagine something even better. "When did you become the sensible one?"

"It's a new thing I'm trying out."

I snuggled against him, disappointment urging me to convince him to turn his impulsiveness back on high. "Your timing is terrible."

His low chuckle rumbled through my chest.

"I want things to go right for us this time around, Harper. We don't have to rush anything."

The warmth of his conviction drowned out any lingering regret. He believed we had time. I would, too.

"But," he added, "I might need a minute in that outdoor shower."

harper

FRIDAY AFTERNOON, I finished the last of my patient notes and cleared my desk in anticipation of the holiday ahead. I'd been antsy and distracted all day, but it didn't have much to do with Christmas Eve tomorrow. Truly, I was surprised I could keep myself focused at all after my night with Sam.

This morning, he'd made us bacon and eggs for breakfast before we said goodbye to the tiny house and headed out. Seeing the place in the daytime, I'd wished we had a chance to enjoy it longer. Surrounded by oaks and ashes, with sweet little walking paths heading deeper into the property, it would have been a dream for a longer stay.

Except for the whole outdoor shower thing.

A knock sounded behind me, and I turned to find him in the PT room doorway. Not that long ago, I would have been mortified at the way my stomach did a loop-the-loop and my heart rate kicked up to high just from seeing him. Now, I relished it, ready for more.

"Hi," he said when I reached him. He put one hand on my waist, the other held behind his back.

"Hi."

We'd been about as eloquent on the two-hour drive back from the tiny house, holding hands and talking nonsense like lovesick fools.

"I wanted to bring you something before I head over to Lotus Flower."

He'd told me he'd offered to cover another instructor's afternoon classes so she could take off early for the holiday weekend. Tomorrow was booked for the same reason. Between his work and the lunch date with Callie I'd arranged, we wouldn't see each other again until the Christmas market tomorrow night. Twenty-four hours already seemed way too long.

"What is it?"

He brought the hand out from behind his back and held it up to reveal a bundle of bright green mistletoe bound with a red ribbon. "One of the guys in the lounge thought I might need it."

"One of the residents gave you that?" Mortifying enough they'd tried to set us up, but trying to finagle a kiss seemed too far. Not a surprise, but too far.

"Good old Frank, my new wingman." He lifted the mistletoe over our heads, wiggling it a little bit. "You don't want to leave anything from your list unchecked, do you?"

I laughed, trying hard not to roll my eyes. "You're really being a martyr, here. This is a *Christmas* tradition."

"I'm willing to make a few sacrifices."

He grinned, his dimples trying to convince me to throw my dignity aside.

"Kiss him already," a voice called.

I hopped back to find Diana peering in at us on her way somewhere, a perfect reminder privacy was in short supply in Fiesta Village. She waggled her eyebrows and shimmied her hips in encouragement. Apparently satisfied she'd embarrassed us enough, she walked away, shooting us one last glance over her shoulder. She probably thought this had all been the result of her pushing us together a couple of weeks ago.

Actually, it kind of was. I owed her a thank you gift.

"My friend Diana gives great advice," Sam said, that grin never leaving his face.

"Everyone in this place will know about us now."

He shrugged. "I'm an open book."

I wasn't. At least, I never had been. I'd always kept my personal life separate from work, sometimes even from family. Then again, I'd never had all that much to hide. And I didn't want to hide what I had with Sam.

Leaning forward, I rested one hand on his chest, drawn to those soft lips still smiling at me. I'd nearly reached them when another knock sounded at the PT door, breaking us apart for the second time. Honestly, we should have soaked in all the privacy we had at the Hideaway, since everywhere else we went seemed determined to interrupt us.

Olivia stood in the doorway, eyebrows raised, no waggle or shimmy in sight.

All my eagerness to have my relationship in the open fizzled out knowing my director had seen us like this. Sam stood frozen with the mistletoe poised above him for another second before he brought his arm down.

"Sorry to interrupt," she said. "Do you have a minute, Harper?"

Sam turned to me, a silent apology in his eyes. "I'll see you tomorrow night."

I nodded as he disappeared out the door, taking the mistletoe and most of my pride with him.

"I'm sorry, I know I shouldn't have been in such a...compromising position here."

Olivia walked into the PT room, brushing off my concerns with a quick shake of her head. "Not an issue. As long as everything's consensual and doesn't interfere with your work, it's not a problem."

"It's very consensual."

"Great." She nodded as though topic closed. "I wanted to talk to you about next week."

I sucked in a breath, disappointment already crawling through me. Her chipper voice somehow sounded like the Grinch rising up to snatch my Christmas break away. Keeping a light smile on my face I didn't feel, I hoped I looked unaffected. "Oh?"

"A few of the residents have expressed concern you won't be available for sessions next week."

"It's a holiday." Futile to point it out, since she already knew.

She ticked her head to the side as though the holiday were debatable. "I was thinking we should let them schedule appointments after Tuesday. Give you Christmas, the day after, then you can come back in. Just for the ones who actually schedule. I doubt it will be many."

I doubted it would be many, too, but the point remained she'd effectively eliminated my time off. Whether it was one patient or ten, coming in to work over what should have been a holiday break meant the same thing either way.

I should have told her absolutely not, that I deserved this time off and the patients could wait a few days. But the fear of letting them down—and finally finding out whether I was irre-placeable here—kept my mouth shut.

"Thanks so much, Harper," she said, her smile shining brighter. "You're really coming through for us. You're part of what makes Fiesta Village such a wonderful place to live."

Then she turned and walked away, leaving me both flat-tered to be needed, and discouraged to have to make yet another compromise in order to stay.

* * *

Ready to drown my disappointments in about a hundred margaritas but figuring it was still too early for day-drinking, I found Callie waiting for me at Lupe's Escape.

"I'm sorry I'm late. Something came up at work, and it kind of threw me off." Probably shouldn't admit I'd sat in a bathroom stall for fifteen minutes processing how easily my Christmas break had been revoked, and how I'd done nothing at all to stop it.

I didn't think Olivia would fire me if I pushed back on her plans...but I couldn't be sure, either. She'd been so worried about keeping up with our rival retirement center, I didn't have a ton of confidence she wouldn't just find someone else more willing to work through holidays.

"It's like five minutes," Callie said with a laugh. "I would have been mad if you'd showed up earlier, I was on a Candy Crush streak."

The waiter showed us to a table, and we settled in. Even though I'd been the one to invite Callie out, it'd been so long since I'd tried to make friends, I suddenly had no clue what to talk about. The weather? Our jobs? How she got her hair to fall in such perfect waves?

"I like your necklace," I said.

She looked down and laughed, jiggling the string of multi-colored raw penne pasta hung around her neck. "A gift from a student," she said with a teasing smirk. "It's a Xander Goranson original."

"That's cute."

"I forgot I had it on. Perils of working with five-year-olds."

The waiter came by with waters and chips and salsa, and took our orders before disappearing again.

"Are you ready to become a regular at Fool Hearted Memory?" Callie asked.

"I don't think my feet could take it." Even if I was really more worried about how my pride would hold up. "It was more fun than I expected, though."

"It all depends on the group. I like to go on Wednesdays, because weekends are usually overrun with single guys looking to take someone home. Coincidentally, that's why my granny and her friends like to go on the weekends."

She made the face of someone who had to put up with the antics of a much-older person. I knew that face well, since I made it every day. "They seemed like they could get up to some trouble. Sweet, though."

She'd introduced us to her grandma and her friends Wednesday night: Suzie, Carmen, Linda, and Rita. Loud and boisterous, they'd finished each other's sentences and bested most of the others on the floor with their dance moves.

"You have no idea." Callie tilted her head, screwing up her eyebrows. "Wait, didn't you say you work at a retirement community? Maybe you have some idea."

"Oh, yeah. People don't always slow down with age the way you might think."

"No kidding. They're like gray-haired sorority sisters, always ready to party." She cringed. "Uh, no offense if you were in a sorority."

"None taken. A lot of my patients are the same way."

"I guess we should all hope to have that kind of energy when we're seventy-eight, right?"

"If only."

She rested her chin on her hand, her pasta necklace clattering as she moved. "What brought you out to the honky tonk if you didn't think you'd like it? It wasn't a meddlesome grandmother."

I ate a big bite of tortilla chip loaded down with salsa. Callie seemed pretty straightforward so far, so might as well just jump in and tell her the truth. In the spirit of friendship, and all.

"I'd made a bucket list of things to do before my birthday."

Her eyes lit up. "And line dancing was on it?"

"Well...sort of." I explained how it counted as conquering a fear, and some of the other things I'd been doing the last few weeks in an effort to add a bit more life to my life.

"I love it. But please, please do not mention your life list to my granny. She and her friends will come up with a list for me, and I really don't want to know the kinds of things that would be on it."

We laughed over that, but from all I'd seen, they'd treated Callie like she was a princess at every turn. They'd been a little pushy about keeping her on the dance floor and nudging her toward seemingly available men, but they'd showered her with obvious affection.

"They seem to want what's best for you."

"They do. We just define that differently. All of the things Granny and I do, the fun little classes and outings, are all so she can find me a man to take care of me."

I couldn't help cringing. "You're twenty-four."

If they thought Callie needed someone to match her up, I must have been a downright spinster in their eyes.

"Right?" She hitched a shoulder, pulling a chip through the salsa, her smile winking out. "I get it, though. I don't have anybody else. My dad hasn't been around since I was nine, and my mom died when I was in high school. Granny doesn't want me to be alone, so finding me a husband is her way of making sure I'm taken care of. She wants me to be happy, but she really only means man-happy."

My heart hurt for her, but shame washed over me, too. I'd been moping around because my closest relatives had found love and expanded our family, meanwhile Callie had lost everyone but her grandma. Kind of put things in perspective. "I'm sorry. That's got to be hard."

"It's okay. I probably shouldn't lead with such a buzzkill conversation starter." She dialed her smile back up. "Who knows, maybe Granny will have better taste in guys than I did. My college boyfriend was not the best." Her eyes went wide. "Sorry. I'm babbling."

"Don't apologize. I've dated some losers, too."

"Sam didn't seem like a loser."

"Oh, he's not my boyfriend." The automatic clarification felt wrong as soon as I'd said it. After everything we'd said last night, my knee-jerk reaction was still denial?

Callie's cynical expression showed I hadn't convinced her, either. "Okay. But the way he watched you all night gave total boyfriend vibes."

I grinned even though I tried to stop it. "We're figuring things out."

"He didn't seem like he had all that many questions."

Giddy happiness fizzed through me over how obvious he'd been. I might have had reservations at first, but Sam sure wasn't trying to hide anything.

The waiter came back with a tray of enchiladas for me and a fat burrito smothered in cream for Callie. The smell of cumin and chipotle had my mouth watering before my plate ever touched the table.

"These burritos are what angels serve for dinner in Heaven," she said after her first bite.

"Lupe's gets all the stars."

"So do your patients try to meddle in your love life, too, or is that just a thing my granny and her friends do?"

"Oh, no, they meddle. Getting fingers in everyone else's

lives is an Olympic sport over there." Had to admit, though, this time around, they'd done a pretty good job.

"Is it bad I'm kind of relieved you can relate?"

"I'm sure they're not as invested as relatives would be, but they do their best to match me up. Even when the guy gives off very *not interested* vibes."

She laughed. "That's good, though, right? It shows how much they care about you. Or at least, that's the way my granny and her friends justify getting their fingerprints all over my life."

"They do care about me." Even if I wasn't supposed to blur the lines of professionalism, many of my patients cared a lot. Like Eliza always said, they doted on me over there.

Callie's eyebrows tugged together. "Why do you sound sad about that?"

I sighed, dragging my fork through the enchilada sauce. "It's wonderful they're so invested, but it makes it that much harder if I ever think of leaving."

Didn't even like to say those words out loud, honestly.

"You want to leave your job?" she asked softly.

"No." I didn't. But deep down, I knew I couldn't keep giving in to Olivia's changing demands. The fear she wouldn't back down and I'd end up losing my whole career in one fell swoop was the only thing keeping me from speaking up about the ridiculousness of her on-call scheme, or how unnecessary spoiling my Christmas break was.

"But..." Callie prompted, sounding exactly like June or Eden might.

"I don't want to leave, but there are some...conditions...about the job I don't love. But having so many people I've grown attached to there makes it harder to look at those issues logically."

Among the people I would disappoint if I left—or was asked

to leave—would be all of my patients I'd dedicated the last three years to. I would let them down if I rocked the boat. And I'd never been all that great at rocking boats.

"I totally understand. I cried for two days straight after my first kindergarten class graduated to first grade. I'd invested so much in them, it hurt to let them go. But I realized that's what I'd signed up for—I'd teach them their basics and get them started in school, and then I had to see them off. But I'd do my best for every single one of them for as long as I had them. Maybe it's kind of the same thing for you and your patients. You do the best for them while you're there, but you're not necessarily meant to stay with them forever."

I sucked in a breath that she could clarify it so easily. I'd been so worried about letting my patients down if I stood up for myself with Olivia, I'd ignored just how much I helped them every day. Like she said, I did my best for them day in, day out —changing jobs tomorrow wouldn't erase one minute of that.

"Or maybe I'm way off base," Callie said with a little trill of nervous laughter.

"No, no, I was thinking you're exactly right. I don't want to leave my job, but if I ever did, I know I've given them the best I could while I was there." It really was as simple as that. "Thank you."

"You're welcome."

"You know, I'm really glad I ran into you at that honky tonk."

"I'm really glad I didn't break your toes." She took another bite and held a hand in front of her mouth while she finished chewing. "Two days before Christmas, obligatory question: what are your plans for the holiday?"

"My parents are hosting a big family dinner party this year. My sisters and cousins and all their partners, my uncle, and my cousin's kids, my grandma." I counted them up in my head.

"Eighteen of us, I think. And that's not including in-laws who might join in."

Pretty sure Booker's parents had said they'd come. Ty's brother, Bret, obviously had not been extended an invite, but I wasn't sure about the rest.

"I love that. I've always wondered what a big family Christmas would be like. It was always just me, Mom, and Granny, and then later, just me and Granny." She made a dismissive gesture, forking up another bite of burrito. "Me and Granny and her three friends now, I guess."

"What do you do for the holiday?"

"We open presents and have a big breakfast, but then I usually escape to my part of the house to watch Christmas movies. Gran and her friends reminisce a lot, and since I didn't live through the seventies, I'm kind of the odd duck out. *While You Were Sleeping* usually gets me through, though."

I sighed. "Great movie."

Her plans sounded lonely. During my DPT program, at the height of my fear of getting kicked out, I'd stayed in my little apartment in Fort Worth for Thanksgiving instead of driving home to take a break. It'd seemed like the smartest option, but I'd missed my family something fierce, and wallowed in my loneliness the whole holiday break. Imagining that for her over Christmas—even with loved ones in the next room—made my heart hurt.

"Would you like to come have dinner with us?"

Callie froze as if I'd suddenly started speaking Mandarin. "Are you inviting me to your family's Christmas dinner?"

"That's weird, I know, but I thought maybe—"

"I'd love to! Thank you, yes. I mean, as long as you're sure it would be okay with your family."

"My mom will be thrilled, she loves playing hostess." I'd

probably get bonus points for bringing her another young woman to fuss and fawn over.

Callie leaned closer to me over the table. "Are you sure, though? I could be a weirdo or a serial killer or an identity thief or something."

"I met your granny. I highly doubt anyone related to her would be any of those things." But now, it was my turn to lean closer, worry probably furrowing my brow. "Will it hurt your grandma's feelings? I can invite her, too."

"Me going to a Christmas party without her would be like Granny's dream come true." She paused a second. "Will any single guys be there?"

"Just one that I know of, but he's, uh, not exactly the most available." Or, to put it another way, Jed was *perpetually* the most available.

"Good. I'll tell her they're all married so she won't get her hopes up."

"Sounds like a plan."

sam

CROWDS STUFFED Center Street's sidewalks, everybody shuffling their way toward the last night of the Christmas market. I wove through couples and families, eager to get to Harper and maximize the little bit of time I'd have with her tonight. After our stay in the tiny house, I was greedy for her.

Closing in on the big tree in town square, I pulled my beanie lower on my head. Memories of the last time I'd been to this Christmas market tried to barge into my thoughts, but I threw them right back out. Still hated the way my parents had manipulated us back then, but holding onto that hadn't done me any favors. I'd resented those memories too long—time to learn from Georgia and find a way to move on.

Anyway, tonight had nothing to do with them—only Harper and me.

The sight of her beneath the tree put all the other lights around her to shame. When her eyes found me, she glowed even brighter, that smile tugging at my heart, urging me to reach her as quickly as possible. I rushed to her, performing a little maneuver I could only hope looked like a jog and not a skip. We stood toe to toe, her delight shifting to confusion to recognition, then the worst—tears sparkled in the corners of her eyes.

She reached up to run delicate fingers over the edges of my hat, looking at it like some long-lost magical thing. Kind of was.

"You kept it all this time."

"It's a good hat."

She sniffed but shook her head a touch. "I missed a stitch here."

Her fingernail lightly scratched my scalp through a hole near the brim. I'd always liked the little mistake because it reminded me Harper had made the hat for me herself.

"Gives it character."

"You are adorable." She threw her arms around my neck and kissed me right in front of the Christmas tree. "I love that you kept it."

I held her close, my heart a jet turbine roaring up to top speed. *I love you.* I wanted to climb the tree like King Kong and shout it to everyone in town square. Probably better if I let her know first, one-on-one. Soon.

I took her hand in mine with no intention of letting it go the rest of the night.

The market booths sat beneath awnings strung with round white lights to show off the goods. We wandered past stalls selling every kind of handmade thing from wooden chess pieces to custom paint sets, candles to knitwear. Harper stopped to inspect each booth, admiring everything on offer.

People meandered down the market aisle, taking just as much time with their booth inspections as her. Every fifth person had the same genius idea to wear a Santa hat, but the effect proved festive. Carols played through loudspeakers, and I found myself bopping along.

"It's not so bad, is it?"

With one arm looped through mine, she smiled so sweetly, I could only give one answer.

Like every other task she'd put on my Christmas experience list, I'd been surprised just how much I enjoyed it. Didn't matter all that much if we were baking cookies or making our way through a crowded market—everything was better with her.

I touched my nose to hers. "Bah humbug."

She tried to glare, but her mouth curled up as if fighting a losing battle against a smile.

"If you two are done canoodling, come check out my soaps," a voice called.

Eliza stood behind a booth stacked with chunky bars in several colors. Forgot she'd said she was a vendor here. Harper looked like she'd rather skip her sister's stall entirely, but I pulled her over to say hello.

"Look at you two, all cozy tonight." She grinned like she could eat us up.

"Market going well?" Harper's question couldn't hide the bright pink patches shining out on her cheeks at being caught *canoodling*.

"Making a killing. And how about for you two? Things going well?" Her voice dropped, and one eyebrow kicked up, giving all sorts of naughty connotations to her questions.

"It's good." Harper picked up a soap bar without looking at it and gave it a sniff, feigning interest.

"How about you, Sam? Are you warming up to Christmas?"

Harper shook her head at her sister's saucy tone. Pretty sure Eliza wanted to know about much more than my opinion on the holiday.

"I consider myself fully warmed." Lifting my eyebrows, I matched Eliza's attitude.

She laughed. "Good to hear. If you need any soaps, I'll give you the family discount."

"Eliza," Harper hissed.

"Sorry. I mean, I'll give you the sister's boyfriend discount. Is that better?"

Harper's glare could have melted all the soaps on the table, but I couldn't keep the smug smile off my face. I put a hand on her waist and nudged her closer. "Sister's boyfriend discount sounds great to me."

"Can I assume we'll be seeing you Christmas Day?"

Harper looked like she wanted to gut Eliza, which didn't give me a whole lot of hope I'd be getting that invite.

"Have I ever told you how much you remind me of Mom?" Harper said.

Eliza gasped. "You take that back."

"If the meddlesome shoe fits..." Harper turned to me, the pink spots on her cheeks even darker than before. "I meant to ask you if you wanted to join us for dinner. I know you've got stuff with your family, though."

"Their big celebration is in the morning. Kids rip open the presents, Ava makes a huge breakfast, and then everyone naps the rest of the day. That's what Georgia says, anyway. I could do both."

"Two Christmas celebrations?" she said, a hint of teasing in her voice. "That's kind of a lot for you, isn't it?"

"I can take it. I have plenty of stamina."

Her glare was ruined by the light of desire in her eyes. If the thoughts in her head were anything like mine, we'd both get coal in our stockings this year.

Eliza snorted, reminding me we'd already made enough of a scene for one night. I didn't care all that much, but Harper seemed to, and that was enough to stop me from pulling her in for another kiss.

A man eased by, two travel mugs in his hands, to reach Eliza in her booth. "Here you go, El. Extra whipped cream."

"Thank you." She lifted her chin for a quick kiss. "I could get used to having an errand boy."

"Good, because you're stuck with me."

After a minute, she seemed to snap out of the dreamy daze the man's appearance had put her in, and focused on us. "Dean, do you know Sam Donnelly?"

"Only by name." He reached across the mountains of soaps to shake my hand. "I think you were in Irwin's talking with my brother Grant a while back."

"We talked a little about his last climb." Grant Irwin had found a balance, getting in climbs on the side while maintaining a good job in the outdoor gear business full-time. I'd hoped to find that kind of balance, too, but it seemed an either/or for me at the moment.

"He said your credentials were impressive."

To someone like Grant, maybe. To any potential employer...debatable.

"That's because Sam's been traveling the world having adventures," Eliza said. "Speaking of, we're going on a hike at The Grotto on Thursday. You guys want to join us?"

"I'm up for that. Harper?"

She looked almost as pained as she had when Eliza preemptively invited me to Christmas dinner. "I don't think I can."

"What? Why not? You've finally got a week off." Eliza's mouth curled again. "Unless you have other plans."

She made it sound like any *other plans* would directly involve me, but I sure hadn't heard about them yet if they did.

"No, it's just...they asked me to come in a few times next week to see patients. So I couldn't do a day trip. Sorry."

"Harper, why—"

She cut off Eliza's question with a sharp look. "I'm not thrilled about it, either, but they need me."

"They don't need you when you're supposed to be on vacation," I said, not hiding my frustration.

I was no doctor, but even I understood that physical therapy wasn't like setting a bone or cutting out a burst appendix. Her patients weren't suffering from emergencies, they simply wanted continuing care because they could get it. Nothing in their concerns should have prevented her from being off the clock all week and taking care of them again next Monday.

"Some of them told Olivia they wanted to see me this week."

"So? You should have told her no."

I hated how easily Olivia could strip Harper of her time off, but I hated even more the suspicion she hadn't put up much of a fight.

"She's my boss."

Her firm tone let me know I was skating on thin ice here, but I kept on skating anyway.

"That doesn't mean she gets to dictate your whole life. First it's evenings and weekends, then it's the crazy on-call idea. Now your vacation. When are you going to put a stop to it? When are you going to choose *you*, Harper?"

If she could have exploded me with her mind, I would have been nothing but bloody bits right then. The pink spots on her cheek flared to red as she glowered at me several long seconds. Finally, she turned to Eliza.

"I'll see you guys tomorrow," she said, before leaving them —and me—behind.

harper

I MARCHED down the market aisle, ignoring the barrage of Christmas cheer all around me and absolutely pretending Sam wasn't walking by my side. Reverting to my old game seemed a whole lot safer than what I really wanted to do. We needed to escape the crowds before I did something stupid like slap him upside the head for his audacity.

"When are you going to choose you?" Made total sense from the guy who'd chosen himself for eleven years straight.

We reached the edge of town square before Sam grabbed my hand, tugging me to a stop beneath a street light. Christmas carols still drifted on the night air, but I didn't feel nearly as jolly as Mariah Carey wanted me to.

"Can we talk about this, please?"

He released me and took a step back as though I might respond with one of the jabs we'd practiced at Rumble Room. Smart man.

"What do you want to talk about?" I asked in a crisp voice.

"How about why you're mad at me right now, Harper. I'm not the one who ruined your vacation."

It wasn't ruined, just...altered. But that didn't sound like a very strong defense even to me, especially when I didn't love the alterations, either.

"You're mad, too," I said instead.

"Yeah, I'm mad as hell, but I'm mad on your behalf. You're not mad at all, and that's just ticking me off more."

"What do you want me to do? Quit my job and go be a nomad like you?"

"No, but I'd like you to fight for yourself. They're taking advantage of you, but you don't want to accept that."

"They're not taking advantage of me." Things weren't perfect, but what job ever was? They were still working out the kinks of the PT program. "Long hours are part of the deal in healthcare."

"This isn't about hours. You're letting them work you into the ground, and you're doing it with a smile because you're so afraid of how it would look if you spoke up. God forbid you realize your own worth and quit to get something better."

My chest heaved, my brain denying his accusations at every turn. He had no idea. None. I couldn't risk my job because of a few small issues. I wasn't happy with Olivia's constant schedule changes, but I'd worked too hard to just throw it all away.

"You keep choosing the safe option," he said. "But is it making you happy?"

Was I happy at Fiesta Village? Most of the time, yes. It fulfilled me, and I took pride in it. I didn't like working weekends or through my vacations, but if it meant keeping a good job, then I would just have to deal. I couldn't quit over an inconvenience. Even realizing yesterday that leaving wouldn't undo all the good I'd done there didn't mean I actually *wanted* to leave.

"What about you, considering a job at your dad's firm because you're too afraid to try for what you really want to do? You're choosing the safe option, too."

His face contorted like what I'd said didn't make any sense. "Harper, I'm doing that for *us*. We can't have a relationship if I'm away all the time on guiding trips. I've seen what that can do to couples, and I don't want to do that to you."

I loved the intent behind what he'd just said, but I didn't want him to give up his dream career because of preemptive guilt. "I'm not asking you to give up what you love and settle for a desk job."

He stepped closer, taking me lightly by the arms. "Do you not understand? I'm settling for the desk job so I *can* have what I love. I love *you*, Harper. I don't think I ever stopped. And I don't want to be with you just on days off, or the rare chance our schedules work out. I want to be with you, always."

Always? My heart trembled, fluttering around like it needed to be free of my ribcage. Sam loved me. I wanted to stop arguing and float around in that knowledge, but I also didn't want him to sit at a desk out of some misguided desire to please me.

I couldn't let him take a job at his dad's business for the sake of our relationship. It'd be as absurd as me abandoning my college plans so I could travel the world with him—it would go against everything he wanted, and he'd wind up resenting me in the end.

"You'll be miserable working a job you don't want to do."

"No worse than being miserable working a job you *do* want to do."

I stood taller, unwilling to give on the point he kept pushing. "I'm not miserable."

"You've been burning yourself out for years, you just don't want to see it. You're so busy taking care of everybody else, you don't know how to do what's best for *you* anymore."

I sputtered over a retort that wouldn't come. Maybe I had been working too hard, but what was the alternative? And he didn't know what he was talking about, anyway. He'd been gone for years, but he thought he had all the answers after being back two months?

"How is that working out for you? Is there *anything* you haven't walked away from in the name of doing what's best for you?"

He stepped back, a grimace touching his mouth. My blood pounded in my ears in the silence that followed, standing off against him beneath a street lamp while *I'll Be Home for Christmas* echoed through the market. He'd just told me he loved me—how had we gone from that glorious moment to this awful scene?

"You're right. I've walked away from everything and everyone that mattered. But at least I'm actually living my life."

Indignation rose up like a huge, ugly monstrosity in my chest. "What is that supposed to mean?"

"Look at your life, Harper. You had to make a list just to remind yourself to have a little fun. That's not really living."

His words hit a perfect bullseye on my heart. I knew it was true, but hated that he'd seen it so easily. But of course he had. Sam's life was all about fun. If anybody knew how to choose what he wanted and opt for some short-lived fun, it was him.

Meanwhile, I'd been running from mess and risk and any chance of making a mistake for years. And why? Same answer. *Sam.* Because I couldn't handle the possibility of my heart being smashed to bits all over again. So I'd clung to routine and plans and safety. My list was supposed to help me break out of that rut, but it sure hadn't stopped me from making mistakes. Falling for Sam again might have been the biggest mistake of all.

"Maybe I should take a page from your book and try walking away."

The air whooshed out of his lungs, the look in his eyes like I'd just landed a roundhouse straight to his chest. He shook his head, disappointment telegraphed in every movement. "You're still not choosing what you want."

"Maybe you don't know me as well as you think you do."

"Maybe I know you better than you want to admit."

I crossed my arms over my chest in a futile attempt to block out the chill. Impossible, since the cold came from my heart now.

"I don't want to do this anymore. I want—" I wanted to go home to my warm house, snuggle under a blanket on the couch, and watch a Christmas movie. I wanted to pretend this whole conversation away. Mostly, I wanted to forget the way he'd sliced straight into the most vulnerable part of me and laid me open.

"What do you want, Harper?"

You. I couldn't even say the word, like it didn't exist in my brain. We'd crashed and burned once before. Who could say we wouldn't crumble again? Even after the last few amazing weeks, we already teetered on the edge of a break. When he left me the first time, it'd wrecked me. I couldn't go through that again.

He took a step closer and kissed me on the forehead, lingering there like he was trying to breathe me in. Releasing me, he sighed, a soft, sad sound.

"Find me when you figure out what you want."

Then, for the second time in my life, Sam Donnelly walked away, leaving my heart crushed behind him.

harper

IF ANYONE'S WONDERING, baking and a broken heart do not go well together.

I'd spent Christmas Eve at my parents' house making pies and cookies, and so far, everything had gone wrong. I'd made a batch of molasses cookies but forgot the molasses, put a pie crust in the oven without poking it first so it puffed up like a football, and left the sugar out of my mom's favorite cranberry orange bread.

Still, my mishaps in the kitchen were a lot better than sitting around watching the love-fest happening in the living room. Booker read *A Christmas Carol* out loud while Eden smiled over his ringing baritone as he did all the voices, their hands clasped between them. Eliza sat in Dean's lap, only halfway pretending to listen to Ebenezer Scrooge's plight while they nuzzled and cuddled each other. My parents had even been out there up until a few minutes ago, snuggling away like lovebirds while Dad teased Mom with a sprig of mistletoe.

I couldn't fathom how Christmas Day would go when we'd more than double the number of painfully happy couples in here. I should probably load one of the desserts with rum so I could drown my sorrows and eat my feelings at the same time.

"Are you still working away?"

Mom walked into the kitchen sounding like she hadn't even noticed I'd been hidden in here all day. Not really the comfort I would have hoped for from my mom.

"I had to redo the cranberry orange bread. The last loaf was inedible." I'd chucked it in the garbage can with a pathetic thud.

"Don't work yourself too hard trying to make a good Christmas for everyone else. You've got to live it, too."

Kind of echoed everything Sam had said last night.

Our conversation had played through my thoughts a thousand times, but I still couldn't figure out where things had gone wrong. How had we moved from making Christmas plans in each other's arms to Sam walking away? And not just walking away—I'd *pushed* him away because...why? Because he knew me too well? Because I didn't want to risk my heart again?

If that was it, I hadn't done a very good job protecting my heart. It'd hurt and squeezed and reminded me of everything I'd got wrong all day.

He thought I was being a martyr about work, that much had been clear. But that he thought he needed to settle down and take a job working for his dad instead of working as a guide? Giving up what he loved made no sense, even if he thought he was doing it for me.

"Did you ever resent all the time Dad spends away on call?" Maybe he'd never spent days out at a time, but he'd had overnight calls through the years, and he'd certainly never kept perfect nine to five hours.

Mom leaned against the counter next to me. "No, because he loves it. It fulfills him. And I'm always here to welcome him home."

I could have done without the saucy wink. I didn't care

what Eliza said, she got about sixty percent of her personality from Mom.

"Why do you ask?"

"No reason." None I wanted to share, anyway.

"Are you sure it's not because they're working you too much over at the Village?"

I tried to play it cool, but I'd apparently lost all ability to hide my emotions. "You think so?"

She scoffed. "I don't know what you girls think of me. Eden pretending she's hiding her pregnancy, and you thinking I can't see you're working yourself to the bone. Baby, it's okay to make time for yourself, too. You don't have to put so much into your job that you don't have anything left for you."

She might have ripped off Sam's speech from last night. "I'm not working myself to the bone."

The defense came on autopilot, like the way I'd been living the last few years. An automatic answer I hadn't fully thought through. Kind of like my argument with Sam last night. Easier to defend old habits than take a long, hard look at them.

She ran a hand along my hair, brushing it over my shoulder. "Baby, you're working yourself down to dust. I don't understand why you think you have to."

Her gentleness loosened something inside me, working past all my defenses straight to my tender center. "I'm afraid if I speak up, I could lose my job."

"Baby, if speaking up is all it would take, maybe it's not the job you thought it was."

I let out a tremulous laugh. "I can't risk my job."

"Why not?"

Her cavalier attitude made me get right to the point. "I've worked too hard to get here. And...I don't want to disappoint you and Dad."

"Oh, Harper." She laid a hand on my shoulder, working her

mom magic until tears sprang to my eyes. "You can't ever do that. We're proud of you no matter what you do. This job, some other job, something else entirely. We just love you, head to toe."

"But—" I turned to make sure Eliza wasn't anywhere near the kitchen. "You pushed Eliza so hard with her soap business because you thought she might fail. Wouldn't you think the same thing of me if I left my job? Or worse—was let go?"

She shot me a quelling look. "I know the women I raised. Eliza needed a push now and then, though I admit, she's pulled her job together, and we're proud of her. You, on the other hand, never needed a push. You did enough pushing all on your own."

Maybe. I'd known what I wanted and went after it. But… maybe I'd been a little overzealous with my efforts. Obviously I had, considering I'd had to force myself to do a handful of things I enjoyed this month. Sam had been right, which somehow both ticked me off and really, really comforted me.

He did know me better than I wanted to admit. The good and the bad.

"What's the worst that happens if you tell your director you're doing too much at the Village?"

"I could lose my job." Fear bloomed to life in my stomach, spreading out tentacles like a giant, unemployed octopus.

She didn't look one bit disappointed or surprised by the answer. "And then?"

"I'd have to find another one."

"Mm hmm. And do you think your three years being the sole PT at a retirement community serving almost a hundred clients would help you get a new job?"

Well…yes. I'd built this job from the ground up, put in incredible patient hours, and would have glowing recommendations. I didn't know who else was hiring, but I could probably get another job as a PT pretty quickly if it came down to it.

"But I don't want a different job. I want this one, just with normal hours."

"So ask for that. You've already realized the worst-case scenario isn't all that bad."

Maybe. I could talk to Olivia, spell it all out for her. Explain her grand ideas to make Fiesta Village more marketable were running me into the ground, and that I needed normal working hours again. And if she didn't like it...well, I could find something else.

I didn't love that last option, but it was still true. I had excellent credentials. And if all else failed, I could always threaten to apply at the new retirement community. That might get my point across to Olivia better than anything else.

"Now. Tell me what's going on with Sam."

My face flushed to life with heat. "How do you know about that?"

"Baby, you kiss a man on Center Street, word is going to get back to your mother."

I exhaled a laugh, unsurprised the gossip had done the rounds. Between the holiday market, the Village, and the tree farm, we hadn't been all that secretive.

How to even explain? "I don't know what's going on. We argued."

"What about?"

"Work. He said basically everything you did."

She nodded approval. "Smart man."

"But it's more than that. He's willing to take a desk job he doesn't enjoy just to try to make a relationship with me work."

"Do you want him to do that?"

"No. I want him to do what makes him happy, even if he'll be gone sometimes, as long as he comes back to me."

She looked about ready to break into song. "And why is that?"

"Because I—"

I loved him. The man I'd resented and wished would go away, the one I'd so desperately hoped I could get over…was also the man who talked me down when I panicked, encouraged me to live my life to the full, and indulged my every Christmas whim. He made my life an adventure, whether that was climbing at the gym or just sitting together watching a sappy movie. I loved him.

He'd told me he loved me last night, and I hadn't said it back. I'd been so afraid of making a mistake if I did or said the wrong thing, I'd done nothing at all. Eden's addition to my Life List ran through my head.

Give yourself permission to make a mistake.

I couldn't predict exactly how things would go between us or guarantee a mistake-free future, but I knew what I wanted.

I wanted Sam.

"I have to go."

Mom's smirk might as well have been six miles wide.

sam

"WHY ARE my romance novels all out of order?" Georgia frowned at her bookshelves she'd arranged by color, their bright covers no longer a perfect rainbow.

I pretended ignorance. Best not to admit I'd flipped through them late into the night, searching for a solution to my problem. Some neat, tidy way to convince Harper to choose me, not because I loved her, but because she loved me. I found a lot of grand gestures, but nothing I could apply to my situation.

Georgia flopped onto the couch next to me. I had one of Dad's financial pamphlets in my lap as though maybe I'd gain insight into the industry by skimming through it.

"Are you seriously going to do this?" She pinched a corner of the pamphlet as though it were trash.

"It's a good job." Or so Dad kept saying.

"You don't want to do it, though."

"No, but I'm running out of options in town."

"Why do you have to work in town?"

I shot her a smile I didn't feel. "Georgia, I just got back. Are you trying to kick me out already?"

She made a face like she wasn't impressed with my act.

"You want me to dumb it down, let's dumb it down. Why would you work in a joy-sucking office with Dad when there's an excellent guiding outfit in Georgetown? Wouldn't be mountain peaks or anything, but you'd be out doing what you loved every day."

"I'd be gone all the time. It'd ruin my relationship with you and Grandpa."

Her laughter didn't sound very convinced. "Are you trying to sell this as worry about your relationship with Grandpa? I've read a *lot* of romance novels, Sam. I know pining when I see it."

I exhaled a groan. "I'm pining for Harper, are you happy? But if I took a job that had me out on multi-day hikes every week, I'd be no better than Dad staying in the office until nine every night."

"Sam."

Wow. My sister's soft, heart-breaking voice brought a lump to my throat like it'd just been waiting to spring into place. I tried to swallow it back, but it wouldn't budge. "Dad did what he wanted without regard for what anyone else wanted or needed. We're pretty similar."

Those similarities had tormented me all night, the fear that maybe the apple hadn't fallen far from the tree, after all. I wouldn't cheat on Harper, but there were plenty of other ways to choose my happiness over hers. I didn't want to be that kind of man. I wouldn't.

"Sam, Dad made his choices. And I'm right there with you, his choices sucked for us and for Mom. But you aren't like Dad."

I'd never thought I was, but lately, I didn't see enough differences. "I left everyone here to go off and do my own thing."

"Do you think those are equal? Dad left his wife and kids for another woman. You spread your wings and left the nest like a normal kid. You didn't abandon anyone or neglect anyone."

Wrong thing to say. I'd abandoned Harper. And maybe it'd been inevitable, maybe we would have broken up then no matter how things had shaken out, but it didn't change my regret over what I'd done.

"And don't work for Dad if you're doing it because you think it will help things with Harper. You want to have a good relationship with her, go get a job that makes you happy. Because then you'll be happy when you're with her, too, instead of always trying to recover from your soul-sucking desk job."

She had a point. Just wasn't sure Harper would see it that way if I was gone all the time.

"I don't even know if I could get that job in Georgetown."

"Boy, love is sure making you a Negative Nelly. What happened to In-Your-Face Sam? To Jump First, Regret it Later Sam?"

"At the moment, he's too busy being terrified he's lost the woman he loves again to be in your face."

She patted my cheek, turning it into a light slap at the end. "So pathetic."

"You're right. You're right." I stood and shook my arms and legs out like I was getting ready to fight the handsy MMA instructor. "I should just phone Pierce Vaughn, apologize for leaving the way I did, and ask for a job recommendation."

"It's not like he's going to say no," Georgia called from the couch. "They want you back, they'll definitely give you a recommendation."

Some of my enthusiasm faded. "Doesn't change the crappy hours I'd have as a guide, though."

I had come back to try to make a real life with Harper. Could I really have that if we were apart half the time?

"Look on the bright side. Maybe Harper doesn't want to spend as much time with you as you think."

"Wow. Thank you. Ten out of ten on the pep talk."

A knock came at her door, and she hopped off the couch. "Just saying." She swung the door open and turned to me, eyes wide. "Or I could be wrong."

Harper stood in the open doorway, all glorious and lovely. She'd tugged a beanie down over her windswept hair and had streaks of something I guessed was flour on her jeans. She looked cold and tired and about as miserable as I'd been feeling, but she was *here.*

"Hi," she said, her eyes locked on mine.

"I am going to go do something in my bedroom." Georgia backed away from the door and slunk down the short hallway to her room.

Harper walked the rest of the way inside, closing the door behind her. I moved closer to meet her, itching to pull her into my arms. I wouldn't yet—I'd messed things up between us out of a desire to let her choose, so I needed to be patient. Why on earth I'd opted for patience now, I couldn't say. I'd never been very good at that, honestly.

"I realized I, uh..." She swallowed, glancing around Georgia's ultra-Christmasy apartment. "I messed up my Life List, and I need your help."

My heart deflated like a sad little balloon. We were back to talking about her list now? "How?"

"Well, it was supposed to just be a few things to shake up my life a little. To rattle me out of my rut. Just some temporary fun, you know?"

My sad balloon of a heart collapsed. Just some temporary fun. I wasn't what she wanted, then. I loved her, couldn't imagine going another day without her, but I was just a way to shake up her life.

"Only, I think I found something permanent." She twisted her mouth, and I might have caught a hint of nervousness in her eyes. "I'm just as bad as Eden, June, and Eliza. I went and fell madly in love with you."

My little balloon heart re-inflated, pressing against my ribcage until it hurt. *Madly in love with you.* Best words ever.

"I'm sorry I didn't tell you last night. I was focused on the wrong things."

"I can relate."

She inched closer to me, and still, I fought the urge to grab her and never let go.

"I'm going to talk to Olivia. If she can't deliver the hours we'd originally agreed on, I'll just have to find something else."

"I never wanted you to quit your job, Harper. I just wanted you to take time for yourself, too."

"I know." She took another step closer. "And I don't want you to work for your dad. I want you to have a job you love. Even if you're gone sometimes, it's okay, as long as you come home to me in the end."

Truly, I was madly, deeply, desperately in love with this woman. I hadn't told her nearly often enough. "I love you."

"I know."

"A Star Wars reference? Really?"

"It fit." She put a hand in her sweatshirt pocket. "We didn't finish my list, you know."

She pulled out a sprig of mistletoe and raised it over her head. "I still need to kiss someone."

My heart pounded out an urgent staccato, desperate to get her in my arms. Finally closing the distance between us, I pulled her to me. "How about the man who is crazy in love with you?"

"The one I'm absolutely nuts for? Yeah, it should be him."

"Later, can we upgrade to naked Twister?"

Her smile turned naughty. "Yes, please."

I kissed her, pouring all my adoration for this woman into every touch and caress. Her hands came to the back of my neck, stroking through my hair until my stomach clenched. I relished her, tilting her chin just right as I drank her in. A perfect start to a lifetime of kisses.

Holding her head in my hands, I pressed my forehead to hers. "I know now it's cliché, but it's always been you, Harper. There's never been anyone else for me."

"No one else ever stood a chance with—" She drew back, eyes open wide. "Wait, how do you know it's a cliché? Have you been reading up on romances?"

I glanced to the side, guilty as charged. "I might have skimmed a few."

"A few?"

"Several."

"I'm going to need details."

"So bossy." I pulled her back to me until my lips brushed hers. I found the little shiver that rocked through her deeply satisfying. "You only need to know that second chance romance is my most favorite trope."

"Mine, too."

harper

WHY DO babies smell so good?

I'd held my cousin Wade's baby, Maisie, at least ten times today, and every time, she smelled better than the last. I couldn't help pressing my nose to the soft little fuzz on her head, her round little cheeks, her adorable button nose. I loved this kid.

Conveniently, she'd saved her diaper blowout for when Jed had been holding her. I liked to think that meant she loved me, too.

"I guess she's pretty cute." Sam shot me a crooked smile while I cooed over the little bundle in my arms.

"Say it louder, and Wade will march you outside," I dared.

He pulled a worried face but smiled at her right along with me.

My uncle Clint came over, arms outstretched. "Mind if I hold my granddaughter?"

I passed her off, letting him and Marilyn take over baby duties. Everyone in the room had taken a turn a time or two while her mother, Annie, napped in Eden's old bedroom. Apparently, Wade and Annie's sons, Dylan and Beau, had woken up at three a.m., ready to rip open presents and eat their weight in sugar cookies.

They weren't the only ones who'd had an early morning.

"How are you holding up?" I asked Sam. "Need to sneak into my old bedroom for a while?"

His grin lit up my chest like a sparkler. "Can't get enough of me, can you, Harps?"

I rolled my eyes, blushing away. "I meant to ask if you're sleepy, but I admit that came out all wrong."

"I think it came out just right."

He'd spent the night at his dad's so he could get the full Christmas experience with the littles. I'd joined them for breakfast, and by the time I got there at nine, the living room had been two feet deep in wrapping paper, the house echoing with the noise of Finn's video games.

"The pre-dawn Santa excitement didn't wear me out," he finally said. "Seeing Willa's face when she got her look-alike doll was worth it. Besides, I don't want to miss a minute of this."

My parents' house had never been so full. Couples as far as the eye could see: sisters, cousins, uncle, and friends. Eden and Booker had made their pregnancy announcement, and the resulting cheers had shaken the floors. Eliza and Dean were practically glued at the hip, and burly Ty acted like if he took his eyes off June for a minute, he might stop breathing.

No surprise, their paired-off bliss was a lot easier to take when I had a match of my own. Now my arms were baby-free, I wrapped them around Sam, ready to nudge him beneath the mistletoe hanging in the dining room. It'd been a popular spot today.

Jed walked by, shooting me an *I told you so* look. Fine, yes. I'd intended to keep him company as the only other single loner of the family, and instead, I'd spent my time tangled up with my boyfriend. I would feel bad about it later. Or never.

"Is it too much for you?" I asked softly. "All of this Christmasy stuff?"

Sam splayed his hands across my back, pulling me close. "I don't mind the Christmasy stuff so much anymore."

"What finally won you over?"

He looked up to the ceiling, pretending to contemplate. Or maybe he was just gauging our distance from the mistletoe. "I think it was the ghost romance."

I laughed against him, ready to lean in for a quick, family-appropriate kiss, when the doorbell rang. Jed was closest, so he pulled it open, revealing Callie standing on the porch. She wore a red sweater with a red plaid blanket scarf, and her light-up Christmas necklace. She also balanced half a dozen plastic containers in her arms. They started to wobble, but Jed grabbed the top layer before they wound up on the floor.

"Thank you," she said, blowing her hair away from her eyes. "I probably should have made two trips but one seemed totally workable, but then I got up here, and nope, not workable."

I rushed over since Jed seemed in no hurry to welcome her in. "Callie, hi, I'm glad you made it."

"Thanks for inviting me."

"Jed, this is my friend, Callie."

He nodded her way. "I'd shake your hand, but..." He lifted the boxes he'd rescued. "What is all this, anyway?"

"Oh, my Granny always says not to go to a place empty-handed, but I wasn't sure what to bring. So I made four kinds of cookies and two kinds of brownies." She grinned at us, out of breath and eager to please. "Hope you like chocolate."

Jed raised his eyebrows and shot me a look like he hoped I knew what I was doing.

"Come on in, we'll get these set up and introduce you to everyone."

I took two of the remaining plastic bins from Callie and ushered her into the house. We trailed behind Jed to the table, where he laid out the goodies she'd brought. He might think her generosity over the top, but as soon I opened the containers, I knew I'd have to hoard some of her cookies for myself, they smelled so good.

Maybe even better than baby.

"Miss Callie?" a little voice called. "What are you doing here?"

"Dylan?" Callie leaned down, hands on her knees, to greet Wade's oldest son. "I didn't know this was your family."

He looked a mix of confused and horrified. "Who's at school watching the kindergarten room?"

"It's okay, little buddy," Wade said, scooping him up. "Your teacher's allowed to leave the school."

I introduced Callie around the room, but when I got to Mom, she took over, sweeping her up like a mother hen. I'd mentioned I'd invited her since she didn't have anybody else but her grandma to celebrate with, keeping what I knew of her losses to myself. But even that much had sent Mom into a frenzy, ready to love on our newcomer before she'd ever met her. And now that she had, Mom might as well have another daughter in the mix.

For her part, Callie didn't seem to mind being thrown into a huge family gathering. She looked right at home, chatting with Marilyn and June, and cooing over the baby.

Sam slipped a hand around my waist. "Looks like you checked everything off your list."

"Yours, too."

"When do we get to exchange presents?"

Looking around at everyone spilling through my parents'

house, I didn't really want to share our gifts with so many eager eyes on us. "Let's go to the porch for a few minutes."

We grabbed boxes from beneath the tree and slipped out the front door to sit on the old porch bench. The afternoon was crisp and cool, with the warm smell of wood smoke on the air. A little chilly for the thin sweater I wore, but we wouldn't stay out here long. Probably.

I passed him his present. He shook it like a little boy, listening to the clinking sound inside. "Mysterious."

He tore open the red and white snowflake paper and eased the lid off the box, revealing a set of six metal loops. "Aw, carabiners. Thanks, Harps. They'll come in handy."

"They're a reminder," I said, feeling weirdly shy. "I won't let you go."

His sweet smile disappeared, his eyes full of so much tenderness, my heart ached.

"I'll never let you go again," he whispered right before his mouth met mine. His kiss practically crackled with electricity, making me ready to forget the Christmas celebration inside and find someplace private.

Around here, that meant my dad's barn, and I didn't really feel like getting covered in hay.

Breaking the kiss, Sam presented me with a box he'd wrapped in cartoony Santa paper. I shook it, but nothing happened. I tore off the wrapping paper, but the thin red box inside gave me no clue. Undoing the flap, I eased a Styrofoam container free.

"Just be more careful with this one, okay, Harps?"

My heart ratcheted up like a little jackhammer, a lump already stuck in my throat. Carefully lifting half of the Styrofoam packaging, I found a perfect snow globe holding a snowboarding Sasquatch Santa. I couldn't look at him long before he went all blurry, the tears in my eyes ruining the moment.

"Where did you find this?"

"I had to do some calling around. This guy was in Astoria, Oregon, if you can believe it."

"I love it." I pulled the globe free and turned it upside down to watch the snow swirl inside before clutching it to my chest. "Thank you. He's going to sit on my mantel all year long."

Sam's pleasure shone out in all its dimply glory. "This is a bad start. I'll never top this Christmas gift."

"Hmm. Maybe another stay in the Hideaway?"

"Oh, Harps, you have the most fantastic ideas," he purred in my ear.

He kissed my face, his mouth trailing along my jaw before finally capturing my mouth. His languid kiss turned me inside out until I had to clutch at his shirt just to steady myself. When he finally pulled back, he rested his forehead on mine, his breathing shallow. "Merry Christmas, Harper."

I kissed him again, grateful this man was finally mine to keep.

epilogue

HARPER

FIVE MONTHS *later*

Sam and I stood on the beach, our toes in the sand, his arms around me as I leaned back against his chest. We stared out at the ocean as the setting sun behind us made the sky burn gold. We'd been this way for a while now, but neither of us had made any move to leave. The sound of the waves washing ashore, the smell of the salt in the air, and the light breeze over us made for ideal snuggling conditions.

"Have I mentioned yet how perfect this is?"

"Five times." He drew his arms tighter around me, resting his chin on my shoulder. "I could stand to hear it again, though."

"I love everything about this trip."

He chuckled against my neck. "We just got here."

"And I love it all."

He'd planned every step of our four-day weekend away, from the flight that got us to Florida to the tiny house he'd rented for us near the beach. I especially liked that little touch. We'd become regulars at the Hideaway, renting it out several times over the last few months for overnights beneath the stars. The tiny house here didn't have a skylight over the bed, but it did have an indoor toilet and shower, which I appreciated almost as much.

"Glad it's a success so far."

"Might be the best yet."

Our schedules weren't perfect, but we'd become pros at maximizing our time off. We didn't have a lot of overlapping days away from work, but when we did, we made the most of them, even if we just stayed in and watched movies on the couch.

I'd talked to Olivia about how her marketing strategies were affecting my work/life balance, and we'd made adjustments. I still worked occasional evenings and weekends, but I'd thrown out the on-call idea, and advocated for more time off. She'd ultimately agreed, and even if she'd been hesitant, we'd had no complaints from the Village residents. No more than usual, anyway.

Sam wound up working a lot of weekends with the guiding outfit in Georgetown, leading multi-day hikes through nature preserves and parks in the Hill Country, but the exhilaration he got out of every trip made the time apart worth it. Plus, our reunions after being separated for three or four days were nothing short of explosive as we made up for lost time. I hoped the thrill of seeing Sam again never got old.

"Any way it could get better?"

I turned my head to try to reach him. "French fries?"

"Within walking distance."

"Board games?"

He sighed, his breath warm on my neck. "I saw a *Sorry* game in the house. Try to show some mercy, won't you?"

"Never."

He shifted one arm away from me a moment before bringing it back, a tiny something perched in his fingertips. "What about if I gave you this?"

I registered what he held and my breath caught, froze, and went on vacation somewhere in my lungs. The small ring glittered in the golden evening light, but my brain had trouble processing it. I pulled his hand closer.

Dark green filaments clouded the center stone, like a drop of paint pulled across oil. Haloed by small diamonds, the ring could only be one thing, but I needed to be sure before I shouted out *"Yes! Yes! Yes!"*

"What is it?" Surprised I could speak at all, really.

"It's a moss agate. It symbolizes friendship."

"It's beautiful."

"Yeah?" His voice cracked on that small word, the first indicator he might be nervous.

I spun to face him, and he dropped down to one knee in the sand, still holding the gorgeous green ring out to me. My stomach flipped, my heart a giant, exploding star.

"Harper, you are my best friend. I want you to be my best friend for life. I've never been very good at thinking ahead, but when I look at my future, my next five years, ten, fifty—all I see is you."

Tears spilled down my cheeks because of course they did, but they came from a place of pure happiness. My smile was probably visible from space.

"What do you say? Will you marry me, Harps?"

I nodded, kneeling down with him as he slipped the ring on my finger. "Yes, I will marry you, Sam."

Blubbered a little, but I got the words out.

He kissed me through my tears, a hundred unspoken words wrapped up in his tender caress. Turning me, he adjusted us so we sat in the sand, snuggled up with his arms around me as I leaned against his chest, the best chaise lounge on the planet.

I couldn't stop sneaking glances at that beautiful ring, reminding myself this was all real, and I would really get to marry him. We breathed in time with the gentle waves as they lapped the beach just feet from our toes.

At my ear, he said, "Of all the places I've been, being by your side is the one I love most."

My sweet, romantic man.

"So stay."

THE END

magnolia ridge

Find out how June got together with grumpy horse trainer Ty in Say the Words.

Read how free-spirited Eliza fell for buttoned-up Dean in Have a Heart.

Discover how Jed meets his match with Callie in Make it Real.

If you'd like bookish emails and sneak peeks of upcoming titles in the Magnolia Ridge series, I'd love it if you signed up for my newsletter here. You'll also get the link to the free novella of Eden and Booker's whirlwind romance, Take the Shot!

acknowledgments

Thank you for reading Stay this Christmas! I wrote this on the heels of moving across the country and I needed to indulge in all my sweetest, snuggliest impulses. Writing this book was a little like hitting all my Christmas romance bucket list moments & I love how it turned out. I hope you enjoyed Harper and Sam's cozy times.

Huge thank you to Claire and Amanda for reading this and giving your thoughtful feedback. You reassured me it did in fact pass the swoon test & encouraged me to share it!

Thank you to my editor, Zee, for pushing me to trust my instincts with this one. Your notes always help my characters become more vibrant!

Thank you to Melody for this beautiful cover and the perfect rendition of Sam & Harper!

As always, I'm thankful for my family's patience and support, from my kids to my parents to cousins and in-laws. You're the best!

And finally, Pete—it didn't take me eleven years to realize I needed a second chance with you, but I'll forever be grateful you were willing to try again. Smoochie smoochie!

Genny Carrick is a sucker for an HEA, especially if there's a whole lot of laughter along the way. She writes romances and rom-coms about stubborn women and the men who fall for them.

When she's not lost in swoony reads, she's probably up to something crafty or trying to get her dog and two cats to love her.

Genny recently moved to Texas after a lifetime in the Pacific Northwest, and lives with her brilliant husband and two hilarious kids.

Stay in the know with book news at gennycarrick.com